No Mans Moor

No Mans Moor

SUZANNE STIRKE

© Suzanne Stirke 2023

Published by Riding North Publishing

www.suzannestirke.co.uk

A CIP catalogue record for this book is available from the British Library.

ISBN 978-1-7390839-0-8 (ePub)
ISBN 978-1-7390839-1-5 (Paperback)

Book layout and design by Clare Brayshaw

Prepared and printed by:

York Publishing Services Ltd
64 Hallfield Road
Layerthorpe
York
YO31 7ZQ

Tel: 01904 431213

Website: www.yps-publishing.co.uk

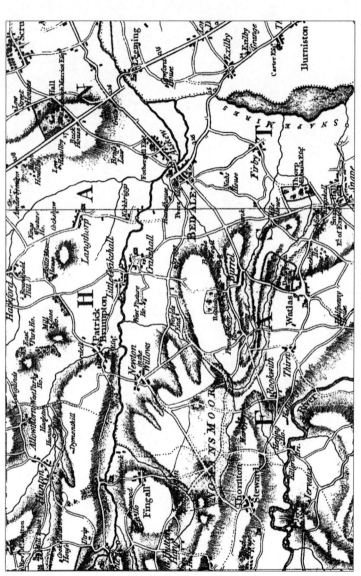

After Thomas Jeffries 1771-75 Survey of York, showing Bedale, No Mans Moor and the surrounding area

CHAPTER 1

"The devil take you," Fordy spat through gritted teeth. Dropping his hammer he stuck his fingers into his mouth and waited for the pain to kick in. Groaning, he tasted his warm blood; it coated his gums like stale ale. Reaching out, he steadied himself against a fence post for a few moments. Daring himself to inspect the damage he took his fingers out of his mouth but couldn't distinguish between raw flesh and oozing blood. He pulled out a rag from his jacket pocket and wrapped it tightly round his hand, attempting to stop the bleeding.

Straightening up he looked back at his morning's work. He'd hoped to get the fencing in this field repaired before dinner time. But he'd been late starting; one of the foals that had been born last spring had refused its early morning feed. The animal had failed to thrive even on its mother's milk and now weaned, it continued to lose ground. He'd mixed cod liver oil with warm bran but had been unable to tempt it to take the smallest mouthful.

It seemed that the world was against him today. Despite being mid-April, the frost was still hard and the fog only just clearing. His hands were numb with cold, hence the stupid accident with hammer and nail.

What should he do? Pack in for now, grab an early bite and get his hand seen to, or struggle on with this thankless task? Another hour would have seen the job finished but there was no rush, there was still no sign of any spring grass; another thing to worry about in this bleak year.

He looked over at the house, his fingers throbbing, and decided on the easy option. Scooping up his tools with his uninjured hand he threw them into his canvas bag then gingerly slid his bandaged fingers through the handle of the bucket of nails, wincing as they took the strain of the extra weight. Blood began to seep through the cloth as he trudged across the field.

"Fordy, Fordy," shouted a voice.

He looked up to see his father at the field gate waving his arms wildly.

"I'm coming," called Fordy, quickening his pace. "What's up?"

"I've got the draymen round t'front; it's news. Philpots 'ave been caught poaching!" Fordy's father gabbled the news as he opened the gate for him. "Heavens, what have you done to yoursel'?" he asked, looking at Fordy's bandaged hand.

"Hammered me damned fingers instead of the bloody nail," said Fordy, dismissively. "Are they still here?"

"Who?" asked Ben, distracted by Fordy's injury.

"The draymen?

"Yes, that's why I was calling you. Come and hear what they have to say."

Fordy dropped his bag and nails beside the fence and followed his father over the cobbled courtyard and round the side of the buildings.

Fordy and his father had several business interests; at the heart of their lives was Worlds End, their home, and an inn. Situated on the edge of No Mans Moor, the hostelry had served travellers and locals for as long as anyone could remember. With Bedale four miles to the east and Leyburn and the Pennines to the west, their situation was remote but the road that passed the property was a busy one. Back in the days before the enclosure of the moor the inn had offered a safe haven from the dangers of wild animals and foot pads. In these days of uneasy peace that followed the final defeat of Napoleon, Worlds End, with Ben Robson's all-embracing hospitality, served locals and travellers well. Offering good ale, hearty food, and a comfortable bed if required, business was always brisk, particularly in the summer months when travel was easier for folk and drovers were on the move.

The weekly delivery of beer and spirits for Worlds End came each Wednesday. Access into the courtyard was through a low archway so the large dray wagon always parked up at the front of the property. It was here that Fordy and Ben found the draymen and the two snorting horses, that were hitched to the wagon, paddling in impatience.

"Malcolm," said Fordy, nodding at the older of the two delivery men.

"Now then, Fordy, y' father'll 'ave told y' bout t'Philpots?" asked Malcolm by way of a greeting, "caught poachin' last night o'er near Leeming."

"I'm not surprised, the man must be out three or four nights a week," answered Fordy.

"You're right, but it's turned nasty. Paul an' his eldest lad are in t'cells at Aiskew. His youngest was with 'em, but he got away. Authorities are out looking for 'im. There's even one of the keeper's sat waiting at their 'ouse in case t'young fella turns up," said Malcolm, taking his cap off and scratching his head.

"Young Mark, on the run? He's barely old enough for that heavy job he's just got at t'mill, he'll struggle being out on his own…" tailed off Fordy.

"It's a bad goin' on. All that bloody land enclosed, a man only wants to snare a rabbit to feed his bairns. He's got plenty, mind… bairns I mean, not rabbits," interjected the other drayman.

"What'll happen to Paul?" asked Ben.

"He's up before t'bench next week. I heard tell a couple of blokes down country got seven years transportation last month and that was just for carrying a couple of traps at night-time. They hadn't even caught owt…" said Malcolm. "Philpots'll be kin of yours?" he added, looking at Ben.

"Aye, on my late wife's side," said Ben.

"I'm sorry to 'ave brought you bad news but we'd best be getting off; got a full day ahead of us," said Malcolm, rubbing his hands down his leather apron before taking it off. "You want the same order next week?"

"Maybe an extra barrel of ale, trade's picking up, or it should do with May round the corner," said Ben. "But I don't know what to make o' this poor weather, I've never known such a late spring."

Malcolm scribbled a note on his pad then climbed up onto the dray cart.

"Can you help me saddle Dapple?" asked Fordy, cradling his injured hand as they watched Malcolm and his team pull away.

Ben stared down at his son's hand, "You can't go now, state you're in."

"Horse knows its way," said Fordy, already heading towards the stables.

"You think young Philpot'll have made his way to Burgess at t'mill?"

"Aye, where else is he going to go?" asked Fordy, watching his father lead Dapple, his grey gelding, out of the stable. While Ben dealt with the horse Fordy found a clean hessian sack in the tack room and cut off a strip with his knife. He wrapped it tightly over the already blood-soaked cloth on his hand.

"You'd better use the mounting block, save your hand a bit," said Ben once he'd saddled up.

"Don't fuss, Father," complained Fordy, stepping onto the block.

"Let me tighten that girth, now you're on. I wish you'd let us have a look at that hand before you go," said Ben, bending to secure the saddle.

Fordy shook his head, "I won't be long, we can have a look at it when I get back."

He pulled on the reins with his good hand and gave the horse a gentle prod with his heels. Dapple needed no instruction and once Fordy was headed in the direction of town the horse led the way. Given to Fordy by his father as a yearling, the bond between the two was strong, built on trust and time. Dapple was the first horse that Fordy had helped break. If Ben Robson was a natural host, his son's talent with horses was proving itself with their growing herd. He could soothe any horse with his placid temperament but, crucially, he had an eye for a well-proportioned animal and potential.

He hoped to build his business and reputation with the increasingly popular Cleveland Bays. The breed was versatile; one day it would be pulling ploughshares and the next, out with the hounds. An ideal mix of attributes in this rural part of Yorkshire.

Fordy and his father had big plans for the future. They'd been promised more land and, with the extra acres, they could expand their horse breeding enterprise and build on their good reputation for producing quality stock.

It was a brisk ride to Aiskew Mill. Through Bedale Fordy kept his head down, in no mood for conversation. Arriving in the mill yard he took a moment; it was quiet, none of the hustle and bustle of the previous market day. Only the flow of water and the deep rumbling of the millstones turning broke the silence.

Fastening Dapple up next to the water trough, he saw John Burgess's foreman walking towards him. "Now then, Matt," said Fordy.

"Are you looking for young Philpot?" Matt spoke quietly, "Good God man, your hand! What…?"

"Never mind that, is he here?"

"Aye, he's in t'boss's office. In a right state, he is, came staggering into t'yard earlier on. I'll take you over," said Matt, already walking across the yard.

In the small room that John Burgess used to run his business Fordy found Mark Philpot slumped in a chair, its size emphasising the smallness of the boy. John was encouraging the lad to take a sip of brandy. Matt followed Fordy in and firmly closed the door.

At the noise of the door John Burgess jumped up. "Fordy, thank God, I'm pleased to see you. You know what's happened?"

"Yes, we heard up at Worlds End, I came straight down," said Fordy as he knelt beside Mark. "How are you, not injured I hope?"

Mark pulled himself up a little. "I've cut me leg, but I'm right enough," said the boy shakily. "What's going to 'appen to me now?" he asked, looking between John and Fordy.

"We can't keep you; I'm surprised they haven't been here looking for you already. Everybody knows you work here," said Burgess.

"Maybe I could take him home with me till this blows over," suggested Matt.

"I'm not so sure this is going to die down, there's a different feel around now, you know," said Fordy.

John turned to Matt and Fordy. "He's right, word is Philpot's to be made an example of," he said quietly, then went to throw a couple of logs on the fire.

Fordy glanced at Mark, who seemed oblivious to their discussion. "Mark, are you fit enough to ride?" asked Fordy. "I'm of a mind to take you back up to Worlds End. We could get you safely away up north with the drovers and there's a friend we 'ave in Scotland who could take you in. It'll be a wrench for your mother but better than what you'd face if you get caught," said Fordy. Prison for a grown man was hard enough, for a lad this age, the consequences were unthinkable.

There was a loud knock on the door, Matt answered it, quietly speaking to the man on the other side without fully opening it.

"I'd best be getting back, we have a load to bag off and they need me," said Matt, touching his floury cap towards Fordy.

Fordy acknowledged him with a nod.

"Will you come with me, Mark?" asked Fordy.

The lad nodded, "But what's going to 'appen to me dad?"

"He'll get a few months behind bars," said John quickly. "Let's not worry about that now."

"And what about me mam? Does she know where I am?" The boy was getting distressed.

"I'll go and see her, tell her you're safe," assured John.

"Get that drink down and we'll be away," Fordy said to Mark.

"What if you're seen?" asked John.

"I'll go round by Firby, cut across the fields. It's a risk, but…"

"I know, anything we do now is risky," agreed John. "Take your horse round the back and I'll bring the lad over.

We don't want him mounting it in full view, anybody could come into the yard."

Fordy left John with Mark in the office, doing as John had suggested. It took them an age to appear, John had tied a hessian sack round the boy, in an attempt to disguise him as a sack of flour. The lad was quiet but quickly jumped up on Dapple behind Fordy.

"Now you hang on to Fordy," John told Mark. "Don't be slipping off…and take care, lad." John rubbed the boy's leg in a rare show of affection.

"I'd say you have your hands full if you didn't have one of them out of action," quipped John to Fordy.

"It'll be the cells that are full if we get caught," replied Fordy grimly, taking Dapple's reins in his right hand. John nodded and slapped Dapple on his rump. "Good luck," he said, as Fordy kicked his horse on.

Leaving the miller's yard Fordy picked his way over the fields and footpaths. The weather hadn't improved, the dreary heavy fog had once again dropped over the land. On this occasion it was a blessing although the chill bit into both riders. As Fordy's hand banged with pain he could feel Mark shivering behind him. But Fordy was in no mood to sooth the boy's feelings as they made their way back to Worlds End.

* * *

"By God, I'm glad to see you two," declared Ben, helping them dismount. "Let's get him into the kitchen; Mary Ann has hot food waiting for you."

The work Fordy had hoped to complete earlier in the day was forgotten as they gathered around the kitchen table to eat. Mark hadn't uttered a word but his appetite was still robust, serving himself a second helping of Mary Ann's beef stew.

"We'll have a look at your hand now you've eaten," said Mary Ann, clearing away the dirty pots.

"It'll be alright," mumbled Fordy. The adrenalin that had kept him going had seeped away. He was feeling cold to the bone and weary, his whole arm ached. He knew more pain was to come.

"I'm away out," said Ben, jumping up, "I've plenty to do in t'tap room."

Noisily scraping his chair over the stone floor, he left Mary Ann to administer to Fordy.

"Squeamish as ever, your father," observed Mary Ann. "Let's get this filthy sacking off your hand first, then you can put it in a bowl of warm water and ease off this old rag." She gently took hold of Fordy's hand then glanced over at Mark.

"If you've finished your food, go and sit in that big chair beside the fire. Cover yourself over with that blanket and keep yourself warm."

Mark did as he was told.

Over by the sink Mary Ann's daily help, little Lucy Tomlinson, was peeling potatoes. She hadn't spoken since Fordy and Mark had come in; always in awe of Fordy even on the most mundane of days, today's activities were too much for her but now she managed a few words.

"I'll cover him," volunteered the wide-eyed girl, wiping her wet hands down her apron.

"Now don't you be telling anyone about all this, will you, Lucy?" said Mary Ann firmly. "We don't want Mark taking to the cells, do we?"

The girl shook her head as she lay the large homespun blanket over Mark.

"I won't say nowt, Mary Ann, honest."

"Stoke the fire up then get back to those potatoes," Mary Ann told her.

"I'll take a swig of brandy before you start, have we any in here?" asked Fordy, watching Mary Ann pour boiling water from the kettle that sat on the stove.

"Lucy," said Mary Ann, "dry your hands and go to Ben in the tap room, tell him I want a large glass o' brandy for Fordy."

Silently the girl disappeared through the door into the hallway that led to Worlds End's tap room.

Fordy sat back in his chair, breathed deeply and watched Mary Ann gently readjust the blanket over Mark, who had fallen asleep. He noticed how she lay her hand on the boy's head, flattening a cotter in his hair. How many times had she fussed over Fordy in exactly the same way?

Mary Ann had cared for him all his life. His mother had suffered ill health after having her only son and Mary Ann nursed her for three years until she died. Fordy and his father had become dependent on her; there was never any question of her leaving. At what stage she had moved into his father's bed was none of Fordy's business but why they didn't wed was a mystery to him.

This kitchen was her domain. The large low-ceilinged room was well equipped for her to cater for any passing travellers and it afforded the family a comfortable homely space into the bargain. Sandstone slabs lay on the floor, covered with multicoloured clippie rugs. The white walls received a fresh coat of distemper every year and the large oak table they sat at was given a regular lathering of bees' wax, the distinctive sharp flowery smell lingering.

Lucy returned quietly with a glass full of brandy. She placed it on the table next to Fordy then scurried back to her work. Fordy picked up the drink and threw it down his throat as Mary Ann placed his left hand in the water. Slowly the makeshift bandages softened and fell away from Fordy's hand to reveal two damaged fingers.

"I don't think you've broken any bones, but these nails are a mess," said Mary Ann, peering at his hand. "Do you want to have a look?"

"No, just wrap 'em up so I can use my hand again." He watched her face as she continued to inspect his injury.

"I'm not surprised this happened. I saw two knives crossed on a table t'other day when I was visiting Mrs Oldham," muttered Mary Ann.

"What do you mean?" asked Fordy.

"Bad luck of course."

"You and your superstitions," dismissed Fordy.

"You may sneer, but I keep telling you to be more careful. The way you conduct your life you're asking for trouble," she whispered at him, not wanting Lucy to overhear her.

"I don't do anything that plenty of other folks do and they all seem to survive," he replied.

"Raking about over t'countryside in the dead o' night when most God-fearing men are safely at home isn't normal," she went on, allowing her voice to rise.

"Everything alright?" asked Lucy, looking up from her work.

"Yes," snapped Mary Ann. "Get that kettle filled up and back on the stove."

Fordy adjusted himself in his chair, he wanted to be out of here. Mary Ann was usually placid and cheerful, but once she got rattled there was no end to her arguments.

"You worry too much; I've no time for this business of ghosts and phantoms," Fordy told her.

"Well, that's as maybe, but Mrs Oldham says she's sure there's a witch living at the bottom of their field," replied Mary Ann, with a grin.

"Now you are having me on."

"Maybe I am, but you should be careful, there's bad

spirits in the countryside these days, evil souls that won't rest," said Mary Ann seriously.

"It's the good spirits I'm interested in," teased Fordy as Mary Ann continued to tend Fordy's injury. "The harmless ones... and the sort you can drink."

"Maybe that's so, and there's plenty of restless souls out there that'll do you no harm but it's the wicked ones you should be wary of," she warned him.

"Life's about the living, I reckon, not vengeful pixies skulking about in hedgerows at night... ouch, that hurt," he cried pulling his hand away from Mary Ann.

"There was a piece of grass stuck in the wound, I had to pull it out," she said, looking up with a smile playing on her lips.

Fordy wasn't sure if she was inflicting a little pain on him in an attempt to make him listen to her. But he could see she was enjoying this task and making the most of having his reluctant ear.

"You love a bit of blood and gore, why can't you give me some sympathy?" moaned Fordy.

"You don't need it, look at that child asleep by the fire, he's the one who needs some love right now."

Fordy turned to see the boy slumped in the large chair, almost hidden by the blanket. Fordy had his hoped pinned on one particular drover to get Mark Philpot out of the area and to safety. Travelling down from Scotland with sheep to be fattened in England, Angus Thurrock had called at Worlds End for over thirty years. All drovers, by the nature of their work were trustworthy. Taking a farmer's stock hundreds of miles, getting a fair price and delivering the money was not a task for a scoundrel. But with the safety of a child at stake, Angus was the man that was needed.

"I'm hoping Angus Thurrock will be passing here soon, we haven't seen him this year yet," Fordy told Mary Ann.

"Does the child know what's going to happen to him yet?" asked Mary Ann.

"Aye, but he might need a bit o' reassurance from you," Fordy looked at her hopefully. "Events 'ave 'appened that quick, I doubt the lad has taken in what my plans are for 'im."

"There isn't a fellow I'd trust more with that bairn than Angus Thurrock, but it could be weeks before he passes through. I'm happy to look after the lad but can we keep his presence here a secret?" commented Mary Ann as she finished dressing Fordy's injuries.

Fordy watched Mary Ann; for a woman who'd never had children of her own she had an ability to show love to anyone who needed it. He knew why she had enjoyed tending to his injured hand, she loved to care for folk. Even little Lucy who helped Mary Ann about the house had blossomed from a stuttering under nourished child to a strong capable lass, although she was still a bit timid and Mary Ann snapped at her on occasion.

"That's you done," said Mary Ann, getting up and taking the bowl of red bloodied water from the table.

"Thanks," said Fordy, flexing his hand, assessing how restricted he was going to be over the next few days. "I'll pop down to t'tap room, see Dad and ask him what he thinks about keeping young Mark here."

CHAPTER 2

Early the next morning Fordy walked quickly from the house across the yard, the cold damp air bit and he hurried into the warm stables. The heat from the horses created a soothing welcome as he breathed in their familiar sweet smell. His hand was still painful from yesterday's accident but the sight of his horses lined up in their stalls lifted his mood.

He went to Dapple first, speaking to the horse as if he were human, "We had a good day yesterday, didn't we, lad?" he said, tipping a scoopful of oats into the horse's trough.

Next, he tended Sparkle, "Alright, fella?" he greeted the younger horse with a firm pat on his neck. As he reached forward to feed him, Sparkle snorted and pushed his head into Fordy's chest. This was one job he could still do with his left hand restricted with its damaged fingers and bandages.

In a stall on her own was Gilly, she was in foal and Fordy eagerly awaited the day he saw her offspring in a few weeks' time. Her foal from last year was the runt, a big disappointment to Fordy and his father and both feared the youngster wouldn't see the summer out. Running a hand over her mane, he whispered sweet nothings in her ear and filled up the hayrack, hoping this year's foal would fare better.

Finally he took an extra measure of oats to their oldest horse Briar, who was paddling impatiently for Fordy's attention and his food. Pushing the animal to one side so that he could get to the horse's manger, he threw the corn into the trough and watched Briar nibble away at his breakfast. Fordy couldn't help but rub the old horse's ears and slide his palm down the silky neck. "Tha's a grand old soul," whispered Fordy. Briar responded by nodding his head up and down. Fordy's love of this horse went back to early childhood; it had always responded by moving his head in this way when anyone whispered in his ear. As a child Fordy had squealed with laughter at this horse's antics and at the same time had secured a place in the family's heart. "Tha'll not be sent t'knackerman," continued Fordy, the horse nodding in agreement. Fordy gave a small chuckle and left the veteran to clean up his breakfast. Leaving the warmth of the stables and the shuffling horses chewing on their hay he went back out into the frosty day break.

Outside he took a moment to survey the scene; their old property had stood here for centuries. Nothing jarred, there was no division between manmade and natural structures. The soft hue of the local stone and cobbles that had been used to build Worlds End blended in with nature's own palette of subdued colours. Fordy glanced around the old courtyard, he had felt this was his whole world for all of his twenty-five years but recently a restlessness had come about him. He thought of Mary Ann fussing over his hand; previously he would have accepted her attention and concern without question, but now… he wasn't so sure. This urge for something else that he couldn't identify was so strange he couldn't sort it out in his own head. Nothing had changed yet everything felt different. How could he be dissatisfied when he had nothing to complain of? His whole life and future was wrapped up with this place and his father, and he was content at that prospect yet still something niggled in his mind that there might be more to life. Was he missing out on something?

He heard a noise from the house and saw his father coming out of the kitchen. He was carrying a bucket and walked over the cobbles towards Fordy.

"You're up early," said Fordy.

"I couldn't sleep," answered his father, coughing up his night's phlegm and quickly spitting it on the frosted stones at his feet. "Here, take this over for t'pigs while I relieve meself," he added, handing over the metal container to Fordy.

Fordy left his father and went across to the pigs which were housed in a sty at the far end of the buildings. "Hoy, hoy," called Fordy, banging the bucket against the wall before emptying the contents on to the floor of the pen. The two piglets came scurrying out of their covered shelter to get their food. Leaning up against a stone pillar he watched them squabbling and pushing one another aside, rooting through the potato peelings and cabbage leaves.

"Penny for 'em, lad," said Ben, joining Fordy.

"Look at these fellas, shoving each other and playing, what a simple life they have. Not a care in the world, they don't have to worry about where their next meal comes from. They don't 'ave to risk their necks and go out poaching to feed themselves."

"Aye, kept me awake all night, that did, worrying about Philpots and how we'll cope with young Mark. Last thing we want is t'authorities landing up and finding the lad here."

Fordy didn't answer, he shivered with cold and plunged his hands deeper into his coat pockets.

"Come on, lad, let's go back inside and see if Mary Ann's got any breakfast for us," said Ben walking towards the house. He stopped, hesitated for a moment and turned back to his son. "Don't dwell on those pigs for too long, they maybe don't have any worries now but they're still facing the chopping block in the back end."

Fordy looked back at the frisky little pigs, his father was right, these fellas would be sides of bacon and salted hams before the year was out, thankfully for them, they were unaware of their fate. 'But then,' Fordy reflected, 'no one knows what's in store for them in the future. Any day could be your last.' At that sobering thought he turned and headed for Mary Ann and her cooking, hoping to find some sausages and eggs on the stove.

* * *

Each day at Worlds End, they waited for the familiar clues of approaching drovers. A cloud of dust on the horizon was the first sign for anyone looking, then the noise of bleating sheep or bawling cattle. Two days after Fordy's arrival with Mark those signs appeared but there was disappointment when Jock Ferguson appeared in their yard; he had 200 lambs with him and was on his way to Boroughbridge. Fortunately two of his men were doubling back the following morning, making their way over to Carlisle. They were agreeable to taking the lad up into the Scottish Borders to Angus Thurrock's home. But they wanted payment.

"What are we going to do?" sighed Ben, when Fordy went to tell his father.

"We could wait till Angus appears and risk having the lad here longer or we just pay them and get him away in the morning," said Fordy.

"What are they asking for?"

"Six pounds of tea and three bottles of brandy," said Fordy.

Ben gasped, "Robbing bastards."

"I know," agreed Fordy, "I'm alright for brandy, I've plenty up in my store, but the tea's a problem, my stocks are low. I'll have to go over tonight and get more."

* * *

Fordy set off as early as he dare, preferring the cover of darkness for his return journey. His destination was the stables of Kings Pasture House, a large property that stood a good three miles from Worlds End. This area of the North Riding of Yorkshire always felt remote but with the main south to north thoroughfare a few hundred yards to the east of Kings Pasture House, known locally as Leeming Lane, London and Edinburgh were only a day or two away on a fast horse.

Riding through the night to collect contraband was usually enjoyable, despite the need to remain alert and vigilant. Although smuggling and dealing was mostly ignored by the authorities, there was no telling when things might go wrong. A bad word at the stables, an accident with his horse or an overzealous customs man with an organised ambush could all lead to trouble. His regular night for a run was a Wednesday; this was Friday so Fordy's sense of anxiety and caution was heightened as he entered the grounds through the little used back entrance. The lane twisted around a couple of fields before running alongside the high wall of the gardens which sat at the rear of the house. To his right a dense line of trees ran all the way to the stables and round behind them.

The secluded location of these buildings made them perfect as a storage and distribution centre for illicit goods. Nearing the stable yard Fordy saw the familiar glow of flaming torches and lanterns; entering the stable gates he could hear the sound of the horses' metal shoes clattering on the cobbles. In the enclosed yard several men busied themselves carrying boxes or pushing barrels, while a couple of men stood with horses. Fordy was always careful not to look too closely at anyone here, always avoiding eye contact. No trader wanted to be recognised.

The exception was Fred Higgins, a local man who oversaw proceedings, his friendly manner at odds with the circumstances. Surrounded by surly fellows who worked for him and grumbling customers, suspecting they were being conned out of a few coppers, Fred Higgins' cheery nature would not have been amiss in a shop selling confectionary.

"Now then, Fordy. What are you doing here tonight, must be short of something, eh?"

Fordy had already dismounted and handed Fred his slip of paper. "I need a bit o' tea, six pounds, if you have it."

"A bit, good God, man, this would keep a regiment going. What you doing with it? Have you turned Worlds End into a tea house?"

"Just as quick as you like, Fred," said Fordy quietly, "please," he added a little more forcefully.

"Right enough, lad, I'll see to this mysel'," replied Fred. "Wait over there," he told Fordy, pointing to a quiet corner before disappearing into the stables.

Keen to get away, he had no choice other than to do as Fred had told him. Fordy moved into the shadows with Dapple and waited.

Fordy had never been in the buildings where the contraband was stored; no customers were allowed near them although it was understood there was a range of cellars below the stables. Many believed that a network of tunnels also existed, running from Kirkby Fleetham Castle over to Jervaulx Abbey, from the days of the monks in King Harry's time. Whether the old tales were true were of no interest to Fordy. These stables, owned by the notoriously greedy Sir Robwyn Stillerton, only had one purpose as far as he was concerned. They provided a hidden location for storing and distributing contraband, but Fordy was increasingly convinced that those at the top of smuggling ring, such as Stillerton, who never got his hands dirty, were the ones who were really making significant profits. The rich facilitated the trading of illegal goods not to help working folk get the odd luxury item now and then but to fatten their own purses. They traded in goods but they traded on the insatiable demand of the population for an affordable packet of tea or a bottle of brandy that didn't cost the earth.

Tonight Fordy's thoughts were consumed by such injustices. It wasn't only the smuggling that benefitted the rich and exploited the poor. The land enclosures were cutting off a vital source of free food for thousands of people and tightening the noose round the likes of the Philpots, along with hundreds of other hard-working families. Men had always caught wild rabbits and game to feed their wives and children… but now, all over the country, grasping landowners were fencing round the common land to increase the acreage of their estates.

There was no doubt the world's a good place if you're rich and have powerful friends but, for the average man, life was a battle just to survive.

Fordy's unease was bothering Dapple, the horse paddling and twitching constantly as they waited. Fred finally appeared with a hessian bundle under his arm. Fordy handed the money to him and the exchange was made in silence. Fred stayed at Fordy's side whilst he pulled himself up onto Dapple.

"You're one of the few honest blokes that comes into this yard, Fordy, I hope everything's alright," said Fred, gesturing towards Fordy's bandaged hand.

Fordy nodded as he pushed the bag of tea down in front of him. He hadn't bothered with his saddlebags tonight. "I'll be away Fred, and thanks."

Getting clear of the stables he settled himself into his saddle and kicked Dapple onto a trot. He felt a little more relaxed now he was clear of the yard although the night temperature had plummeted, he was feeling the cold and his damaged fingers throbbed. Another hour should see him home, but there would be little sleep tonight. The drovers would need paying and Mark would have to be prepared for his journey north. Mary Ann had nurtured the child over the past few days, feeding him up and reassuring him that he'd be able to see his mother in a year or two. The boy was terrified but she had told him that living with the Thurrocks would be just like living at home. There was a houseful of children and a farm to roam around on. Not that anyone at Worlds End had ever seen the place but Angus told stories of his home and large family on his many visits.

The plan was a good one apart from the obvious flaw that Angus knew nothing of it and they were trusting the safety of the boy with two unknown fellas who could easily take their payment and desert the boy on some open roadway. Or, worse, hand him over to the authorities for a reward. There was no choice. Fordy was going to have to trust them to take the lad up into the Borders and explain the situation to Angus.

Fordy imagined droving would be a good life but he could never substitute cattle or sheep for his beloved horses. There was soon to be a new foal at home and the thought of fresh life comforted Fordy; there was no better sight than a new-born foal, hot and steaming from its mother's sac, taking its first snorting breaths, and the startled contentment of its mother's attention. With those thoughts he breathed a little more easily for the first time since hitting his fingers, stroking Dapple's neck with the back of his bandaged hand. As he did so Dapple stumbled and roughly swerved, throwing Fordy forward as he tightened his grip with his legs, just managing to stay in the saddle.

"Woo, steady lad," soothed Fordy. Taking control of Dapple, he tried to look around him. But the darkness he had craved for the journey was now his enemy. He pulled Dapple up, not sure if he should make his escape but fearing the horse may be injured. Had he caught a stone in his hoof?

Dismounting, he laid his bag of goods on the road and began to run his uninjured hand over the horse's legs. He could hear a high pitch whimpering close by, a small creature laid on the road, he guessed. Straining his eyes in the dark night, he dimly made out a lump just ahead of him.

"Bloody rabbits," he swore, taking aim to kick it into the hedge.

"Sir," a voice behind him shouted, "move away from my dog."

Fordy swung round ready to fight, his first thought that he had walked into a trap. But it sounded like a woman's or a child's voice. He peered into the shadows; a figure emerged, female from what little Fordy could see, moved towards the dog and picked it up.

Fearing an ambush with the girl as decoy, Fordy retrieved his bundle of tea and went to remount Dapple.

"Help me; my dog is injured. I need light," the girl said.

"I have no light; I must be on my way," he shouted, putting his boot into the stirrup but Dapple moved and Fordy lost his footing. His bandaged hand made him clumsy. He hopped nearer his horse and pulled his foot out of the stirrup. The girl was at his side.

"The least you can do is assist me," she said.

"Are you alone?" he asked, looking down at her dark form.

"Of course I'm alone; why else would I ask you to help? Come with me."

The girl appeared ignorant of his dilemma as she walked towards the double gate that led through the garden wall. He felt responsible for injuring the damned dog but had no wish to involve himself further.

"Come on," she said, standing at the gate.

"But I have my horse," he replied, hanging on to Dapple's reins; the horse was jumpy and pulling away from him, unsettled by the sudden noise and commotion.

"There's a tree you can tie it to," she said.

"You mean I should follow you into the gardens. Are you bloody mad, woman?" he called at her.

"You're the one responsible for the injury. You must help me," she said as she walked back to him. "Please come."

"No, I'm not coming in. I can't. I'm needed elsewhere." He stood his ground.

"If you won't come with me, will you wait while I get my lantern so we can examine my dog here?"

"Very well, but you must be quick," he told her. His heart thudded loudly through his chest. If this was a trap, he was in it.

In a moment she reappeared through the garden gates, holding up a fluttering light with the dog tucked under her other arm.

"Put the dog down. I'll take a look but my left hand is injured. You'll have to help," he snapped at her.

She placed the dog and the lantern on the dusty road. Fordy's hand and eyes inspected the wriggling body of the terrier.

"Look, here, there's a cut on its back leg. There's no bones broken as far as I can tell, bathe it well and it'll be fine," was Fordy's brisk analysis. Lifting his eyes from the animal to its owner he gasped. This was no child. As her shawl fell away he saw her well defined features and her hair gathered with clips that glittered in the lamp light. She looked him straight in the face, her confidence challenging Fordy. If only he had time to stay, if the circumstances were different, he wouldn't brush this beauty off so quickly.

"Are you sure?" she demanded.

"As sure as I can be, in the dark. Bathe it like I said," answered Fordy, aware now of her nearness. She wore a perfume unfamiliar to him, a rich deep aroma, unlike the cheap rosewater most of the country lasses used.

"Where do you live?" He peered into her face.

"In there," she answered, nodding towards the high garden wall. "I've seen you before, coming down here on a night."

"You watch me?" he asked, standing up.

Her tone lightened, "Yes, usually on a Wednesday, and with two horses. You must be up to no good."

Fordy thought he heard her laugh but he couldn't see her face to be sure. It was tempting to linger.

After the moment of hesitation he spluttered, "I'm away. Your dog'll be fine."

Fordy picked up his bundle and pulled Dapple close to him, preparing to remount the horse. She was at his side again. "Will you be back next Wednesday?"

"Yes."

"I'll watch for you," she said, adding, "I could offer you refreshment to thank you for looking at Jasper."

Settling himself onto his saddle, he looked around for her, wondering what, if any, reply to make but he didn't need to say anything: she had disappeared.

"Damned woman and her wretched dog," he muttered to himself. His father would be wondering where he had got to; they must get Mark away tonight. He urged Dapple on again into a quick trot, but his thoughts remained with the girl. A fine-looking lass, of that there was no doubt, but who was she? And might she be more trouble than she was worth?

It was past midnight when he neared home and the gentle shimmering of torches appeared up ahead of him. The drovers had settled in for the night, although they would begin stirring before dawn in preparation for continuing their travels.

"Where 'ave you been?" was Ben's greeting to Fordy as he jumped down from Dapple. He threw the bag of tea towards his father, before leading the horse up to the stable. "I'll tell you about it when I get in," Fordy called over his shoulder.

Mark was abed when Fordy got in from settling Dapple and he joined his father and Mary Ann around the kitchen table for a pot of tea.

"I've no idea who she was but she fair gave me a fright with her wretched dog. There wasn't much I could do for it with my hand," said Fordy, holding up his injured limb, as he told of his trip to Kings Pasture. "I think I'll away to bed," he announced, "I've no wish to be here when the lad goes."

Mark would need preparing for his departure and his forthcoming ordeal. It could be a difficult parting and Fordy had already decided to leave it to his father and Mary Ann to see the lad through his last hour under their roof.

"Off you go, we'll manage," said Mary Ann. "You've done your bit for him and I know you aren't one for sentimental goodbyes."

Fordy went upstairs, leaving the tea and brandy on the kitchen table for the drovers who were taking Mark up to Scotland.

He threw himself onto his bed fully clothed and thought on the day. It was a relief to shut his eyes. His shoulders relaxed and the day's images flashed through his mind. The Philpot situation could go either way, no point getting vexed about it.

He thought on the lass and her dog.

'Have I missed my chance with her?' he asked himself. 'I might not see her again, but I needed to get back home to Dad with the tea.'

He pictured her crouching on the ground, tending to her dog. He reminded himself of the pleasant surprise when he saw her face… and of her perfume as it wafted over him.

'Should I have lingered?' he asked himself again. Involuntarily he curled up his damaged fingers, the sharp pain that shot through his hand made him wince.

"No," he said aloud, "I was right to get away, I'd 'ave looked a clod with this useless bandaged hand."

Rolling over, sleep was slow to come. Eventually he got up again and clumsily undressed for bed. The girl was proving difficult to dismiss from his thoughts, those words of hers played over, "I'll watch for you."

CHAPTER 3

Tuesday morning found Fordy driving Dapple, harnessed to the flat cart, down to Bedale market. Clad in two overcoats to protect against the cutting easterly wind that had been present all spring, he reached behind him for the rug that Mary Ann had given him and pulled it over his legs. His hands were oddly matched, on his right he wore one of his usual lambskin gloves but on his left he sported a rough sewn covering that Mary Ann had made for him. His hand was on the mend although a nuisance at times as well as being a reminder of what a rotten day last Wednesday had been.

It was three days since Mark had been taken north by the drovers; there had been no news, as yet, of his safe arrival at Angus Thurrock's in the Borders. Nor had any further information reached them about Paul Philpot and his eldest son; as far as Fordy knew, they were still in the town jail. He'd pick up any gossip or new developments in town today.

As worrying as these matters were, there were other irritating problems for Fordy to contend with this morning.

Driving into Bedale he passed the Hall on his right and made for the railings near the church where he tied Dapple and the cart. His first job was to secure an order of vegetables from a stall near the cross. Fresh produce was scarce at this time of year but, confident of getting a basic selection of potatoes, carrots, onions and turnips, he was surprised they had a few cooking apples left too. Mary Ann would make the most of them. After a brief word with the stall holders, reassuring them he would pick up the purchases once his other business was concluded, he settled up with them and went into the noisy taproom of the Royal Oak.

"Fordy, over here," a voice called out.

Sat beside the fire were Abe and Chalky.

"I thought it might be quiet in town today after the excesses of last week," said Fordy, pushing through the jostling crowd. The previous week had been the Easter Fair, the first livestock market of the year when farmers and dealers traded horned cattle and sheep.

Hundreds of townsfolk and villagers had flooded into the town to take advantage of the stalls selling all manner of goods and to meet up with friends after a long winter of isolation.

The low room in the Royal Oak was warm and full of smoke. Overcoats were beginning to steam as bodies heated up and the smell of damp clothing clogged the air.

"Have you seen Jane yet?" asked Chalky.

"I've just got here," said Fordy.

"She's looking for you and she's as mad as a cat that's lost a mouse," laughed Chalky.

"Hell, I knew there'd be trouble today. I was late getting off this morning. I've an ailing foal. I know the damned thing's gonna die but I keep trying with it, it's making me late for everything."

"Stay and 'ave a pint," suggested Abe.

"I'll nip out; see if I can find her. I'll be back in later," said Fordy.

"See you about one," nodded Chalky.

Fordy turned left out of the Royal Oak towards where Jane's father had his butcher's shop and, within seconds of setting off, he saw her walking towards him, her diminutive figure belying her strength of character.

"Where've you been?" she said, once Fordy was in earshot. "I expected you an hour ago. Now Father has sent me out on some errands."

"I'll walk with you. What's the matter?" asked Fordy.

"I haven't seen you since last week. Where were you on Friday?"

"We were busy."

"You would've made the effort once," she spat back. He glanced down, her mouth was nipped up. The fiery spark, which had at first been attractive, had become irritating.

"Don't be like that. You've got your dad to help and I have so much work on up at Worlds End. What with one thing and another."

"It's that 'one thing and another' that bothers me."

She was a bonny lass and had been lots of fun at Christmas but as the weeks had passed by she'd become moody and possessive. He'd tried several times to shake her off but she wasn't for letting go.

"There's some funny talk going round about you," Jane said.

"What do y' mean?" Fordy glanced around, aware of the looks they were getting from folks on the street.

"Like what you get up to in the middle of the night," she answered.

He looked round again to see if anyone heard, grabbed her by the arm and dragged her into the nearest alleyway. "You should know better than to talk like this."

"And you should be careful, Fordy Robson; I know more than you think."

"What's your point?"

She dropped her head and took hold of his hand. He noticed how cold her fingers were and saw they were swollen and red. He guessed she'd been salting hams; involuntarily he pulled away from her.

"Don't be cross with me, Fordy. It's just… I thought me and you would…"

"You're getting ahead of yourself," Fordy said quickly.

"We've been courting since Christmas, are you telling me you've just been passing time?" Her voice was getting louder again.

"I haven't time for this, I'll be down on Friday, we'll talk then," he said, taking hold of her shoulders. She nodded but said nothing and he left her standing alone as he strode back to his horse and cart.

Untying Dapple, Fordy stood there for a while, stroking the horse's nose and gathering his thoughts.

"You still on for Sunday?" a gruff voice asked over his shoulder.

Fordy replied without turning round, "Aye, Jack, I'll be there."

"We've got some good birds lined up. It'll be quality not quantity this week." Leaning closer Jack continued, "I wanted to have a word with you about that stuff from…"

"Not now, I'll have a word with you on Sunday, I've got to get to the mill," said Fordy.

"Alright, lad. Some 'at up?"

"Women!" Fordy paused and grimaced, "You know?"

"Tha'll learn one day." Jack was already walking away and Fordy could see his shoulders shaking with laughter.

He clambered up onto the cart and headed down Emgate, splashing through the ford before turning right down the track that led to Aiskew Mill. John Burgess had done well out of his years grinding corn. He also farmed fifty acres of land and had a good reputation as a trustworthy businessman. Above all, Fordy and his father trusted him.

In the miller's yard, trade was brisk, John busy with a couple of customers. Fordy pulled up alongside the covered area and tossed a couple sacks of corn into his cart. He stayed with his horse until John stole a moment and ran over.

"Everything alright?" asked John, quietly.

"It's too busy to talk today, and o'er risky. Mark's away with drovers but no more news," said Fordy, under his breath. "I've put a bag of wheat flour and one of rolled oats in the cart," he said, raising his voice and nodding over at Matt who was loading up another cart. "We'll need a full load of 'orse oats at the end of the week." added Fordy.

Reaching down at the front of his cart he pulled out a small bundle wrapped in an old flour bag. Without a word he handed his goods to John, who accepted the package with a smile and a nod.

"All quiet down here?" asked Fordy.

"So far. You'll have heard that Philpots are to be taken down to York?"

"No," replied Fordy, taking a deep breath, "it's a bad job."

"There's a few folk trying to pull some favours but it's not looking good for 'em."

"I'd like to stay and talk but I'll have to get off, it looks like rain," said Fordy. "I'll see you on Friday… for the oats."

"Aye, and you still fit for our journey on Monday?"

"Definitely, I'm all fixed for that," nodded Fordy.

The miller disappeared into his buildings with the bundle under his arm as Fordy secured his load, covering it well.

He returned up Emgate, tied Dapple back to the railings and re-joined his friends in the Royal Oak. The day had lost its shine for him as he took a seat by the fireside.

"Did you find her?" asked Chalky.

"I did. She's too bloody keen for my liking," said Fordy, taking a bite out of his pie.

"It's your own fault," Abe said.

"I don't know what you mean," said Fordy as he let the contents of his tankard slip down his throat. The ale tasted sour today.

"Somebody'll catch you one day, be it a lass or her irate father," said Chalky.

Fordy laughed, shaking his head.

"Aye, or the excise man," said Abe, in a low voice.

Fordy ignored this remark. He was in no mood for idle banter and wanted to go home but knew he must share a few words with the brothers.

"What are you lads busy with for the rest of the week?" he asked, attempting to appear courteous.

"I'm here at the shop with Dad, and Chalky's off up t'Redworths at Huntby," answered Abe.

Fordy nodded.

"Aye, we've made a pair of fancy gates and a length of metal railings for t'new entrance, I'm off up to fit them. Should be there till end of the week," confirmed Chalky.

"You stopping up there?" asked Fordy. He knew of the Redworths, they lived about five miles away towards Richmond, one of the wealthiest families in the area with the unusual reputation for treating their tenants and staff well.

"You'll get looked after, up there," said Fordy, without waiting for an answer.

"I know," agreed Chalky. "Last time I was there doing some work for 'em I got fed in the kitchen and was even offered a proper bed when I had to stay over. Old Mr Redworth's a kindly sort, he alus comes out to see what his men are doing and to 'ave a friendly word."

"Is that why you're always so keen to go up to Huntby when they want work doing?" snipped Abe.

"Or is there a bonny willing lass over there?" added Fordy quickly.

Chalky shrugged and took a drink without responding to their questions.

Fordy took the opportunity of the break in the conversation.

"I'd better be off now, lads," he said. Taking the last mouthful of ale from his tankard and getting up from his seat, he wiped his hand over his mouth. "I'll see you Sunday night."

"Expect so. We should be off too, Abe. Father'll be getting agitated," said Chalky. "You know he gets niggled if we leave him alone too long on a market day."

Fordy's mood was as cold and wet as the weather on his way home. He'd been a fool to let this thing with Jane run on. Then there was her father, who hoped for a wedding. Tom Dennison was undoubtedly the best butcher in town; he was also handy with his fists. He'd be nearing fifty now but Fordy knew he'd be no match for Tom should he feel his daughter had been treated badly.

* * *

At home Fordy found his father in the tap room with all the windows and doors open. During the winter, folk gathered around the large fireplace that filled the narrow internal wall. Now that the warmer months were approaching the room could be opened up again and the travellers dining area needed freshening up.

"Spring cleaning?" asked Fordy, as he came into the tap room. He ran his hand over one of the large oak tables which, despite being covered in dust, felt smooth and warm.

"I bloody 'ate this job, but she said it had to be done," muttered Ben.

Fordy glanced at his father and stifled a laugh, a tangle of cobwebs trailed down the back of his head. With his fair hair and blue eyes the familial resemblance to his son was clear although Fordy had inherited his mother's height.

Ben Robson had lived all his forty-eight years at Worlds End, marrying a local farmer's daughter when he was twenty-three and never travelling more than twenty miles from the inn. While not exactly lacking in ambition he had been content with his lot, still proving himself astute when it came to buying and selling horses. He took satisfaction from Fordy's interest in the horse trade and his hopes for the next few years were high, facts he made no secret about.

"You get on alright in town?" asked Ben.

"Saw Burgess, he said there's word that Philpots are to be taken down to York."

"Bloody hell, somebody's trying to make a point."

"I know, but there isn't anything we can do when it comes to the courts."

Ben had stopped his sweeping, "Did you see that lass of yours?"

Fordy walked across the room and aimed a kick at the pile of wood next to the fire grate, sending several logs tumbling over the hearth rug.

"Trouble?" asked Ben.

"She's not the one for me, Da, but I don't know how to make her understand."

"Just tell her, lad."

"It's not that easy. She's keen to be wed, she could make trouble for me."

"What does she know?"

"Nowt, but she's the sort who'd spread a rumour out of spite."

"You could do a lot worse than marrying a butcher's daughter," Ben chuckled, watching his son's miserable face.

Fordy wandered back outside to his horse at the water trough. Taking the damp reins, he shuffled Dapple and the cart over to the back door and unloaded the provisions for the house.

"I'll take those carrots straight into the kitchen," said Mary Ann, who had come out. "What's mithering y'? Your hand?"

Fordy shrugged his shoulders and screwed his face up.

"You'll be giving Dapple a rub down once you've unloaded the cart?" she asked.

He nodded at her.

"I'll bring you a mug of tea out," she told him.

A damp drizzle continued to fall and Fordy took Dapple into the stable after unhitching the flat trailer. After throwing him an armful of hay and filling his water bucket, Fordy wiped the horse down before brushing him.

His thoughts were interrupted by Mary Ann peering into the stable, "I'll pop this mug on the windowsill. What's the matter?"

"It's Jane. I've 'ad enough of 'er."

"Just tell her it's off. She'll get over it in a week or two."

"If only it was that easy," moaned Fordy.

"She's not breeding, is she?" asked Mary Ann.

"Good God, Mary Ann, what a thing to say to me, and no, she isn't. I've not made that mistake."

Mary Ann shrugged, mumbled, "I was just wondering," and headed back to the kitchen.

With Dapple groomed and fed, Fordy tended to the other stabled horses. His last job was to feed the ill foal which had been taken into a loose box. The space made it easier for Fordy to tend the animal and he hoped the fresh straw and airy building might boost its health. Before mixing its drink he went to check on it. Fordy's heart sank; it lay lifeless on the bedding. He knelt down, gently placing his hand on its neck. The animal gave a small shudder and a short exhalation of breath. He waited a few more minutes, hoping it might take another gasp, but the poor thing was dead.

After the loss of the foal and his unpleasant exchange with Jane, Fordy longed to ride over to Kings Pasture House and reacquaint himself with the intriguing dog owner; time in her company might be a pleasure to counter the disagreeable day but caution and the rain got the better of him. It would have to keep till tomorrow.

* * *

Fordy's dilemma the following evening was whether to take two horses with him over to Kings Pasture. He was low on stock and could do with a good top-up but was reluctant to take Sparkle, one of his other horses, with him. The horse was well suited to the job, steady on the lead rein but his hand was still bandaged and he didn't want to be fighting on with two horses without full use of both hands if he saw the girl again. Not that there was any guarantee that she'd be there.

As dusk fell, he left home, turning out at this time of night with his saddlebags on meant only one thing for Dapple. The horse set a brisk pace down through Newton and over Hollow Moor. It was slightly shorter to go by Crakehall but an ambitious customs man had moved into the village before Christmas. Fordy thought it wise to avoid the place.

In the grounds of Kings Pasture, Dapple quietly picked his way along the road. Fordy took his hat off so that he might hear any movement or a voice as they passed by the garden wall but the gates were closed, there was no indication she was there. "I'll watch for you, I could offer you refreshment," had been her words, but where was she?

He felt deflated, he had hoped she'd be waiting for him.

"Get on," he urged Dapple in annoyance. Latching onto flippant words from a woman was ridiculous. How many throwaway comments had he made over the years in the hope of a kiss or a tumble?

In the stable yard the air was tainted by the fumes from the pitch which burnt to give light. There was no wind to lift the acrid smoke away and, as it settled in the confines of the yard, it caught in the back of Fordy's throat. His business was quickly concluded and, after stowing his goods securely in his saddlebag he was bending down to inspect Dapple's girth when he heard two raised voices at the stable door. He looked up to see Higgins marching across the yard.

"Now then, Arnie, what's going on?" shouted Higgins.

Fordy watched; Arnie Fuller would be trying to get his goods on the tick.

"I were just tellin' this fella o' yours that you let me 'ave a bit o' stuff on account, you know. But he's startin' to get rough wi' me," bellowed Arnie, believing everyone to be as deaf as himself.

"Alright, Picard, I'll sort Arnie out. Go and fetch more crates of gin," Higgins told Picard; one of the two unsavoury characters Higgins employed to do the heavy work. Picard and Rennie had worked for Higgins for a couple of years; they claimed to be Flemish but there was much speculation they were Frenchies who had deserted Boney's army. Both spoke with heavy accents and would settle a disagreement with a punch rather than a word.

Picard shuffled off, muttering to himself, no doubt feeling Higgins had deprived him of a bit of sport at feeble old Arnie's expense.

Fordy pricked his ears; he could hear Higgins and Arnie coming to an arrangement. Men usually took a beating for non-payment but Arnie was Higgins's uncle by marriage.

* * *

Leaving the stables, he was still hopeful the girl would appear. Approaching the gates, he hesitated, peering at them through the dark, but they were closed. He pulled Dapple to a standstill for a moment then slowly moved on.

"Hello," called a voice as a light appeared over the wall. Fordy halted Dapple and looked up. There she was, holding her lantern high; he felt she had caught him off guard somehow.

"Hello again," he replied.

"Have you time to come in this evening?" she asked.

"Yes," he answered. Moments later he could hear the bolts being drawn back on the gate. She stepped through the opening, "Bring your horse in here, there's a tree you can tie him to."

Hearing her clipped accent and observing her confident manner again, Fordy began to doubt his decision to accept her invitation. She already seemed to have the upper hand. If this wasn't the trap he had initially feared, his new concern was she may belittle him and amuse herself by making him look like some sort of country fool. Thank God he'd only brought one horse, it was one less thing to worry about, he thought as he followed her into the walled garden.

CHAPTER 4

Securing Dapple, Fordy followed the girl to a door, which she unlocked and opened. "Come in," she said over her shoulder.

He closed the door behind him and watched her quickly move around the room, turning up the lamps and lighting a few candles. His eyes adjusted to the light. He could see fine furniture, curtains at the windows, ornaments and books; they had nothing as fine as this at Worlds End. Near the window was an easel covered with a pale sheet and, to the side, a small table haphazardly piled with paints, brushes and cloths. He felt less than comfortable in these unusual surroundings,

"You are my first official visitor," she said. Running his eyes over her he saw she wore a threadbare cotton dress with a faded floral pattern. She removed the thick shawl she had worn outside and replaced it with a colourful flowing silk scarf. She was just as attractive as he remembered. With brown eyes, curling hair and a strong jaw line she wasn't like local lasses. But it was her bearing that struck Fordy. He had worn his cleanest leather jerkin and given his hands an extra scrub before setting off this evening but still he felt like an oaf set against her delicate build and light step. His mind raced, attempting to assess this strange situation while trying to maintain an air of nonchalance.

His initial impressions of her social superiority were immediately confirmed but what were her circumstances? Perhaps a lady's maid, genteel by birth, possibly impoverished, waiting for her mistress to arrive at Kings Pasture?

Whoever she was, she had been oddly keen to ask him to come in here. Why was she making such an effort to be friendly when, as a high-ranking servant in the big house, she was of a far finer class than he?

He stood watching her. He was well acquainted with gentlefolk. His father was respected in the neighbourhood and had business dealings with many of them but never had he or his father been on intimate terms with them. Doing a spot of business in the yard or sharing a glass of refreshment was common enough. His father's friendship with the Duke of Malbury went back forty years but he doubted his father had ever been in the Duke's drawing room up at the castle.

"Jasper is totally healed, he doesn't even limp," she said, picking up the dog.

"Let me look at the little fella." Glad of the distraction, Fordy took him from her, a bundle of curls with a reddish tinge, no doubt the origins of his name. The animal wriggled as Fordy felt its legs and he quickly put it back on the floor, his best jerkin now covered with dog hair.

"Please, sit down," she said, filling two glasses from a pewter jug, as Fordy sat. He recognised her hospitality as that of a congenial superior which was at odds with her eagerness for him to join her in this garden room. She was trying to greet him as an equal but her well-mannered attempts to make him feel at ease only emphasised the difference between them.

"May I sit with you?" she asked, as she handed him the drink.

"Of course," he answered. "What's your…?" he coughed. "What's your name?"

"Anna, what's yours?"

"Fordy, well, that's what people call me," he replied. His usual easy manner with women was inadequate here. Any reference to daily life would highlight the gulf between them.

As she sat beside him, he was aware of the intoxicating perfume he had smelled last time he saw her. Was she stealing her mistress's perfume or did she have money to buy her own?

"I'm pleased Jasper is fully recovered. Had he escaped when he ran across the road?" he asked, taking a sip from his glass, wondering if this wine might also have been pilfered from the big house.

"He was chasing rabbits and squeezed under the gate. It was my fault but it's rare that anyone uses the lane, especially late at night." She raised her eyebrows and smiled at him.

"I can imagine, it was unfortunate," Fordy replied. "Do you spend a lot of your time down here, er, in the garden?" He knew he sounded stilted.

"This building was the head gardener's but now that there's no longer a head gardener, I've made it my own. I bring bits and pieces from the house to try to make it cosier."

"You're allowed to do that?"

"Do what?"

"Take things from the house."

"Of course, I can take anything I like." She shook her head and drew back her hair. His mouth went dry. He got up and went and stood by the fire, he could see she was enjoying his discomfort.

"Where are you from?" she asked. Fordy didn't answer. If she wasn't so pretty, he wouldn't have risked this meeting.

His glass was empty, normally he'd have helped himself to more.

"You tell me where you live and I'll tell you where I live," he said.

"I live here of course." Her eyes sparkled as she returned his gaze.

"In the big house?"

She nodded.

"You work there?"

She shook her head.

"So who are you?"

"I'm Annabelle Stillerton."

Fordy's heart thudded. This was even more tricky a situation than he has supposed.

"Sir Robwyn's daughter?" he asked, but he already knew the answer.

She nodded.

Although Sir Robwyn Stillerton owned this small estate his reputation as a spendthrift was something of a local joke. Everyone knew he was a man with fancy ideas but lacked the means with which to fulfil his ambitions.

Several years ago, this house had been one of the foremost in the area. Sir Robwyn and his wife, Lady Mary, had employed dozens of staff both in the house and the gardens; they had entertained at the highest level and were frequently away in London and Italy. Since the death of Lady Mary ten years ago, Sir Robwyn no longer had the means to live the lavish lifestyle he once enjoyed. It was well known locally that he spent most of his time in Durham, pursuing a wealthy widow. Kings Pasture House had been shut up for the past few years, with only a housekeeper installed to keep an eye on things. No one had seen Stillerton's daughter locally since her mother's death.

It was also common knowledge that Sir Robwyn had jumped at the chance to use his buildings as the centre of this local smuggling ring, the funds it brought in were sorely needed.

Fordy swallowed hard, "I wondered… but word had it you were in Italy. Why are you even talking to me?"

"I'm lonely," she said, lowering her head. Her hands knotted together on her lap. Her show of bravado dropped.

"But why are you here?" he asked.

"To be guarded."

"From what?"

"Prospective husbands," she said.

"Why?"

"I get my inheritance from my mother when I'm twenty-five, or when I marry, but my father is keen to secure it for himself. He's penniless; he's gambled his way through all of Mama's money that he could get his hands on."

What could Fordy say? How could he offer words of consolation to a woman like this? No doubt these kinds of people had a way of comforting each other in troubled times, but he didn't have the refinements or grace to ease her pain.

"How long have you been here?" he asked, taking his seat again, moving a little closer to her.

"Four months; I was living in Florence with my aunt but when a suitor asked for my hand, my father whisked me away and incarcerated me here with only Mrs Dinsdale, the housekeeper, for company."

"Is there no one in the neighbourhood who visits you?" asked Fordy.

"No one knows I'm here; I think Father has told everyone that I'm still in Italy."

"But surely, someone calls…"

"Why would they? Father spends his time up in Durham, courting Mrs Holden. He comes back here occasionally to check on me and the house. Anyway, who cares? I am of no consequence apart from being the link to Mama's fortune."

Fordy listened to her story intently, taking a few moments to reply. "I shouldn't have asked but I wanted to know because I was worried you were going to bring the law down on me," he said.

"For what?"

"Dealing in contraband."

She shook her head and got up to bring him a tray of bread and cold meat.

They sat in silence together on the couch, picking at the food. The Stillertons may be impoverished but the belongings in this room reeked of money and quality. Fordy ran his hand over the arm of his seat, a dry callus on his palm snagged on the velvet pile and he glanced at the grubby bandage that covered his hammered fingers. He pulled both hands towards himself in embarrassment.

"So, where do you live?" she asked, eventually.

"About three miles away, over on No Mans Moor. You know it?"

"No, I've roamed the fields around the house but with no friends or money I don't go away from here."

"It's out towards Masham, it's called Worlds End. We have an inn; it's a busy spot," Fordy added.

"You live with your parents?"

"My father and Mary Ann, our housekeeper; my mother died when I was small."

"We are both motherless then," she commented.

"Yes and no, Mary Ann has looked after me since we lost Ma. She is the kindest woman I know. Did you not have someone that cared for you… after…?"

"A couple of nursemaids; no one ever took Mama's place," she tailed off, leaving a few moments silence.

"And you supplement your income with a bit of trading?" she asked.

"You could put it like that. It's more the excitement than the money if I'm honest."

"You should try living here, then you'd really crave a diversion," she said.

"Well… I'm glad we've met, even if Jasper did get injured."

"It looks like you've been in trouble too," she said, nodding towards his bandaged hand.

"It's nothing, banged it with a hammer, that's all," he answered, sliding his hands away from her view again.

Their burst of frank exchanges died. Fordy started to feel uncomfortable once more as he searched his brain for something to say.

"Tell me about Worlds End, what it's like to live there," she said, as she leant back on the couch.

Fordy told her about the old house and buildings that he called home. He told her about his horses, the foal that had just died and another that he hoped would be born in a few weeks. He brought to life his daily routine and his work with his horses. He described his father and Mary Ann, who always made friends and strangers so welcome at the inn.

His unease fell away as he described his life to her. She listened, asking questions, even laughing at times. With her encouragement he found conversation easy and they quickly fell into a relaxed exchange. It was easy to forget their different stations in life, even that she was a woman. He'd never talked so freely and frankly with any other lass that had taken his fancy.

"And then of course there's my two friends, Abe and Chalky. They're blacksmiths in Bedale…" he hesitated.

"Tell me about them," she insisted.

"We go cockfighting every Sunday night, at Newton. We have some rare nights out," he chuckled.

"And no sweetheart living in Bedale?" She eyed him carefully.

"I never seem to find the time for women," he mumbled, his cheeks burning with the lie. "There was a lass but… well…"

Once again Fordy was at a disadvantage; he got up out of his chair to avoid her eyes. He walked around the back of her chair and stopped by the easel, "Do you draw?" he asked, scrambling to change the subject.

"Yes," she said, getting up and moving to his side. "I paint as well, watercolours, look." She lifted up a small half-finished painting of her dog.

"You found time to visit me, didn't you, Fordy?" she asked, returning to that sensitive topic.

She was too close and much too bold for comfort.

"Well, I was passing," he replied, inhaling her perfume again.

"And you'll be passing again, won't you?"

Fordy swallowed hard, "Aye, I will."

"Next Wednesday?"

"Yes," he said, "that's my regular night."

"If I leave the gate unlatched you could come straight into the garden. You know where to tie up your horse?" she said, turning a statement into a question with her tone.

Fordy knew she was being forward but still he nodded.

"Forgive my presumption but I am so lonely here," she added.

"There's nothing to forgive, I've enjoyed m'self. I'll see you next week."

* * *

Riding home Fordy dwelt on Anna's situation. Captivated by her, he found it difficult to imagine that she might think him in the least bit interesting. But she had made a definite point of asking him to call next week. There was no doubt in his mind that he would visit her again. Deep in thought, he was brought back to reality by the familiar restless bleating of sheep as he neared Worlds End. Was it Angus?

"Come on, fella," he urged Dapple on, the horse less than keen to pick up the pace loaded down with goods.

Flares had been lit along the grass verges, illuminating the resting sheep. Fordy had experienced this scenario many times, yet he still took comfort knowing hundreds of animals temporarily used these wide grass verges as their resting place. He could hear them shuffling and breathing, some chewed their cud noisily and others slept on silently. Nearing the buildings of Worlds End he saw a small huddle of men round a fire.

"Are you Thurrock's men?" Fordy called down to them, bringing Dapple to a halt.

"Aye, Angus is inside teking a dram with y' fatha, if that's Fordy I'm talkin' to," came a broad voice out of the dark.

"It is. Have you travelled safely?" Fordy asked the anonymous voice.

"We 'ave, we're away down to York, come sunrise," was the reply.

"I'll leave you to your meal," Fordy replied as several voices grunted their acknowledgement of his presence. "Wrap up well. There's a frost in the air tonight," he added as he walked into the yard at Worlds End.

Despite his eagerness to see Angus, Fordy took Dapple back to the stable and unloaded him. Settling the horse, he carried his heavy saddlebags over to the house. There was no need to hide his activities to anyone here tonight. Angus

Thurrock had called on the Robsons for over twenty-five years and of all of the travelling Scotsmen he was the one who Ben Robson called a true friend. Moving cattle and sheep down into England each year from the highlands of Scotland the drovers had a reputation for hard work and honesty. With the responsibility of a farmer's whole year's work in the form of livestock, these droving men were trusted to treat the cattle well, sell them at a good price and to give the farmer his fair return.

Covering hundreds of miles on foot they travelled light with a satchel over their shoulders filled with a few handfuls of oats and a bottle of whiskey, they lived off the land and the blood of their cattle and sheep for many a long week. Despite the rugged lifestyle and appearances of being unaccountable there were more rules and regulations around the occupation of being a drover than almost any other rural way of life. With yearly licences issued and a raft of sponsors and references to be maintained, this wasn't the work of rogues, Fordy reflected.

* * *

In the tap room Angus and his father had already taken drink, and his father was looking worse for it.

"Fordy, lad, it's grand t'see y'," Angus Thurrock said, taking hold of Fordy and giving him a tight bear hug. The ginger-haired Scotsman released his grip and held Fordy at arm's length. "Let me look at y'," he added, inspecting Fordy from head to toe.

"It's good to see you, by God we thought you'd never appear," said Fordy. "Have you got young Philpot at your home?"

"Aye, there's no need to fret o'er him. We passed the two fellas you sent him with over at Carlisle. I told 'em to tek the lad up to my place. He was fair bewildered but he'll settle. Your father's told me about what happened, I hear Philpots are still awaiting a hearing."

Fordy nodded, confirming his father's report.

"Never mind your young friend, Mark, and your poaching friends, what I want to know is where did this lad get his good looks from, Ben? Certainly not you. You still not wed, Fordy? How do you manage to stay single?" Angus had taken hold of Fordy again and was shaking him by the shoulders, not giving Fordy or his father the chance to answer his string of questions.

"I just lead a quiet steady life, Angus, you know me," laughed Fordy.

"What have ye' done t'your hand?" cried Angus, noticing Fordy's bandage.

"Ah, just a clumsy accident," said Fordy, pulling his hand behind his back. "It's nothing."

"Well, have a dram with us," suggested Angus.

"No, I've seen the damage it does to Father, I'll stick with me ale."

While Fordy went behind the bar to pour himself a drink he listened to his father and Angus discussing the weather.

"The flooding up north is a terrible sight to see. Thousands of acres of grazing land stood in water not to mention the winter corn that's rotting in the wet ground."

"Surely it'll start to pick up now that we're nearly into May," said Fordy.

"I see all sorts on my travels and I can tell you there'll be plenty of folk starve in the next year or so," said Angus, taking a drink.

"Aye, and for all the talk of peace there's still that damned war to pay for. I tell you, it's not the landed folk who'll have that debt to settle... or who'll go hungry," agreed Ben.

"They might tell us we had a victory last June at Waterloo but for folk like us the battle goes on and the biggest one will be to stay alive. People are restless, you know, the government might choose to ignore the hardships but they can't hide from it for long. They can tell us Boney is locked away and is no longer a threat, but there's still plenty of starvation and danger in this country."

"You're right, Angus, and a man can't even go out and snare a rabbit for the pot like he could in the old days. I know it's over ten year since they enclosed this moor but folks still resent it," added Ben.

"These new corn laws don't help matters either," said Fordy, joining in the conversation. "I can't work out what it all means; they tell us it's to protect our farmers but as far as I can see the only group it protects are the landowners and those who can afford high prices for grain. What's a man to do these days to feed a family?"

"And what would you know about feeding a family?" Angus roared with laughter at Fordy.

"Make fun of me as much as you like, Angus, it's still a fact: there's too much wrong in this world of ours but there's a fat lot we can do about it. Those buggers in Parliament keeping grain prices artificially high won't harm them; it's our friends and neighbours who'll pay the price."

Ben muttered his excuses as he shuffled outside to empty his bladder.

"Enough of the politics," said Angus, throwing his arm over Fordy's back, "tell me now, is there a lassie you visit on the way home from collecting your contraband?"

Fordy gave a low chuckle.

"I tek that t'mean a, 'yes.' Is she bonny? Is she free wi'her affections? Och, lad, I wish I were young again," Angus said, raising his glass to Fordy.

"What's she called?" he pestered further.

Fordy looked back at the door to make sure his father hadn't returned. "She's called Anna, I've only seen her twice…" he stuttered, immediately regretting confiding in Angus.

"A local lass?"

"Sort of… well, not really. It's nothing… she's maybe a bit grand for me. I think she's bored and amusing 'erself with me. Her father'll take her back to London soon so…"

The door banged. Ben was back, fumbling with his trousers and muttering about the cold. The moment for confidences was over and Fordy straightened himself up. He was beginning to feel the effects of the fire and the lateness of the hour and he could see neither Angus nor his father were ready to turn in.

"I reckon it's time to call it a night, I've a long day ahead of me tomorrow and I'm not made of your strong Scottish fibre," he said, as Angus rose to shake his hand.

"Aye, good night, lad. We'll be away afore you rise but it shouldn't be long before we pass by again. Good luck to y', lad," said Angus, with a wink, "I'll look for'ard to catching up wi' your news next time I'm passing."

Fordy left his father and Angus to the fire and their drink and crept upstairs knowing Mary Ann would be asleep. He took off his outer wear and slid into the cold sheets of his bed. Angus's words about the weather and the unrest that appeared to exist in the country ran through his mind. The nation was divided and, to some extent, so was his life. It didn't matter how much he liked the idea of Anna, there was never going to be the chance to court her properly, the differences between them would see to that. As much as he might welcome the chance to see her again it wouldn't surprise him in the least if she was no longer at Kings Pasture House the next time he went over there.

These unsettling thoughts added to the sense of dissatisfaction he had been feeling for some time. Was the world changing or was it him that was different?

CHAPTER 5

Friday's trip to Bedale held little attraction for Fordy. He knew Jane was going to prove difficult. He had harnessed two horses to the cart, the journey back would be heavy, fully loaded with oats from the mill.

Mary Ann accompanied him, sitting next to him at the front of the cart. "I need to visit the tailors and I promised old Nelly Stubbs I'd call in on her next time I was in town, her legs are that bad now, she never gets out of the house." Mary Ann chattered, pulling at the blanket that was slipping off her legs. "And don't forget to leave that basket of food at the Burgesses for Mrs Philpot," she added.

Apart from a young lad leading a cow in the opposite direction the road was deserted until they pulled onto the main road from Bedale to Leyburn.

Fordy had little to say until Mary Ann dug him in the ribs. "What's bothering you this morning?"

"I'm trying to work out how to tell Jane I'll not be calling on her again. She can turn nasty so quick," replied Fordy.

Mary Ann shook her head. "She'll have a few harsh words for you no doubt, but you'll survive."

"We've only been walking out since Christmas, four months and she's keen to be wed." He shrugged and silence fell between them.

When they arrived in town, the high street was quiet. Fordy dropped Mary Ann off at the cross and passed her basket. "I'll do my jobs then wait for you at Nelly's, I can keep a watch out for you from her front room."

"I don't want to be hanging around after I've spoken to Jane, so keep your eyes peeled," were his words as he left her.

* * *

Down at the mill he loaded up with oats and accepted John Burgess's invitation to share a glass of ale. Fordy settled himself into the chair next to the fire in John's office. "At least we know Mark's safe, one less worry," Fordy sighed. "I'm on my way to see Jane now, I've got to tell her it's all over. Not sure how she's going to take it."

"I'd not worry too much; word has it that she's been seen about with Andy Hawkins."

"When did you hear of this?" asked Fordy, sitting up.

"Only yesterday, I wasn't sure what to make of it; I thought Andy was all but wed to Elsie Smith. He'd be a fool to throw over Elsie in favour of Jane but what would an old fellow like me know of such things?" John laughed and took a loud slurp of his beer.

Fordy hesitated before speaking, "Isn't Elsie due to get her uncle's farm when she marries?"

"That's right. Like I say, Andy would be mad to let her slip through his fingers, even if she is built like a bull," John snorted.

"I certainly wouldn't fancy waking up next to her every morning, but by God, a hundred acres of good land isn't to be sniffed at," said Fordy, shaking his head.

"Jane has her charms too, a pretty face and probably the family butcher's to take over, what with her brother, Nathan, being as he is," said John.

"Aye, you're right Nathan's not up to the job, but I wouldn't be a butcher for anybody," said Fordy forcibly. "Imagine, half your week killing livestock and the other half trying to keep the women of the town happy as they pick and poke over their meat."

"You like a good steak pie," answered John.

"I know, but I'd rather be doing the eating, not the butchering."

Silence fell on the two men for a few moments, each staring into the fire.

"Are you still on for Monday?" asked John. "If we leave early afternoon we should have plenty of time to get to Skelton before nightfall."

"Yes, it's all sorted with my father, he can manage without me for a couple of days."

"We should be back on Tuesday night. I'll not keep you now, we can talk on the ride over," said John as Fordy took to his feet.

"See you Monday... and good luck," John slapped Fordy's back before heading towards the mill.

Fordy jumped onto his wagon and returned to the high street. With it being quiet he was able to pull up outside Jane's father's shop.

Taking his cap off, he wandered in to find her father, Tom, cutting up a side of beef. The damp metallic smell of raw meat in the butcher's shop had become sickening over the weeks, as the rot set in between him and Jane.

"Ah, it's you, lad, you'll be wanting Jane?" boomed Tom, his round red face beaming from ear to ear.

"Aye, can you spare her for half an hour?"

"Jane, your young man's here," Tom shouted down to the back of the shop.

Fordy inwardly groaned; Tom had high hopes of a wedding and wasn't going to stop his daughter stepping out. He looked around the shop with its stained chopping blocks and sides of beef stacked against the back wall. Huge ox kidneys sat in a large, glazed bowl, oozing blood, waiting to be bought.

Hung up behind Tom were half a dozen sheep's heads with lifeless blue tongues lolling out of their open mouths. One head would provide a welcome meal for a poor labourer's family and Fordy knew the Scottish drovers favoured them. It made an easy dish whilst on the move, a sheep's head with a handful of oatmeal and root vegetables could be boiled overnight on an open fire. Fordy was thankful it was not a dish that Mary Ann served at home.

He thought of John's challenge about his love of a good steak pie; he had no objection to the food on the table but found the idea of spending the day handling cold lifeless slabs of meat repulsive. He'd rather be dealing with living animals, creating new life, watching young limbs grow.

"Hello, Fordy," shouted Nathan, Jane's halfwit of a brother.

"Nathan," nodded Fordy, "you busy?"

"Aye," he shouted in reply, "killed two pigs this morning, didn't we, Dad, didn't we, Dad?"

"We did, son, now get yourself down the back and start swilling the floors down," said his father who was making short work of slicing through a shoulder of beef. Fordy watched Tom at work. The soft flesh offered no resistance to his sharp narrow blade and bones were quickly sliced through with his small but vicious saw.

For a moment Fordy was captured by the scene; it only served to add to his low mood. Before taking up with Jane he'd never considered the work of a butcher. Not in the slightest bit squeamish or overly concerned for the fate of the animals, the business of butchering was as unappetising as spending time with Jane.

Interrupting his miserable thoughts, Jane came through from the back, wiping her hands on her apron. What had possessed him to let this relationship run on? A vision of Anna flashed through his mind. Struggling to dismiss it he greeted Jane with a nod.

"Hello," she said, smiling at him.

"I had to come down for a load of oats, thought I'd try and catch you. Fancy a walk by the beck?"

"Is that alright, Dad?" she asked, whisking off her apron and grabbing her shawl before Tom had time to answer. She darted round from behind the counter.

"I'm never sure what you are going to do, Fordy Robson. One minute you haven't got time for me and the next you're coming into the shop to take me out," she said, clutching at him.

"I told you on Tuesday that I had to collect some oats today from John Burgess," he mumbled as they walked out of the shop and down Bridge Street towards the beck.

Squeezing his arm, she huddled to him. "I love it when you come and surprise me, like I'm important to you."

"Jane, this isn't what you think, I've a lot to deal with now."

"No more than anybody else, surely?" she snapped.

"There are things I do to make a bit of extra money, you know to set myself up for…" he stopped, he hadn't wanted to make reference to his exploits or his future plans.

"Set you up for what? Isn't Worlds End enough for you?"

"I'm grateful for what my father provides but I don't want to be stuck behind a counter my whole life," he replied.

"Well, it's good enough for your father and mine," she said quickly. "You never mentioned this before."

Fordy had said too much already. She had this annoying way of trying to wheedle information out of him. He hadn't shared any details of how he dealt in contraband and had resisted telling her about his ambitions to breed horses or that he might soon have chance to take on more land. She knew little of what drove him.

"Well, it's not good enough for me," he replied, "I want more from life." He glanced at her; he could see her trying to work this out.

"You mean more than living up there… alone?"

She was smiling; she'd got the wrong idea. He turned away from her. Couldn't she take a hint? The previous slow burn of Fordy's emotions exploded. An image of Anna standing close beside him as they looked at her drawings, her self-assured manner and the memory of her perfume engulfed him. His temper flared. "This is impossible; you've let this plan of marrying run away with you."

Her smile disappeared; her colour rose. "You've no intention of us getting married, have you?"

"I've never mention getting wed. It's you that…"

She stopped and stood her ground. "Alice Bedford said she'd heard that you were seen…"

"I don't care about your friend's tittle-tattle," he retorted.

"My dad says I need to pin you down. He thinks you're messing me about; he says…"

Fordy had known this was going to go badly but there was no halting it now. "I'm not interested in what your dad says either," he snapped back. "Jane; it's over. In truth, it never really started. I've tried to tell you before but you don't listen."

Jane pushed at his chest with her clenched fists and marched past him back up towards the high street.

She stomped several yards then spun round, "You wait till my dad hears about this, and the rest of what I know about you," she shouted at him.

He sprinted up the hill behind her, he wanted to get the horse and cart away before she could tell her father. He didn't fancy a black eye today. As Jane ran into the butcher's shop, he jumped onto the cart.

"Get on," he said, flicking the reins to encourage the horses into a trot, panic spreading hotly through him. If he had to wait for Mary Ann there was no doubt that Tom Dennison would be at him here and now. Praying she would be ready he pulled up outside the row of houses where Nelly Stubbs lived. Not sure which one it was he scoured the small paned windows of the short row of cottages.

He looked back down the high street to see if he was being pursued and thankfully heard the sound of a door being banged shut. He saw Mary Ann with both hands full of shopping.

"Quickly, Mary Ann, here pass me your bags. I told Jane it's over and she's gone in to tell her father."

A load roar went up down the high street; Fordy looked back but couldn't see what was happening.

Mary Ann handed up a wicker basket. "Do you think he's going to come after you now?"

"Yes," said Fordy, "stop talking, hurry up."

"Oh dear," she said, passing up a brown paper parcel to Fordy and fumbling with the remaining bags. "I've bought some extra onions too…" As she passed the string bag up it slipped from her hand, the onions cascading over the cobbles.

The noise from the down the street was increasing; Fordy glanced up from helping Mary Ann. Tom Dennison was marching along the street followed by a noisy gang.

"Leave them," shouted Fordy, "he's coming, get up now, leave the bloody onions."

She gave a small shriek as Tom Dennison strode towards them.

"Take my bag," shouted Mary Ann, "look at him, I think he's going to kill you." She fumbled with her long skirt, preparing to climb up onto the cart. Fordy threw her bag behind him, risking another look at Tom's progress.

He was now in full view, striding toward Fordy and Mary Ann, bellowing curses. His face looked fit to burst, his blood-splattered apron adding menace to his intentions, not to mention the meat cleaver he was waving over his head. The crowd behind him were in high spirits; nothing broke the boredom of the day like a fist fight, especially when both combatants were known to everyone.

"Heaven preserve us," whimpered Mary Ann. "Fordy, help me," she said, grasping the side of the cart.

Jane was beside her father, screaming at Fordy, but the noise was so loud he couldn't make out what she was saying, although it wasn't difficult to guess. As Fordy reached down and dragged Mary Ann up, Tom Dennison reached the cart and he took hold of it at the back on Mary Ann's side, trying to prevent Fordy from driving off. Dapple and Sparkle were getting skittish, eager to move away from the commotion. Suddenly Jane was at Fordy's side shouting at him to get off his cart, hands clawing up at him. Luckily she couldn't reach.

Fordy grabbed Mary Ann's arm to be sure she was securely up onto the cart and, before her bottom had touched the leather seat, Fordy clicked the reins and shouted at the horses to move on. They took off, leaving Jane clutching at an empty space and Tom unable to keep his grip on the cart as he shouted a torrent of oaths at Fordy.

Once past the church, Fordy turned back and saw Tom had stopped. He was bent double, obviously trying to catch his breath. The crowd had gathered around him, onions rolled at their feet. He could see Jane was stood slightly apart from the group around her father, with her hands on her hips, as she watched him drive away.

Fordy slowed Dapple down, "Sorry, Mary Ann, are you alright?"

"A bit dishevelled," she said, between her gasps. "He'll be after catching up with you next week on market day, you know."

"Aye, but I'll be away with John then, it might give him a chance to calm down," he mumbled, not convinced that a few days would be enough. He'd have to find a way of avoiding town for a while.

"I've never liked Jane Dennison; I'm pleased you've broken with her. Now all you need to do is find a nice young lady," said Mary Ann.

Fordy's heart rate slowed down as he recovered from their ordeal but Mary Ann's words did little to settle him. He had found 'a nice young lady', but would it work out any better than this fiasco with Jane Dennison?

* * *

The following morning, after Fordy had seen to his horses, he went to help his father in the forge at Worlds End. Ben had picked up an old flat trailer from one of his neighbours; it had been cheap on account of needing substantial repairs. They had already replaced the rotted wood and it now needed firming up with metal straps. They rarely lit the forge fire these days but it was handy having it there if needed. Ben's father had been a blacksmith by trade and all of his tools remained in the smithy.

"About what happened in town yesterday…" said Fordy, throwing a rotten piece of wood into a basket. "How long do you think it'll take Tom Dennison to calm down?"

"A week or so, he'll be happy once Jane finds herself another fella," said Ben, working the bellows on the forge.

He peered at the red-hot coals. "They're about ready, pass me those two straps."

Fordy picked up the lengths of iron and placed them at the side of the fire.

"It's a blessing I'm off with John on Monday, not that our business in Saltburn is goin' to be without its problems," said Fordy, watching his father pushing and settling the metal into the heat of the coals.

"You shouldn't have let this thing with Jane go on if your heart wasn't in it. It's not fair on the girl," said Ben, pushing the straps into the coals.

"It all happened so quick. She was the one that was pushing, and with such a temper on her," said Fordy.

"Like her father then."

"Aye, I know. She was hinting she would drop me in cos of my trading but I'd rather face up to the law than be shackled to her for life."

"She'd not tell on for dealing contraband, do you think?"

"I don't know. There's more to do with Jane Dennison than you'd think."

"How do you mean?"

"I'm not rightly sure. She implied she has a hold over me with what she knows but I've told her nowt then Burgess tells me she's been seen with Andy Hawkins, who's meant to be marrying Elsie Smith. Jane's up to something, I'm certain."

Ben stopped his work as he listened to Fordy. "Andy Hawkins? You sure?" asked Ben.

"Aye, that's what he said."

"Come on, lad, let's get this job finished. It'll be dinner time soon. Mary Ann said she's doing fried mash and tu'nip with that cold beef. I'm hungry already. By God, I'm glad Tom Dennison's not our butcher, he'd be sending up a rotted carcass now you've ditched his daughter."

"Don't jest, Dad, have you seen the way he throws a side of beef onto his chopping block? It could be me on the receiving end soon."

"She'll find herself another bloke soon enough, that sort always do," replied Ben.

"Before we go in," said Fordy, laying his hand on his father's sleeve, "you, er, you haven't told Mary Ann about my involvement in John Burgess's dealings over at Saltburn, have you? You know how she frets."

"I've said nowt, lad. We'll keep that to ourselves. If it pays off, you'll be well placed to take on that land later in the year. But it's best she doesn't know. Now come on, my belly's rumbling."

CHAPTER 6

Sundays at Worlds End revolved around Mary Ann and her church going. Her preferred place for weekly worship was St Mary's at Thornton Watlass, and its distance meant most of her morning was taken up with the business. Fordy had prepared the small cart for her earlier, before continuing his preparations for his journey over to Saltburn with John Burgess the following day. When he finished checking Dapple's hooves and shoes he cleaned the horse's tack. He would have been happy to spend all morning pottering around the stables and horses but there was a job to do that couldn't be put off any longer. The dead foal needed burying, the corpse was so small the knacker man wouldn't have thanked them for the trouble of collecting it.

He threw the carcass on a sled and quickly harnessed up Sparkle to drag the foal and his tools to the fields. There was a piece of soft land beside a small copse where he could dig a hole big enough for the tiny animal. There was very little about this cold wet weather that was beneficial, but it would make digging the grave an easier task.

Marking out an area, he began to dig. It wasn't long before he cast his coat and hat onto the ground. The physical exertion was welcome and this simple task, although one he would not have chosen, was straightforward and allowed him time to reflect on the previous fortnight that had turned into a damned nightmare. Life was precarious at the best of times but how quickly had matters spiralled into chaos.

Despite all the pressing problems at hand such as the bad weather and Philpots incarceration, he was finding it difficult to keep his mind off Anna and her strange predicament. He tried to imagine what she would be doing at this very moment. Playing with her dog or sitting and talking to Mrs Dinsdale the housekeeper. Perhaps she would be painting: in reality he had no idea how a girl like Anna would pass her time.

He had hoped to find this part of the field easy to dig but when the spade kept hitting the same stone, he resorted to his pickaxe. Working his way round it, it was clear he had no chance of removing it on his own. Stopping for a breather, he stared into the shallow grave and thought about this foal he was burying. He'd had high hopes for it, a well-bred sire coupled with one of his mares should have produced strong healthy offspring. He had used the same stallion again on Gilly, this foal's mother. Hopefully, the weakness in this dead animal was a fluke but he knew all the planning in the world couldn't defeat nature. It was the same with the law, or those who administered it. Philpot's fate sat at the whim of men whose priority was maintaining their hold on the people and they were as fickle and unpredictable as the natural world.

Returning to his work, Fordy increased the size of the hole, working round the obstruction. Once he had finished he rested against the sled and took out a flask of ale. He'd broken into a sweat as he'd been digging but in a matter of minutes the sharp wind chilled his damp skin. There was no pleasure in taking any further rest; he threw the flask onto the grass, grabbed his jacket and slid it over his shoulders, shaking his upper body to warm himself again.

Returning to his task he found the foal was stiff with rigor, and manoeuvring it into its grave was proving difficult. Fordy tugged and pushed at the forlorn carcass, eventually wedging it in the hole. He arranged it so that its body lay around the large cobble that he had been unable to move, its front and back legs framing the dirty stone lump in the ground. Once he had it placed to his satisfaction, he spent a moment looking at the dead animal, his disappointment both for himself and the foal was real enough. He allowed himself to remember the hopes he'd had for it. There was nothing he would have wished for more than to have saved it from the wasting illness that had taken its life. Whatever disease it had suffered from, it had deprived the foal not only of its future, but also Fordy's pleasure in working with it as it grew and the financial return they had banked on. Dismissing such thoughts, he wasted no time in returning the soil to the hole. There was nothing to be gained in loitering and he guessed that Mary Ann would be home soon; he was ready for his dinner.

Sat in the kitchen with Mary Ann and his father, Fordy listened to Mary Ann's account of her visit to church that morning. Gossip was circulating about their exploits in town on Friday. Tom Dennison had started telling his customers that same afternoon about what a rogue Fordy was and how broken-hearted Jane was.

"What can I do?" asked Fordy. "No one's going to listen to my side of the story, I don't know why she's making such a big thing of it…"

There was a loud rapping at the door that led through to the tap room.

"More ale, landlord, if you please," a deep voice bellowed. Ben jumped up; a large party had called in for refreshments earlier. "I'll see to these fellas, pour me a mug of tea, I'll be back in a minute," said Ben, pushing away his chair and stuffing the remainder of his bread into his mouth.

"I saw Betsy Williams at church, she said I could have half a dozen hens. I was telling her about the fox getting mine. Would you have time to collect them from her next week?" asked Mary Ann, pouring out tea.

"I'll be back from Saltburn on Tuesday night, I'll pop over on Wednesday for you," answered Fordy.

"I don't know why you have to be raking all the way over t'Saltburn with John Burgess. What's it all about?"

"It's John's business. Asked me to go with him as company."

"What's he want company for? He's a grown man," queried Mary Ann.

"It's a long way I suppose," muttered Fordy, "I'm off out, better make sure your chicken run is safe if we're getting more hens."

"Before you go, did you throw a penny into that foal's grave when you buried it this morning?" asked Mary Ann, stopping Fordy's escape.

"No," he said, signing, knowing that more sharp words were to come.

"It's bad luck to bury an animal wi'out a coin, you're tempting all sorts of evil spirits to come a-visiting," she muttered, shaking her head. "I'll go up and push one into the soil this afternoon. Where did you bury it?"

"Next to the copse, you'll find it easily enough," said Fordy, heading for the door; he didn't want to get caught by any more of Mary Ann's questions.

* * *

If Sunday mornings were all about Mary Ann getting to church, for Fordy, the evenings were taken up with cockfighting. Leaving his father and Mary Ann looking after the Sunday night drinkers, he set off for Croft Farm which lay about a mile away from Worlds End. Its isolation made it the perfect location for a cock pit, no neighbours to complain about the noise and rowdy behaviour that usually accompanied an evening of cocking. Generally, a few local breeders would take along a handful of birds, offering a bit of sport and the chance of a wager. He felt sure that Tom Dennison wouldn't come looking for him out here. His father had agreed that Tom was more likely to tackle Fordy on the off-chance rather than go looking for him.

Riding down to Croft Farm, Fordy nodded in recognition to a group of village folk on their way to a Methodist meeting. Their surly response confirming Fordy's opinion that the more devout a man became, the more miserable and unfriendly he was.

In the yard at Croft Farm, Fordy tied Dapple up next to a few other horses; he could hear the noise of the early arrivals through the open door. Carrying in his saddlebags, he adjusted his eyes to the light of the barn and saw Abe and Chalky leaning up against the makeshift bar.

"Fordy, lad, over here," Jack Simms called. "'Ave y' got me those couple of bottles I asked for special?"

"Have I ever let you down, Jack?" Fordy greeted the owner of Croft Farm.

"You're a real regular lad when it comes to gin but I wouldn't like to think I were one o' your lasses waiting." The blokes in earshot laughed and Fordy had no choice but join in.

Jack Simms's larger than life character was the main reason the Newton Pit was so popular, which was fortunate as he had thirteen children to support and the income it generated was crucial. A circular raised platform was all that was needed for the birds to fight, with a low barrier running around the stage to stop the birds falling off. Fresh sand was scattered over the fight area, it helped the birds get a grip and soaked up the resulting blood.

Several benches encircled the pit, for the older punters, but most preferred to stand. The building was large enough to accommodate a substantial gathering, but tonight was a small local affair, there were no more than a couple of dozen men there.

Fordy had already scanned the room for unfamiliar faces; Jack's somewhat incriminating greeting confirmed that everyone was known to him and trustworthy.

"Here you go, Jack, your bottles. I've got tea here as well if anyone's interested."

Fordy delved into his bags and a small crowd gathered around him. Although the men favoured alcohol many took home a bag of tea to keep their wives sweet. Once his goods were sold, he threw his saddlebags aside and went over to Abe and Chalky; a tankard of ale was waiting for him.

"What was going on with you and Dennison on Friday?" asked Chalky eagerly before Fordy could draw his drink to his lips, both brothers struggling to hide their grins.

"I told Jane it was finished; I knew she'd cause a fuss. Fetched her bloody father but I managed to get away before he got hold of me," said Fordy, grimacing.

"He'll catch up with you one day," remarked Abe, shaking his head.

"Bloody man. I tell you, I'm giving up on women."

Chalky spluttered on his beer. "Aye, and you'll find me at the Methody Chapel this time next week," he said.

The bell rang for the first match, or 'main' as the cockers called them, as four gentlemen walked in. Jack was at their side instantly, making way for them to get to the bar and ensuring they had a space at the ring.

The roar of men cheering and exchanging insults over by the pit made conversation impossible; Fordy, Abe and Chalky stayed beside the bar. None of them had placed a bet on this fight, preferring to place their money on the bigger birds that fought later on in the proceedings, so were indifferent to the outcome.

Birds were matched by size and much attention was paid to the accuracy of each bird's identity. Every entry was scrutinised by the referees; notes were taken regarding its colour, markings, weight, name and ownership to avoid substitution. Once in the ring the referee's word was law. The bloody nature of the sport was at odds with the gentlemanly conduct exhibited by the cockers.

At the back of the building several men worked on their birds, trimming their feathers before weighing them. The business of cockers was a secretive world; owners and trainers guarded their methods closely. Much attention was paid to the bird's diet; the ritual that preceded a fight often meant the birds were starved for twenty-four hours before doing battle. For the punters it was an evening of pleasure but for the cockers it was a serious business: for the birds it was life and death.

The call went up for the next classes and the friends made their wagers. Fordy fancied the outsider, refusing to listen to the brothers' reasoning that the favourite bird was proven, although they appeared to be well matched in size.

As they were set beak to beak, the cocks arched their necks, drew their bodies up to their full height and engaged in their battle. It was a close-run thing as the two combatants jumped and flew at each other. Both were successful in drawing blood. The excitement grew in the crowd as shouts of encouragement and despair became more frequent. Each bird was tightly trimmed to stop its opponent latching on to it, even the combs were cut back, a tear in the flesh around the face would bleed profusely, affecting the birds' sight and make for a sticky dirty fight.

After several minutes of intense combat, the favourite bird was struggling. He stopped to gasp for air, his beak stretched wide; he stood for a moment panting as his opponent prepared to make his final lunge. Before they engaged the vanquished owner shouted, "Submit," indicating his acceptance of a defeat, and jumped into the ring to retrieve his bird as the referee proclaimed victory for the remaining cock.

The crowd split in two. The jubilant waved their chits in the air; the disgruntled shuffled over to the bar to replenish their tankards. Fordy felt his inside jacket pocket again, always conscious of his money bag, even though he was among friends.

"How much did you win, bloody crafty beggar. Who slipped you that tip?" asked Chalky.

Fordy tapped his nose.

"I've a dead cert on the final main," said Abe, "come and look at the creature." He led the way over to the tables where the birds were shown off before fighting.

Fordy felt a tap on his shoulder. It was Jack Simms.

"You got a minute?" he whispered in Fordy's ear.

Fordy followed him to a dark corner.

"Do y' know yon excise bloke from Crakehall 'as been on the prowl again? Seems like he's been given word to break a smuggling ring round Bedale."

"How do you know this?"

"Some of the lads," Jack said, nodding to the other side of the room. "Don't ask me the details but you need to be careful. Say nowt and stay sharp."

"Thanks for the word, Jack," nodded Fordy. He followed the brothers to look at the birds for the next main but neither of them took his fancy.

"Come on, Fordy, stake some o' that money you've just won," urged Abe, "I tell you; I've been told yon bird'll win by miles."

"I'll sit this one out, watch you win this time," Fordy acceded, stepping away from Abe.

As the fight progressed it was clear things weren't going well for Abe's bird, when the owner suddenly jumped onto the ring and snatched his injured bird. There were shouts of foul play from both the punters and the owner.

Fordy made for the back of the room and picked up his empty saddlebags as the commotion over the outcome of the main grew. He saw Chalky talking to one of the four well-dressed gents that had come in earlier. Fordy was reluctant to approach them, you never knew what deals people were striking, but he raised his hand towards Chalky and gave his companion a nod. Chalky stepped over to Fordy's side.

"You going?" he asked.

"Aye, I've had the best of the night, leave these idiots to scrap it out. Look, I've a spare wrapper o' tea here. Tek it for your mother," said Fordy, handing out a small brown packet.

"Thanks, Fordy, she'll be glad of it."

"Who's the bloke?" asked Fordy quietly, nodding over at Chalky's neighbour.

"It's Giles Redworth from Huntby Hall. I'll introduce you," offered Chalky to Fordy's surprise.

Chalky gestured to Redworth who walked over to them.

"Giles, this Fordy Robson. He keeps Worlds End hostelry o'er on No Mans Moor with his father, but he's a horse man at heart," said Chalky.

The use of this gentleman's first name wasn't wasted on Fordy and he looked closely at him as he offered his hand in response to Giles's open palm.

"Fordy, this is Giles Redworth. You remember I told you I was doing some work up at Huntby this week?"

"How do you do?" said Giles, with a friendly smile.

"Hello," said Fordy, with a small deferential nod.

"Chalky told me there's usually some good sport here on a Sunday night so we thought we'd take a look. He was right, there's been some good birds put through their paces, and I've won a guinea or two."

As friendly as Giles Redworth might be the gulf in their social standing was clear, even if Chalky was addressing him by his first name. Redworth's clipped manner of speaking and his fine clothes separated him from Fordy and Chalky but the cock pit was often a place where folks of diverse social standing rubbed shoulders with each other. The usual class barriers might drop for an hour or two but they were soon re-established once out of the heady confines of the gaming enclosure, Fordy reminded himself.

"Horses, is it, that interest you?" asked Giles, keeping the conversation going.

"Yes, sir. Trying my hand at a bit of breeding," replied Fordy, unsure why this man should be interested in him. He turned to Chalky, "I need to be away now," he explained.

"Of course," said Chalky, rather awkwardly.

"Pleasure to meet you, sir," said Fordy, turning to Giles Redworth again. They gave each other a quick nod before Fordy made to leave. He glanced across the room to see Abe was still in the middle of the disagreement about the outcome of the fight and, as Fordy made for the door, he saw that Abe's 'dead cert', now lay twitching on the pile of the evening's fatalities.

Their scrawny crumpled bodies, no longer full of bold aggression, now were fit only for the dung heap. An image of his stiff dead foal flashed through his head. The stench of death and blood caught in the back of Fordy's throat as he walked past the pile of carcasses and out into the fresh chill of the night. He hesitated and took in a few long low gasps of air. He had never felt the atmosphere of a cock pit to be oppressive before but tonight there was no pleasure in the half-lit den of sport.

His mood was low on the short ride home. Jack Simms's words played in his head about the excise men wanting to crack the local smuggling ring. Fordy knew he was as dispensable in the game of smuggling as a defeated cock at the pit. A concerted effort by the local militia could easily disrupt the local trade. A few fellows would be brought before the bench and made an example of. Just as Philpots had been seized, now incarcerated in York Gaol, facing a hopeless future.

Even Anna's fate was out of her own hands, women fared poorly against men. Her father could easily control his daughter's destiny, should he put his mind to it. Fordy knew women were forced into marriages against their will. The chances of Anna being removed from Kings Pasture House as quickly as she had arrived were very real. Anna was as trapped as the Philpots, and Fordy could feel the threat of unfair justice at his door for the first time in his life. He knew that Sir Robwyn, and others of his standing and connections, could and would ride well-shod over anyone of inferior standing to suit their own purposes.

Lights moving across an open field caught his eye; he pulled up Dapple as he watched two glowing dots bob along over the hedge. Who on earth would be travelling over the fields with lights? Certainly not poachers, it was barely ten o'clock. His first thoughts were that it was a couple of characters up to no good. For a moment he remembered Mary Ann's words about evil spirits. He gave a quick snort of amusement. Mary Ann and her superstitions might be enough to make some men stay at home all night, but Fordy wasn't going to fall under her fanciful wives' tales.

Watching the flickering lights disappear in the near distance, Fordy shivered, and felt for the hard coins in his breast pocket again, they gave him a fleeting sense of security. He buttoned his coat up and gave Dapple a kick. Despite his bravado he knew home was the safest place tonight.

CHAPTER 7

Halfway up the hill Fordy stopped to take his breath. The effort of walking on the light slippery sand was unexpected; progress was further impeded by the annoying coarse tufts of reeds that grew everywhere. He placed himself on a level piece of ground as he regained his composure. The wind did its damnedest to knock him over.

Down below there were two rough looking fellows, watching him, pointing and laughing. Spurred on, he continued his climb.

At the summit, this unfamiliar environment assaulted his senses. Gasping for air through the icy gusts that blew in from the sea, he stood tall, taking in the view. The vastness of the ocean was unbelievable. As the wind took his balance again, he laughed out loud. Fordy realised that no one could hear him over the roar of the sea and he let out several more whoops of delight.

In the distance he could see a couple of large schooners out at sea that were fighting the weather. Nearer, on the shoreline, a small rowing boat was being dragged out of the swirling water by several men.

Directly beneath, he saw the purple slate roof of the Ship Inn, situated on a piece of slightly raised ground. From Fordy's vantage point at the top of Nab's Head there appeared to be nothing to stop the sea flooding straight into the inn at high tide. To the south, sheer cliffs rose up, encircling the vast sandy beach. Northwards the bay opened up and sand dunes swept back into open countryside.

This was Saltburn, well known in the northern counties for smuggling but few people ever penetrated the security that guarded this remote coastal village. Lookouts were always strategically placed along the exposed part of the bay; any unwelcome visitors were intercepted long before getting close.

Contraband had been brought over the North Sea from the continent and landed on these long shallow beaches for decades. At present the business was controlled by Jim Adams, the tentacles of his enterprise reached far inland.

Many had thought the trade would die out once hostilities with the French had concluded. But the debt from the war was enormous and taxes remained high. There was no will in the country to stop the trading; every strand of society was involved, womenfolk looking for tea and perfume, the working man searching for liquor, even the gentry demanding silks.

Fordy was killing time waiting for John while he conducted his business with Jim Adams. That morning, after a hurried breakfast, they'd left their lodgings in Skelton, setting out in good time for Saltburn. About a mile away from their destination they were challenged by a couple of men who were well equipped with sturdy staffs and a gruff manner. John had dismounted and spoken to them quickly and quietly, confirming who he was and his reason for visiting Adams, explaining that Fordy was his friend, there to help. The men nodded and waved them on.

Riding into this unsettling environment, Fordy had heeded the advice that John gave him earlier.

"Don't say anything and keep your eyes down," was John's directive. "As soon as we arrive they'll take the horses off us."

"I'm not so sure about that," said Fordy.

"You'll have no choice; they'll only give us the horses back once the business is concluded to Adams' satisfaction."

Fordy didn't answer, involuntarily stroking Dapple's neck.

As predicted, their horses were taken the moment they dismounted. Before being led away, John told Fordy, "While you wait, climb up there," pointing to the small hill that sat behind the Ship Inn. "The view's spectacular."

Fordy had taken John's suggestion; this vantage point was the perfect place for a stranger to understand why Saltburn was so successful as the hub of the smuggling enterprise. Perhaps more important for Fordy was the revelation of the alien landscape. As the seagulls swooped above him Fordy's thoughts soared too. What a contrast this was to Worlds End. He crouched down on his haunches, holding onto the dry grasses to prevent being blown over. He tasted the salt on his lip and felt damp air that seemed to cling to his skin.

He thought of the cockfight two days earlier and the growing sense of unease that had overcome him that night. It would have been easy to give John backword and not accompany him on this trip. But it was as dangerous for John as it was for himself. And, apart from his loyalty, he too had money resting on this venture. They had agreed from the onset that Adams wasn't to know of Fordy's involvement. As far as Adams knew, it was Burgess who was helping underwrite this risky business.

Several shiploads of luxurious goods were being brought in from the east later in the year. Silks, perfumes and spices, not your average fare for the north country dealers. Money had been needed upfront and John Burgess had been approached to support the venture. When Fordy had heard of the scheme he was keen to put some cash up himself. Standing here and understanding the enormity of this enterprise, Fordy couldn't understand why he hadn't asked John for more details but his trust in John was so complete he hadn't thought of questioning it.

What would Anna think of his involvement in this scheme? He would see her again tomorrow night. The thought thrilled him. He must remember to comb his hair and wash his hands before setting off to Kings Pasture. Recalling her cosy retreat in the garden, he pictured himself sitting on the soft chair, drinking wine and watching her playing with her dog.

There was movement and noise below; John and a group of men had come out of the inn.

Fordy immediately descended the steep hill and found John, accompanied by a small man, on the shore looking out to sea.

"This is my trusted companion, Fordy Robson," said John, emphasising the word trusted and holding out his hand, encouraging Fordy to join them.

"Hello, Robson, I'm Jim Adams, good to meet you. Burgess's friends are my friends," said Adams, taking Fordy's hand and smiling, but avoiding Fordy's eye. With the firmest of handshakes, this man had intimidation mastered.

"Glad to meet you, Mr Adams," said Fordy, trying to stop from swallowing too hard.

"We'll be away now, I hope all goes well next month," said John.

Adams shot Fordy a sharp glance before turning back to John, "Don't you worry about that, my friend, it's all taken care of," he said, as he raised his arm towards his men.

One of Adams's lackeys brought their horses forward; they had been fed and watered and even brushed down. John and Fordy mounted without hesitation but when they turned to bid their farewell, Adams had already disappeared.

Climbing up out of Saltburn they passed several men who gave them a curt nod before quickly looking away. On the only road out of the place they wove and twisted their way up, away from the coast, passing a large white house on their left as they ascended the hill.

"That's where Adams lives; they reckon there are tunnels going all the way down to the Ship Inn from here. It's how they get the contraband up from the beach," said John, as they maintained their pace and their horses took the strain.

Inland the weather started to close in. Their journey took them over the open expanse of the Cleveland hills, skirting along land just south of the River Tees. Passing through isolated villages and hamlets, the sleet that had initially hampered them turned to steady snow on the higher exposed ground.

Despite the harsh conditions they rode hard for several hours and spoke little other than acknowledging fellow travellers.

Back on familiar territory they found that snow had engulfed the bridge over the Swale at Catterick. Fordy and John's horses slowly picked their way over the low rise. As the heavy flakes swirled, Fordy and John's white hunched figures could easily have been mistaken for restless spirits from the dead patrolling the river crossing. One moment visible, the next, disappearing into a snowy world.

John glanced up and reached out to Fordy, tapped his shoulder and pointed. Fordy nodded and together they rounded the front of the building that had appeared through the filthy weather.

A young man rushed out to them, a hessian sack pulled tight over his head. "You here for the night, gentlemen?" he shouted, taking their reins with his spare hand as the travellers dismounted.

"No, we're here to thaw our bones, should be away within the hour. No need to unsaddle 'em, a bite of hay will put them on till we're off," replied John.

"Aye, sir; do y' know y' way to t'tap room?"

"We do, lad, many thanks," said Fordy as they headed for the entrance.

Guttering torches, offering almost no light, were mounted at either side of the main door into the George Inn. The men pushed open the large studded door into the warmth; once it was firmly shut; each raised himself up to his full height and shook like waterlogged dogs. Splashes of muddy sleet covered the floor as they removed their full-length oilskins.

John rubbed his arms in an attempt to bring life back to them. "We'll take a drink and a bite," he said to Fordy. Neither of them noticed the landlord over by the fireplace, stoking the embers and observing their noisy wet entrance.

"Is it John?" asked the landlord from his fireside spot.

"Aye, it is," answered the older man looking over to the source of the voice as he removed his scarf and flattened his hair.

"I thowt I rec'gnised that voice o' yours."

Reaching his hand out to the landlord, John greeted his old acquaintance, "Good to see you, Alf, we've ridden over from the coast, I know we're only five miles from home but by God, we're in sore need of refreshment."

"Tek a drink first, then I'll have a word in the kitchen. They've been cooking chickens this afternoon," said Alf, moving towards the tap room.

"That'll be grand, a couple of glasses of wine with the poker in 'em would be most welcome. This is Fordy Robson, I think you'll know his father, Ben, from No Mans Moor," said John, turning to his young friend.

Alf reached out his hand and took Fordy's with a strong grip. "Aye, lad, I know Ben. How are things up at Worlds End?"

"We're all well, apart from this damned weather," answered Fordy, cupping his hands to his mouth and gently blowing on them. Both men stood over the fire taking in the heat.

Alf poured two glasses of red wine and took them back to the fireplace. He pushed the long poker into the heart of the fire then pulled two chairs up to the hearth, "Here, sit down and warm y'selves through."

Both men did his bidding and willingly availed themselves of the warmth the burning logs offered. Alf called over to a girl in the corner, "Jenny, take these gentlemen's hats and coats and hang 'em next to the kitchen range." Turning back to John and Fordy, he added, "They'll not dry out, but it might take the edge off 'em a bit before you set out again." He took the red-hot poker out of the fire and plunged it into each goblet of wine until steam rose from them.

"There you go, get them down you, you'll feel better in a few minutes," said Alf, handing over the drinks and heading for the bar, shouting as he went, "Jenny... Jenny, we'll have a capon for each of these gentlemen."

"I'd have kept going if I was on my own," said Fordy, "but I'm glad we've stopped. I thought my hands were going to drop off." He looked down at his swollen red fingers. The two fingertips that he'd hit with the hammer a few weeks back throbbed with the cold.

"If I'd known the weather was going to turn bad again I'd never have taken this journey," said John. "You know the problem with stopping off here?"

"What?" asked Fordy.

"We'll be asleep before we know it. It's going to be a real wrench going back out into that snow and riding up to Bedale."

"You daft bugger, that's why I'd never 'ave stopped in the first place," remonstrated Fordy.

Both men were silent for a while as they stared into the amber glow of the high-banked fire, the warmth stinging their eyes.

Trying to stop himself falling asleep, Fordy moved his legs and glanced over at John, who had given into the heat, his eyes shut and body slowly sliding down his chair. Fordy smiled at John's comical position but slowly he began to drop off and slide down too. Both men were asleep when Alf brought their food.

"Come on now, lads, food's here," he boomed, clattering two plates onto the table. "Let me refill your glasses," he added.

Neither man spoke as they ate. Washing his final mouthful down with a drink of wine Fordy resumed their conversation.

"How did you first come across Adams? What induced you to chance your money with a man like that?"

"His Grace," replied John, in a matter-of-fact voice.

"Duke of Malbury?" asked Fordy, raising his eyebrows.

"Aye, his Grace and Adams make odd bedfellows," laughed John.

Fordy shuffled in his chair and stared at John, "Why didn't you tell me this before?"

"You didn't ask," answered John, "you didn't need to

know. These fellas at Saltburn don't hesitate in silencing a loose tongue."

"But the risks…" muttered Fordy.

"Course they're high, you damned fool, but so are the returns…if the plan goes well."

"Do you trust Adams?" asked Fordy tentatively. "He smiles too much for my liking."

"Aye, he does," said John, nodding in agreement. "I don't trust him. But he has his Grace breathing down his neck and he'll not dare cheat me."

"You sure about that?" asked Fordy. John didn't reply. Fordy hoped John's optimism was well placed.

"We'd best be off, lad, or we'll be here all night," said John, emptying his glass and slowly lifting himself out of his chair. "I've about seized up after all that riding." He carefully straightened himself up.

Fordy's youthful body had coped with the rigours of the day with comparative ease. His biggest complaint was leaving the comfort of the fireside.

"I'll settle up with Alf," said John, going in search of the landlord.

"Hello," said a breathless female voice behind Fordy. He turned to see the girl Alf had told to hang up their coats. She was struggling with their steaming garments, trying to lay them over a chair.

"Hello," said Fordy, with a nod, "let me help you," he added as his own coat dropped to the floor.

"Are you not staying the night?" she asked with a sly grin.

"Er, no, we're off now," said Fordy, shaking the garment out.

"If you're ever passing again, ask for me, Jenny's my name," she said, swinging from side to side and biting her lip.

"Right, thanks, I will…"

"Fordy, come on, let's be on our way," called John.

"If you'll excuse me," said Fordy, backing away from her, buckling up his coat. She stood and watched him, ignoring someone who was calling her name from a back room. Pulling his hat on Fordy gave her a nod and followed John outside.

"I've never seen owt like it. You and women…! It hurts an old man like me to watch you rebuffing them."

"I didn't rebuff her, she's a fine-looking lass."

"Wait till you get a broken nose, then the lasses might not fancy you so much."

"Why would I get a broken nose?" demanded Fordy as they made their way round to the yard where their horses were waiting.

"You've already got Dennison after your blood. You've done well not to get a good hiding the way you go through the lasses."

Fordy gave the stable lad a couple of coppers before mounting his horse. They left the inn in haste; soon the bitter cold would bite into their bodies again. The snow was still falling as they headed down through Catterick, which sat eerily quiet in contrast to its usual bustle of activity.

Three miles down the road at St. Anne's Cross they pulled up their horses. Fordy reached out his hand and shook John's.

"I'll see you next week," he said.

"Aye, thanks, lad," said John Burgess, squeezing Fordy's hand tightly.

John's firm handshake brought reassurance, in contrast to Adams's chilling one.

The snow was now inches deep as Fordy completed the final part of the journey alone. The country had endured several hard winters in Fordy's lifetime but this one just didn't know when to end.

At the bottom of Bowbridge Lane Fordy passed the stone-pillared entrance to Kings Pasture House. Where would Anna be now, surely not in the garden shed? He pictured her sat in front of a roaring fire with Jasper snuggled at her side. By God, he'd give a month's supply of tea to be with her.

The snow suddenly stopped, the clouds cleared and the moon shone, its translucent light reflected by the layer of pure white snow. He turned down over Hollow Moor. Wet marshland with stunted trees and stagnant ponds lay on both sides of the track. In the summer hundreds of bulrushes grew here, but tonight all that was hidden under inches of snow.

The reassurance and warmth he felt when he left John Burgess had ebbed away, the cold was piercing his bones. Dapple was exhausted and his progress was slowing. Fordy didn't have the heart to kick the horse on after such a long ride.

Eventually he reached Crakehall. The large village green now resembled a huge white blanket, tucked in on all sides by houses of various shapes and sizes. Most folks would be abed by now and many houses sat in darkness. His silent vigil was broken by laughter and lights from the Bay Horse Inn.

He thought of his father and Mary Ann back at Worlds End. Fordy had no idea of the hour; he knew they would be worried about him.

"Now then, lad, where you off to on a night like this?" A shadowy figure lit by a lantern appeared at Fordy's side.

"Now then, Joe," replied Fordy, recognising Joe Ellis.

"Thou must be courting to be out on a night like this, Fordy, lad." Joe gave a loud throaty laugh.

Fordy didn't answer and watched him shuffle away through the snow to the inn. Nosey old fool, why couldn't folk mind their own damned business?

"Come on, Dapple, not far now," he urged his horse on, squeezing his knees into the animal, hoping the horse might respond with a quicker pace. "There'll be a tub of warm oats and a rack of hay for you when we get home."

The horse's ears pricked and he seemed to quicken his pace a little. Fordy kept the conversation up, encouraging the horse and keeping his thoughts off how cold he was.

Finally, Worlds End came into view. Silhouetted by the light of the moon the sight lifted both the horse and rider's demeanour; there was no need to encourage Dapple now. Rounding the end of the building they turned in through the archway into the open yard.

"Heavens above, lad, where have you been?" cried Mary Ann, holding a lantern aloft.

"What are you doing outside?" Fordy asked her, as he dismounted.

"We've been out looking for you," said his father, also holding a lantern in his hand.

"We were slowed down by the weather, you shouldn't have worried," explained Fordy.

"We've been worried sick here. Ben, take his horse while I get this lad into the kitchen," said Mary Ann, taking Fordy by the arm, leading him into the warmth.

CHAPTER 8

With no cloud cover through the night the temperature had plummeted. By morning the previous day's snow had become a crisp slippery nuisance. Inside the stables at Worlds End, Fordy took refuge from the cold. Tending the horses, he noticed Dapple was playing with his hoof on the floor. With closer inspection he saw the front right shoe was loose.

"Damn it, it must have come loose with that long ride yesterday," muttered Fordy, laying a steadying hand on the horse's back. That buggered his plans for the day. He'd have to use Sparkle for the day's work.

Ben was already at the breakfast table when Fordy went into the house, it had been a late start on account of Fordy's delayed return home from Saltburn the previous night.

"Would y' have time to take Dapple down to Bob Sparrow's this morning?" Fordy asked his father.

"I've got my beer delivery later and I wanted to see them lads, I need a word wi'em; that last leg of ale was like vinegar at the bottom of the barrel," answered Ben.

"That's alright, I'll do it this afternoon. I promised I'd get Mary Ann's chickens this morning," said Fordy, stretching back in his chair and yawning. "By God, Dad, it was a real eye opener over at Saltburn yesterday. You've never seen owt like it, the sea stretches for miles and miles. And the wind, it fair whips through you…"

Mary Ann plonked their plates down in front of them. Fordy was pleased to see the usual thick fatty slices of bacon had been supplemented with a couple of sausages on this wintery morning.

"Thanks, Mary Ann, this is a right plateful, I'm starving. When we got to Saltburn…" Fordy was interrupted.

"I still don't know why you had to go traipsing off with Burgess, we've plenty to do here," snapped Mary Ann. "Your poor father had to go to Bedale yesterday and I had to serve on in the tap room…"

There was a loud splash at the sink and Mary Ann looked up. "Lucy, what in heaven's name are you doing with that ham? I told you to change the water…" She went over to Lucy who was struggling with a joint of meat almost as big as herself.

"Something's rattled her this morning," grimaced Fordy.

"Best to avoid her today, I think." Ben glanced up, making sure Mary Ann was out of earshot. "How did the business go?"

"Fine, as far as it went, I left John to handle the matter, it's all still on course, they've got plenty of backers now so it's a waiting game. Hell, they're a rough crowd over on the coast, there was even…"

"What are you two whispering about?" Mary Ann cut in, "Fordy, are you off to Thirn for my chickens?"

Both men ate up their breakfasts quickly before sidling out whilst Mary Ann was in the pantry, reprimanding Lucy for some small misdemeanour.

In the yard Ben helped Fordy get ready to go for Mary Ann's poultry. "Can you give me a hand, lad? My fingers are as numb as carrots this morning," asked Ben, trying to fasten the small straps that secured the basket behind the saddle which would carry the chickens.

"Let me 'ave a look." Fordy's extra height gave him a better angle to complete the fiddly task. "How did Bedale go yesterday? Did you share a jar with Abe and Chalky?" Fordy asked.

"I did, and I called in to see their father, his 'ands are fair buggered now, in a worse state than mine, he can't even hold an 'ammer."

"Anything said about Jane?" asked Fordy, adjusting the stirrups.

"Chalky said she's not been seen since last Friday when Tom chased you down the street. Folks are still laughing 'bout that," Ben gave a chuckle. "Tha'll know 'bout it if he gets hold o' you."

"He'd do well to rein that girl of his in, rather than bothering me," said Fordy, giving the girth a final check before mounting Sparkle. "I'll be off now, Dad, shouldn't be too long." Fordy nodded to his father, turning the horse towards the arch that led out of the yard.

The roads were quiet, the unexpected snow and the piercing cold deterring travellers.

He daren't kick Sparkle into a trot, the ground was too hard and slippery. Thirn was only a mile away but he could carve a few hundred yards off if he took the footpath past Thirn Grange. Somebody had already been up the track, the snow showed signs of a horse and cart, so Fordy knew the route was passable.

Fordy's thoughts drifted to Anna and his meeting with her tonight. How cosy it would be in her garden room, she'd have the fire lit and wine waiting. It was far more comforting to think of her than the many troubles that had occurred recently. He was even beginning to think fondly of her small dog, if only he could remember its name…

"Fordy Robson." A voice boomed out.

"Fordy Robson, Fordy Robson." A second voice echoed the first.

Fordy looked up ahead, Tom Dennison and his gormless son Nathan blocked his path. He'd been distracted with his daydreaming and hadn't seen them approaching.

Fordy pulled Sparkle to a halt, quickly looking behind him in the hope that someone else was on the road. No such luck; he was alone with the two Dennisons. They were out on their deliveries; boxes were piled up in the cart behind them. Fordy pulled on Sparkle's rein in an attempt to turn round and get away from them, but the ground was so slippery that the horse skidded and was unable to get a secure footing. Nathan had quickly jumped down and ran along the snowy roadside towards Fordy, avoiding the icy road. Lurching forward he caught hold of Sparkle's reins. For being such a numb skull, the lad could move quickly enough if he wanted thought Fordy. This was all happening too fast.

"What do you want? What are you playing at jumping on me like this? Get off my horse, Nathan," yelled Fordy, trying to jerk the reins out of Nathan's grip. Seconds later Tom was at Fordy's side, clutching at his leg.

"Get off me," Fordy shouted as he tried to kick Dennison off his keg while urging Sparkle to walk on. He might have stood a chance of getting away on Dapple, but Sparkle was young and flighty, he started to rear backward, alarmed at the wild noisy behaviour of the Dennisons.

"We want a word with you," said Tom Dennison.

"Yeh, we want a word with you," Nathan repeated, copying everything his father said.

"What about?" Fordy knew if he got off his horse he'd take a beating so he tightened his grip round Sparkle with his legs as Dennison kept tugging at him. "Get off me. If you've got something to say get on with it," said Fordy.

"I've got something to say," Dennison shouted, "our Jane's having a baby."

"Jane's having a baby, Jane's having a baby," bellowed Nathan, spraying Fordy with spittle as he jumped up and down with excitement, flapping the horse's reins.

"That's nothing to do with me," said Fordy, doing his best to steady Sparkle. The icy conditions weren't helping, the horse struggling to get a good grip on the road, as Nathan hung on. He was a big lad, all brawn, he'd won the town's strong man contest at the last two summer fairs; with no brains, folk smiled kindly on the lad and his meagre achievements. But today Fordy cursed him.

"She told me last night that she's having a bairn. You've bin courting 'er since Christmas. You take me for a fool?" demanded Dennison, still trying to dislodge Fordy.

"Courting since Christmas, courting since Christmas," Nathan shouted.

It was too much for Sparkle; the horse swung to the side. Nathan lost his footing on the ice and Sparkle dragged the bulky butcher's boy across the ground. The movement was so sharp that Fordy lost one of the stirrups and began to slide off his saddle.

If Nathan had let go of the reins, Fordy may have been able to right himself and move Sparkle away from them but Nathan had wrapped the reins around his hands and his weight was enough to restrict the horse.

Dennison saw Fordy slipping over and lumbered around the horse to grab him by his arm. With nothing to get hold of to steady himself, Fordy was easily brought to the floor by Dennison.

"I've got you," spat Dennison as Fordy landed on the hard icy road with a thud. "You o'er-sexed young stallion."

Nathan could hardly contain himself, "Young stallion, young stallion."

"Shut up, Nathan," shouted Dennison, hauling Fordy to his feet. "Make sure you keep hold of his horse," he commanded his son.

Dennison took Fordy by the collar and pushed his fist up under Fordy's chin. Moving in close Dennison said in a low voice, "We was on our way up t'see you at Worlds End so it's lucky we've bumped into you."

Fordy tried to pull Dennison's hands off but the man's grip tightened.

"I don't know anything about a baby, it can't…." Fordy tried to answer.

With that Dennison aimed several fierce punches at Fordy's stomach which robbed him of his breath. He took the blows to his body like a rag doll.

Dennison stopped, his grip on Fordy still iron tight. "I'm giving you one week to recover from this beating. Then you'll come down to Bedale, ask Jane to marry you and get a license sorted."

He then aimed a final blow at Fordy's head. Fordy fell to ground and Tom Dennison finished his assault with several kicks in the chest. Fordy's crumpled body offered no resistance.

When Fordy came too he was alone. He could hardly breathe and the pain he felt when he tried to move was excruciating. He lay there, on the freezing grass verge, in and out of consciousness until a farm boy came past. The lad was reluctant to approach Fordy at first.

"Where are you heading?" gasped Fordy, through shots of pain.

"Up t'farm, I work there," said the lad, raising his head towards the house and buildings on the near horizon. The boy was jumping from foot to foot, eager to be away.

"Tell your master to come and help. Quick!" Fordy groaned with the effort of speaking.

Blackness overcame Fordy again, the next thing he knew he was being lifted none too gently onto a flat cart.

"You're alright, Fordy, we'll get you home," said a local voice. Fordy turned to see Ged Lowes who farmed Thirn Grange and was one of the Worlds End regulars.

Fordy was conscious but dazed by the pain and shock, vaguely aware of the movement of the cart and the brightness of the sky. At one point he thought he heard men and women shouting as he was pulled off the sacks he had been laid on. Rough hands grabbed at him, the loud voices continued, the movement was different now but the pain was constant.

* * *

When he awoke he found himself in bed propped by half a dozen pillows. He lay in a daze, not sure what day or time it was until the door latch gently opened and Mary Ann appeared carrying a tray.

"Hello, have you woken at last?" she asked gently.

"I'm not sure I can move," said Fordy, shuffling in the bed.

"Were you set upon by footpads?" Mary Ann asked, as she laid the tray next to the bed, fussing over his hair and stroking his bruised face.

"Sort of. What time of day is it?"

"Just turned eight, come on, let's try you with the broth."

"Morning or night?"

"It's heading towards night, you've been here all afternoon."

Fordy tried to edge himself up the bed as pains shot through his chest, "I can't move, Mary Ann."

She picked up another pillow and helped him to sit up a little. As he groaned with pain his father appeared at the door.

Together they slid a protesting Fordy into an almost upright position.

"I'm glad to see you're awake lad, what happened?" asked his father.

"It was Tom Dennison. He's got it into his head that I've given Jane a baby."

"What? Have you?"

"No, I never bedded her."

Mary Ann gently spooned the now cold liquid into Fordy in silence, forcing him to finish every last drop. Ben paced around the room, waiting for Fordy to finish his food.

"I'll go and get you a cup of tea," said Mary Ann, lifting the tray from Fordy's lap and leaving.

"Alright lad," said Ben, coming close to Fordy. "As long as I have your word that the bairn's not yours, I'll back you all the way. I'll go down to Bedale in the morning and have it out with Dennison. I don't care how big and strong he is I'm not having him attacking you like this."

Fordy stifled a laugh but the pain was excruciating.

"What you laughing at?"

"You… getting so cross. Please, Dad, don't get into a fight with him, he's dangerous."

"He won't hit me, don't worry," said Ben.

Fordy lay back against his pillows; every action brought pain, even sighing. He closed his eyes and fell asleep. He was woken almost immediately by footsteps on the stairs. Mary Ann was followed by Dr Hewitt into the bedroom.

"Well, Fordy, what have you been up to?" the doctor asked as Fordy tried to lift himself up a little.

"I met with a disgruntled fellow, so it seems." Fordy looked over at Mary Ann who hovered beside the bed. The doctor checked every limb and ran his hands over Fordy's head.

"Have you passed any blood or coughed any up?" His manner was brisk.

Fordy looked to Mary Ann for the answer.

"No, Doctor, nothing at all."

Running his fingers gently over Fordy's torso, the doctor gave his verdict, "A couple of broken ribs here, you'll be in a fair bit of pain for a week or two."

Fordy groaned.

"Mary Ann, wrap a tight bandage round him, for support, and I'll give you a small bottle of laudanum, to ease the pain."

Looking at Fordy, he said, "Get out of bed tomorrow, I know it'll hurt but you'll mend all the quicker."

"When can I get on a horse?" asked Fordy, thinking of his arrangements to meet Anna that evening.

"Try getting downstairs first, then see how keen you are to be on horseback," said the doctor curtly.

"Would you take a cup of tea, Doctor?" asked Mary Ann.

"No, I'll be away. Iris Thomas is having trouble, on with her tenth. I told old Arthur to leave her alone but it's like talking to a stone wall. She'll do well to survive this," he mumbled to himself. "Good day to you, Mary Ann, I'll see myself out." With a nod of his head he left the room.

"That's a relief, I'm sure." Mary Ann sat on the bed and took Fordy's hand. Fordy relaxed back into the mound of pillows. "Who would have known broken ribs could be so painful," he moaned. "I reckon Tom Dennison knew exactly what he was doing. But I'll not marry Jane, even if he breaks all my limbs."

Ben had disappeared down to his customers in the tap room. Mary Ann gave Fordy a few drops of medicine and sat with him till he dozed off.

At first Fordy slept well but he was woken by the pain.

Mary Ann had left another dose on his bedside table; with effort he reached for it and drank it. The effect was immediate, his body felt light and the discomfort subsided.

He worried that he'd let Anna down. What would she have done tonight? How long would she have waited for him? Had her anticipation turned to anger as she listened for his knock at the door? He pictured her trudging through the gardens in the snow, with that dog tucked under her arm.

How was he going to explain his injuries? Would he ever get the chance to see her and talk to her again?

In the night Anna came to him in his dreams. She sat at the low window seat and watched while he slept. As he became restless she sat on the bed with him, taking hold of his hand and soothing him.

* * *

The following morning Mary Ann was insistent that he get out of bed. With his ablutions seen to and a breakfast of scrambled egg, Ben and Mary Ann helped him up.

They positioned a chair to face the window and managed to install him in the seat. His view stretched out over the flat horizon towards the hills that he and John Burgess had travelled on their journey to Saltburn. To his right he could see the road that led to Bedale and the rising land where Kings Pasture House was. Would Anna keep looking out for him? Or would she dismiss him as a ruffian and forget him? Exhausted from the exertion of moving he soon found a comfortable position and drifted off to sleep.

A clattering at the door woke Fordy; his father had brought a pot of tea up.

"How are you feeling?" asked Ben.

"Sore," said Fordy with a grimace. "How did your trip to Bedale go?"

"Interesting," said Ben, as he pulled up a stool.

"There's no doubt about Jane, she's starting to show. After he'd given you the good hiding he'd gone back home and asked her if she was certain the child was yours. But she wouldn't answer; now Tom isn't so sure."

"I wish he'd been bloody sure before he knocked seven bells out of me."

"I said the same to him, he could have killed you. But he assured me he only wanted to crack a few ribs. He says you'll be up and about in no time."

Leaning back into the cushions Fordy let out a long slow sigh. "So who is the father then?"

"Not a clue." Ben shook his head.

"Am I safe now?"

"Yes, and he sent me away with a basket full of meat by way of apology."

"What a dolt he is, I'd rather not have had the beating."

CHAPTER 9

Sitting by the open window of his bedroom recovering from his injuries, Fordy had plenty of time to consider the events of the last few weeks. Anna had never been far from his thoughts but the erratic behaviour of Jane was troubling to him. It was easy to understand she needed a man to wed if there was a baby coming. But who was the father? If Andy was the father, why wasn't she expecting him to marry her? Was there another man in Jane's busy life? Nobody could keep a secret like that for long in a place like Bedale. The matter would unravel itself in time.

Jane bothered him during his waking hours but Anna invaded his dreams. She hovered around his room as he slept, sometimes she lay beside him, other times she sat in his chair, watching him or gazing wistfully out of the window.

His obsession with her was heightened by the fear he may never see her again. Tom Dennison had said he would give Fordy a week to recover and go to Bedale. He hung onto these words, although Kings Pasture would be his destination not the butcher's shop.

After a couple of days confined to his room, he attempted the stairs, gingerly at first but with growing ease as the days passed by. Taking on light jobs around the house, Fordy felt his body begin to heal and his mobility improve. Pushing himself harder than he should, he held on to the goal of being able to ride by Wednesday.

* * *

Ben took care of the weekly trip to Bedale on Tuesday but news had been hard to come by. There was no word about Jane and still no news about the fate of the Philpots.

On his father's return from market, Fordy helped unload the provisions from town. Unhitching the flat cart from Dapple, Fordy took the opportunity of asking his father if he would help him mount Dapple.

"What's the hurry?" asked Ben.

"I can't mope around here any longer, Dad. I need to get over to Kings Pasture tomorrow for some bits o' stuff," he hesitated to see how this was received but his father remained silent. "And there's the other business, I haven't seen John Burgess since our journey to Saltburn, I must call on him soon… and I need to be fit for Yarm Fair in two weeks' time. It's a long ride and I hope to be bringing a couple of 'osses back with me."

"Aye, maybe you're right," answered Ben reluctantly. "Come on then, we'll throw Dapple's saddle on, you can see how it feels."

Fordy nipped his mouth together to supress any groans of pain as he mounted his horse. He felt hot and dizzy but kept his discomfort to himself. It didn't matter how much pain he was in; he was determined to get to Anna.

* * *

The following night Fordy had to ask his father to help saddle up Dapple. Ben held the horse steady while Fordy slipped his foot into Dapple's stirrup before he tentatively threw his leg over the horse's back. He landed in the saddle with an involuntary grunt.

"Don't you be calling off to see one of your pals… or a woman," said Ben, watching his son struggling.

"Why do you say that?" asked Fordy, catching his breath in an attempt to disguise his pain.

"I know your weaknesses, son; a jar and a bonny lass are too much for you to resist. You don't share all your secrets with me, and why should you? But just be careful… please."

"I'll not be long, Dad, honest," replied Fordy. A mouthful of sticky phlegm rose in Fordy's throat, he leant over, spitting the foul-tasting liquid onto the ground. "Sorry, Dad," he said, looking at his father. Fordy had never felt disloyalty towards his father before.

"As I said, be careful," repeated Ben.

Darkness was falling as Fordy left, Dapple setting his regular easy pace. By the time they reached Kings Pasture he was shivering with pain, sweat pouring off him. He tried to conclude his business in the stable yard quickly but Fred Higgins wanted to know about Tom Dennison and why he'd punched Fordy.

"I can't linger, Fred," said Fordy. "The ride's fair taken it out of me. I'll tell you next week."

"Fair enough," Fred said, "I'm right glad to see you up and about again though. Didn't want to be losing one o' me best customers."

"I'll use the blocks to get back on the 'oss, if that's alright wi' you?"

Fred nodded. "See thee next week."

Once Fordy was through the stable gateway and out of sight he pulled Dapple to a halt, taking time to steady himself. The effort of the journey had left him lightheaded and trembling. He fumbled for his hip flask and swallowed a mouthful of brandy. He'd already taken a dose of laudanum before setting off. He sat a little while longer before having another swig. The alcohol eased the pain but increased his dizziness and a feverish heat flushed through him. He kicked Dapple on.

Approaching the garden gates Fordy looked into the darkness for any sign of movement. There was nothing. Unsure if the gates would be unlocked, he pushed at them; to his relief they opened. Taking a moment, he strained his ears for any giveaway sounds. Again nothing.

Sliding gently off Dapple, he tried to tie the horse to the tree but his hands and fingers fumbled with the leather rein. His heart was thudding from the mixture of alcohol and opiates; coupled with pain and anticipation they created a dreamlike state for Fordy. His eyesight blurred and his legs shook like a dish of tripe as he stumbled towards the garden shed.

He slumped against the door and banged on it. It opened and he fell through the doorway, Anna leaping backward to avoid him landing on her.

"What's the matter?" she cried. "What's happened?"

Fordy shuffled his way inside and collapsed onto the couch.

"You're in pain. Can you speak?" She stood over him as he tried to find a comfortable position.

"Give me a few moments," he gasped, laying his head back and closing his eyes. Slowly the shaking and trembling stopped and his body began to cool. "I'm sorry, I was injured last week, this is my first time on a horse."

Fordy recounted the events, omitting the crucial fact of why Tom Dennison had hit him. She poured him a glass of wine and sat opposite him on a low stool. Leaning forward, with her arms wrapped round her knees, she listened intently to his descriptions of events.

"But why would this man want to attack you?" she asked.

"It's a misunderstanding," replied Fordy.

"About what?"

"Let's not talk about him, I want to know how you are," he said, reaching out to her. She took his hand with both of hers, gently squeezing it.

"Oh, Fordy, I felt sure something awful had befallen you." She got up and moved to the couch next to him.

"I felt dreadful last Wednesday night, thinking of you here, alone," he said.

"But your injuries… you shouldn't have risked riding just to see me. You poor darling, you're in pain."

"I couldn't bear the idea that you might think I had deserted you," he told her, wincing from his injuries and flooding with delight; she had called him 'darling'.

"I just want to hold you and make you feel safe," she said, kissing each of his hands. Fordy tried to lean forward but the pain stopped him, "Oh Anna," he sighed.

Still holding on to his hands they stayed there, silently, for some time. The room was warm and Fordy felt at ease for the first time since his encounter with Dennison. But he soon started to ache and shuffled uncomfortably. "I know I've not been here long but I must go. My father was concerned about me coming out; they won't rest until I'm home."

"Yes, of course, you must go now. Your poor father and Mary Ann will be worried sick whilst you are away. Let me assist you." She took his arm and helped him stand. They were stood close; he could feel the warmth of her body, she raised her head, "Do you feel steady or…?"

He leant closer and gently kissed her. It was a spontaneous action; if he'd had to think about it or build up courage to embrace her, it would have been clumsy. As he lingered on her lips, he pressed harder, kissing her with a little more urgency. She responded, clinging on to the back of his jacket she met his embrace with equal desire for a few seconds before pulling away.

"I've never been kissed by a man before," she said shyly.

"Well, you have now, and there's plenty more to come, but not tonight unfortunately," he said, momentarily mesmerised by her dark eyes and consumed once more with the smell of her perfumed body. "That scent you wear, what is it?"

"Lily of the Valley, but there are more urgent matters now," she said, untangling herself from his arms. "Come on, we must mind your need to get home. I'm coming with you, to hold Dapple, and close the garden gate."

She carried a lantern and held it high as Fordy untied Dapple. "Is there something I can use to help mount him?" asked Fordy.

"We've a block here, next to the garden wall," she said, leading the way through the darkness. Before getting on Dapple he turned to Anna and kissed her again.

"Next week?" he whispered in her ear.

"Yes, next week," she replied.

He braced himself against the pain of mounting Dapple. Knowing she was watching him, he kept his face fixed and teeth clenched, absorbing the agony of the awkward actions of getting onto his horse. Taking the reins, he quietly nudged Dapple on and, with a smile, mostly from the relief of getting on the horse without making a fool of himself, he waved Anna goodbye.

Every muscle in his body was aching, the stabbing pain in his ribs that jolted through him with every stride Dapple took affected his breathing. Tom Dennison's sharp cleaver came to mind, although a blade would have been the end of him. Despite his discomfort Fordy was happy; not only had Anna waited for him but she had also shown she cared... and kissed him.

Taking deep breaths to help with the throbbing he filled his thoughts with Anna. Her beauty, her grace and kindness. His mind off his injuries, he settled into the steady rhythm of Dapple's walk. All Fordy had to do now was sit still, the horse knew the way home.

At Worlds End Ben was watching for him. He helped Fordy off Dapple and took the horse's reins.

"I didn't expect you to wait up," said Fordy.

"I could see you were struggling when you set off. If you'd been another half hour, I was coming out to look for you. Now I'll see to the 'orse and the goods. Get up to bed if you can," said Ben.

"Thanks, Dad," said Fordy, shuffling away to the house.

"And I'll see to the 'orses in the morning. I can see you've overdone things," called out Ben.

His father's kindness was appreciated but would he be so considerate if he knew what Fordy had been up to? Again, he felt a twinge of guilt, but it was nothing in comparison to his elation and eagerness to see Anna again.

* * *

"I don't see why you had to go over to Kings Pasture last night," said Mary Ann.

"I can't sit around forever," answered Fordy, taking a mug of tea off the kitchen table. He had slept till mid-morning and, despite feeling stiffness and a few aches, he felt fit and ready for work.

"Work's one thing but going over there among those ruffians at Kings Pasture House, there's really no need," she complained.

Fordy laughed as he went to her, put his arms round her and kissed her on the cheek. "Don't fret so, I'm fine. I know you worry but, really, there's no need."

She pushed him away.

"I'm not best pleased wi' you. You go off to Saltburn on a whim and nearly freeze to death riding back in that blizzard. Then you get a thrashing off Dennison for messing about with his daughter and still you don't know when to stay at home. Raking over the other side of the county for a bit of tea, you should have more sense…"

"Kings Pasture is not at the other side of the county," he answered, "and I'll not sit at home like some bloody milksop."

Mary Ann didn't answer, keeping her head down over her work at the kitchen sink. Fordy sighed heavily. "I'm going to clean out the tack room," he said to her turned back.

Fordy slowly wandered outside, fingers pressed into his ribs. There was a soreness that lingered, bending sideways he stretched out his muscles to ease the discomfort. As he passed the stables he looked in at Gilly, their expectant mare. He saw she was in the early stages of labour, sweating and pawing at the floor. She glanced up with wide eyes and gave a low snort. He went into her and stroked her face and neck, offering her reassurance; the horse responded, pushing her head into Fordy's chest.

"Now then, lad, you up and about? How you feeling?" asked Ben, walking up to Gilly's box.

"Better than I expected, bit stiff, that's all," replied Fordy, quietly withdrawing from Gilly. "She's started, I see."

"Aye. I gave her some bran and oil first thing this morning," said Ben, "it should help her labour."

The pair of them left Gilly to it, knowing horses preferred not to be disturbed while they were giving birth, and walked over to the field where the rest were grazing.

Leaning over the fence, both men cast a quick eye over each of their stock, checking every horse looked well and contented.

"They make a grand sight," said Fordy, admiring their animals. "Do you think we should still get two more fillies from Yarm? I know it's what we've talked about for the past year but, with the late spring, grass is going to be short."

"I think we should keep to our plan," replied Ben. "Prices could be down at Yarm; everybody'll be worrying about the lack of fodder. We run a tight ship here, we al'us get by."

"I'll certainly not pay over the odds."

Father and son stood watching their livestock for some time before Ben straightened up to move away. "What are you doing today?" he asked Fordy.

"A bit of tidying up in the tack room."

"Well, don't be throwing anything useful out," answered Ben, leaving Fordy to his thoughts over the field gate.

Everything looked different today for Fordy, even the sun was managing to shine weakly through the cloud that never seemed to lift this spring. In his twenty-five years, Fordy had never experienced what he was feeling. Was he in love? Did love exist?

Whatever it was, it made him feel that the world was his to conquer. Always an optimist, this new emotion made him feel like a king. This morning his troubles became irrelevant, the Dennisons had no hold on him and the venture with John Burgess must surely come good before Christmas. They had done their best for the Philpots, although the wait they faced before their trial was a worry. Fordy was full of hope for the coming months and years and his step lightened as he made his way across the cobbled yard.

In the tack room, Fordy began laying out old leathers that had been kicking about for years. His father never threw anything away. In the old smithy all the tools that had belong to Fordy's grandfather were still hung up around the walls. Ben was obstinate, "You never know when it might come in 'andy," was his answer every time they tried to throw something away.

But the situation in the tack room had become unmanageable, with no space for new leathers or replacements. Fordy pulled up a tall stool and began to sort through the rubbish, saving any items that still had some life left in the hide.

Again his thoughts slipped to Anna; where was all this going to lead? How long would her father allow her to stay at Kings Pasture?

He could hear Gilly over in her stable, gently whinnying and snorting during her labour. With a new foal about to be born and the possibility of another couple of fillies from Yarm, their need for more grass was growing. They'd rented twenty acres off a neighbour for the last couple of years but needed something more permanent.

His Grace, the Duke of Malbury, had promised Ben that there'd be a small farm coming up next year, which he would get first pick of. By then Fordy should have the money from the Saltburn deal, making the risk of expansion of the business less fraught. For now they had to make do.

The Duke owned several thousand acres in the North Riding of Yorkshire and his country seat, at Hackforth Castle, near Kings Pasture House, was his home for a few weeks each year. When he was in the district, he took a keen interest in his tenants and friends but the day to day running of the estate was left to Mr Peterson, his agent. Many a promise of the duke's was broken once he had disappeared back to London or the Continent. Peterson would make his own decisions, often lining his own pocket at the same time.

Fordy's thoughts ran on, it was a common enough story; the gentry took their pleasures and their wealth with leisurely assurance that their position in society was as secure as God in heaven. Fordy had no personal complaints about His Grace; Fordy's father and His Grace had played together as boys. Neither man forgot the friendship, despite the social divide.

Feeling frustrated with having to wait for their plans to become reality, Fordy pondered the alternatives. How he would hate to be a tied man; seven years apprenticeship never appealed to him nor did labouring to make another man a profit. He was happy to take the risks he took, confident they would pay off in the end. But he was still dependant on others; success was not totally in his control. A man needed luck to succeed, when the weather and the world could be quick to turn against you.

His good spirits began to ebb. Feeling uncomfortable and in need of stretching his legs, he went over to see how Gilly was getting on. Her waters had broken and two creamy brown hooves had begun to emerge. Not wanting to shout or make a noise, Fordy ran for his father; he found him in the tap room and told him the news.

Quietly they returned to the door of the building where Gilly was. It was rare to see a foal being born and an even better treat when they saw it was another filly.

"Come away, lad, leave 'er be. She'll want to be left alone," said Ben, taking hold of Fordy's arm.

CHAPTER 10

After the thrill of seeing Gilly's foal born, the week dragged for Fordy. His injuries healed and he kept busy with work at Worlds End. The usual Sunday night of cockfighting made for poor sport. Abe and Chalky were not there and, with little appetite for taking a gamble on any of the birds, he took himself home once he had completed his business.

Catching up with the two brothers on his weekly visit to Bedale, he confirmed their plans for the following week. They would travel to Yarm together, leaving Bedale on the Wednesday afternoon for the Ascension Day Fair at Yarm.

Down at the mill, Fordy found John in his office, fighting with his weekly accounts and orders.

"By the saints, you're a sight to gladden the heart!" John had not seen Fordy since his encounter with Tom Dennison. "So, tell me what it's like to be done over by Dennison, he won some big fights at the fairs in his youth."

"It was bloody terrifying, and that clod of a Nathan, Tom has no damned control over him. Not that he handles Jane any better. Both of his children are bloody feral."

John poured two beakers of ale. Handing one to Fordy, he returned to his seat behind the desk.

"You're as safe as 'ouses. Dennison's a fool, the whole town's laughing at him and his slut of a daughter."

"Abe and Chalky say she's not been seen," said Fordy.

"I'm not surprised."

"And they say she's going to wed Andy Hawkins," added Fordy.

"I saw Andy's father down at Leeming t'other day and he's not happy with things. Especially when Andy had already set the day to marry Elsie Smith and her hundred acres."

"I don't know what to make of it. Andy'll rue the day he marries Jane," said Fordy.

"I can see Jane's attraction, she's a bonny lass. But give her a few more years and a gaggle o' screaming bairns, I reckon Elsie and her dowry might look a darned sight more appealing."

"Enough blethering about her." Fordy emptied his drink. "What's fresh wi' you?"

"You'll be going over to Yarm next week for the horse fair?" John answered with a question.

"Aye."

"I've a favour to ask."

"Go on," said Fordy.

"I've had word that Jim Adams is looking for more money for this venture of his. Seems like someone let him down. I'd like you to take a message to him… in Yarm."

Fordy heart sank but he wasn't about to show John his reluctance. "I can do that." Fordy had found his last encounter with Jim Adams unsettling, but at least he had been with John. The prospect of having to see Adams on his own was unnerving.

"He uses one of the public houses as his base in the town, the Ketton Ox. All I'm asking is that you hand him a letter."

"Alright, I'll collect it next Tuesday."

"I'm sorry to ask you to do this. I'm increasingly uneasy about this business with Adams."

"Are you going to put more money up for Adams?"

"No, but I need to see His Grace; I've had word from his man up at the castle that he expects the Duke of Malbury to return from the Continent in June. He's the only man that can bring Adams to heel."

"Why the unease?" asked Fordy.

"When I was first approached to put money into this, His Grace assured me he would be back in Yorkshire by May but he hasn't appeared."

Fordy nodded, aware already that the Duke's absence was conspicuous.

"I was also told I would begin to see a return on my money by September but now Adams tells me it might be after Christmas. It was a risk from the start and, without damned Malbury here, Adams will feel free to ride over everybody's back," said John, looking into his empty beaker.

Fordy watched John. This old office had always felt like a refuge to Fordy, he'd known it from being a child, visiting the mill with his father. With just enough room for John's big oak desk and a couple of chairs, Fordy had always thought that the world was in order in here. Old ledgers lined one of the walls and a high-banked fire always glowed in the winter months. For the first time in his life, Fordy saw John was under pressure.

"You must have known it was risky," said Fordy, "I mean, Adams has…"

"Course I knew, don't take me for a bloody fool. I would never have entertained such a scheme without Malbury's encouragement. Adams would have no qualms about cutting the throats of everyman that's put up collateral and keeping the money for himself if he didn't have to answer to Malbury."

"Why didn't you tell me at the start, when you first suggested that…"

"Because I had Malbury's word he would have a hand on Adams but the bastard's not here to keep Adams in check." John smashed his clenched fist onto the top of his desk. "Adams is completely without honour; I wouldn't like to be the fella who's changed his mind about going in on this venture. He'll be lucky to be walking now… that's if he is still alive."

"What's the connection between His Grace and Adams?" asked Fordy.

"It's been going on for years. They hunt together with the Cleveland and His Grace even acted as Adams's sponsor when he joined the local militia," John laughed.

"How can Adams be in the militia when he controls the smuggling?" asked Fordy.

"The country's corrupt… you know that. But Malbury could bring him down quicker than a scented fox."

Fordy thought on this news before chancing another question.

"Do you know who else has put money up for this venture?" he asked.

"If I did I wouldn't tell you. You should have more sense than ask."

Fordy's dislike of Adams was based on his first impression of him and, given a choice, Fordy would never see the rogue again. Why hadn't John seen the dangers involved in this business? Fordy watched John get out of his chair and go to the dusty window that looked out onto the miller's large open yard.

"Why did you get involved with Adams and the Duke if it's so risky?" asked Fordy, eager to know more but conscious of John's mood.

"Bit like you and your cocking or selling your contraband. It adds a bit of excitement to life… and the possibility of earning extra money… without being taxed to rags."

John continued to stare out of his window and Fordy saw that John's shoulders had slumped as he stooped forwards into the depth of the window frame. Fordy held his tongue. He was sure there was much more to this story than John was prepared to tell but he dare not probe further.

Fordy sat quietly while John collected himself and was relieved when John turned around with a happier look on his face. "Enough of my troubles, why don't you tell me about the latest young lassie you've got your eye on?"

Fordy flushed.

"By Christ," said John, "what's up with you? 'Ave you gone soft on a lass? Not that wench up at the George at Catterick, is it?"

"No, it's not her…"

"You young devil, tell me who she is and I can warn her about your reputation for breaking hearts."

"A gentleman never divulges," answered Fordy, raising his brows.

"I'll drag it out o' you one day, after you've taken too much ale," replied John, replenishing their drinks.

* * *

With the nights pulling out it was impossible for Fordy to conduct his contraband dealings under the cover of darkness but as he set out for Kings Pasture House the last thing on his mind were the risks associated with handling smuggled goods. He had only a short list of items needed; his heart had gone out of trading. The petty detail of selling half a pound of tea or a bottle of brandy to a neighbour had lost its appeal. He wasn't sure if it was Anna's influence that had made him question his lifestyle but he knew his outlook on life was changing. He had no clear idea of who he was or what he wanted now but he had to collect something from the stables tonight as an excuse for making this trip.

After their exchange of kisses last week Fordy wondered where tonight might lead with Anna. He still wasn't sure of her but the uncertainty added to the anticipation; her spirit made her bold and her social superiority made her unpredictable. Passing the garden gates on his way to the stables there was still a small doubt as to whether she would be waiting for him.

In the stable yard Fred Higgins monopolised Fordy, still eager for an account of his altercation with Tom Dennison. Fordy obliged, quickly relaying the ambush tale and describing his injuries. As he was leaving Fred followed him outside the stable gates, checking around him before speaking,

"I saw Jane Dennison up here a few days ago," said Fred.

"Where?"

"O'er by Bowbridge Beck, heading out to Leeming Lane."

"What was she doing?"

"I don't rightly know, I was on my 'oss, I could see her through the trees talking to somebody. I couldn't hear what she was saying and when she saw me looking at them she jumped behind a tree."

"Who was she with?" asked Fordy eagerly.

"I not right sure, I couldn't see, but I reckon it was a bloke," said Fred, looking over his shoulder. "I'll have to get back to t'stables, those two thugs, Picard and Rennie take some watching. They'll 'ave somebody's eye out if I'm not there. But I wanted to tell y' bout Jane, 'specially as you took a beating for 'er." Fred put his hand on Fordy's shoulder. "Now you watch you'sel', Fordy," he added, before hurrying back to his work.

Fordy didn't bother to mount Dapple, he walked the couple of hundred yards from the stable gates to the wooden doors that lead into the garden. Why would Jane be in this part of the county? Despite his best efforts to forget about her, she kept cropping up like a smell from the outdoor privy. What was Jane up to? Was he a fool to have missed any clues? Not that he had taken much notice of what she said or did; after the first couple of weeks of seeing her, he'd spent most of his time trying to shake her off.

Leaving Dapple at the usual tree, Fordy tried to dismiss any thoughts of Jane, but his eagerness to see Anna had been blunted by Fred's gossip.

"Hello, you look deep in thought," Anna said, walking over to greet him. Surprised, Fordy looked up. He watched her approach, carrying Jasper under her arm. She had curled her hair and run a ribbon through it. Her dress was different, not the old faded blue frock she always wore, but a bright yellow one that rustled as she moved. Fordy noticed the low cut of the garment and while his eyes lingered over her breasts he saw the fabric was covered in small sparkling beads. He'd never seen a woman dressed like this before.

Fordy widened his eyes, "You look fit for a ball." He lay his hand on her shoulder and kissed her lightly on the lips. Jasper began to wriggle between them.

"Let me put this creature down," she said.

Fordy took a deep breath, his heart fluttered, sending a tingle through his body, she was enchanting. How was he going to be able to hang on to this woman? His confidence ebbed, unsure once more of the social etiquette, of her expectations. His usual easy way with women was inadequate, he felt clumsy and out of his depth again.

"What's the matter?" she asked, anxiously scanning his face.

"Nowt... er... nothing, just... well, you look so lovely."

"I've been looking forward to this evening. I couldn't resist dressing up for the occasion. Come, Fordy, shall we walk?"

"Won't someone up at t'house notice?"

"Who cares, I'm so happy," she said, spinning around and leading him towards the orchard.

Fordy was not so sure about her carefree attitude. If seen by the wrong person, Picard or her father, there would be plenty to worry about.

The night was a little warmer than usual as they strolled amongst the fruit trees. Jasper trotted along behind them, sniffing through the grass for rabbits.

"What have you been up to? You seem quiet," Anna asked.

"I haven't been up to anything," he said, rather too quickly.

"That wasn't an accusation," she said with a smile.

"Ah, you mean back at Worlds End? We had a foal last Thursday, a strong filly, we still have to name her, maybe you could help with suggestions."

"That would be fun. What else have you been doing? Do tell me, life is so boring here."

"It's been an odd week but there is something I need to tell you. I won't be able to visit you next week."

"I thought you seemed quiet tonight. Have I upset you?"

"No, Anna, nothing like that. It's my work, I'm away to Yarm, the 'orse fair. I'm looking for two more Cleveland Bays."

"How exciting. I wish I could come with you."

"To Yarm, to buy 'osses?" he laughed. "You're the first wench I've ever known to show an interest in 'orse trading."

Fordy stopped and broke off a branch. The leaves were stunted and brown around the edges and, where the blossom should have sat were the shrivelled remains of discoloured petals. The late frosts had decimated any chance of fruit forming.

"There'll be no crop from this orchard this year," Fordy commented.

"In London the stalls are always full of fresh produce. I'd never thought about where it all came from."

"Mark my words, even y' fancy stalls in the city will be struggling to find fruit and vegetables come the back end."

"What's the back end?"

"After summer, when it starts to cool down, that's the back end. I suppose it's the back end of the year."

"You mean autumn?"

"Probably." Fordy turned away. She didn't have a clue about real life, getting your hands mucky or worrying about hunger and a failed harvest. What was he doing strolling around this fancy garden with her?

Anna took his arm. "What's the matter? What have I said?"

"Nowt, lass, it's just you'd be better served by young Lord Alverton up at the 'all. He'd know how to talk to you and the right things to say."

"I don't want young Lord Alverton. I've spent too much time with the likes of him; you are the first man I've met that makes me feel alive." She stopped walking and turned to face him, reaching up to kiss him with firmness and desire. She held on to Fordy until he responded, his reservations melting away. He ran his hands over her, moving from her waist over her breasts and around her neck.

"It's no good out here," he muttered, "it's too wet, dew's fallen." He took her hand and led her back into her garden shed.

In the fading light of the evening, Fordy sat her down on the settee and they kissed again. "Are you sure about this? he asked, cupping her face in his hands, still unsure of himself.

"Here." She turned her back to him. "Unlace me."

With trembling fingers he worked at the laces and eased her out of the clothes.

"You've done this before?" she asked.

"Aye, but that's not important now."

"I'm glad, at least you know what to do." Her eyes brightened and her smile grew as she began pulling at his jacket.

Naked, she was just like any other girl, she responded to his urgency, allowing him to lead the way, surprising him with her eagerness. With their bodies united, there was no social divide.

In the neglected gardener's shed at the back of the grounds of Kings Pasture House Anna lost her maidenhood and Fordy lost his heart. If Fordy remembered his Bible, he may have considered that Anna was his Eve. In the garden, he had been led into temptation with forbidden fruit. But Fordy didn't care for the Good Book. He was a willing lover, and the apple trees, this year, were barren.

* * *

Fordy woke with a jolt, a scuffling noise at the door disturbed him. Anna had dozed off and he gently lifted himself up from the couch. The scratching sound came again. The candle they had lit earlier guttered weakly, offering little light. Finding a lamp, he lit it and went to the door, opening it slowly. Jasper pushed past Fordy, ran over to Anna and threw himself onto her. She woke with a cry; the animal was wet and cold and she knocked him roughly onto the floor.

Fordy went to her and sat beside her. "I'm sorry about that," he said, gently holding the light high so as not to dazzle her. "He was scratching at the door, we forgot about him." He ran his fingers over her face, her hair was crumpled and one of the ribbons she so carefully arranged was loose and tangled on the cushion next to her.

Anna stared at him. "You're going now, aren't you?" she asked, breaking the spell.

"I'm sorry but I must, I can't be seen leaving here as dawn breaks."

"I know, and two whole weeks till I see you again." Her voice cracked.

"Don't upset yourself, please." He stood and began to dress. "We must be cautious, if we're reckless this will be over before it has even begun. Be patient, once I'm back from Yarm, I'll be able to see you every week."

"You promise, every week?"

"Of course, I'll not let you down. I'll be here for you for as long as you want me."

"My father could whisk me away at any moment, I may not even be here when you come back."

Fordy took hold of her hands, "I know that. I would stay if I could but you know I can't." He kissed her.

"Oh, Fordy," she began to weep.

"I know this is hard, my dearest Anna, but be strong."

She lifted herself from the couch, wrapping the shawl around her. Fordy busied himself with collecting his clothes, trying not to be distracted by Anna's shivering and her forlorn face.

"I'm off," he said.

"I'll come out with you," she said standing up.

"There's no need, its freezing out there."

She didn't answer but followed him to the door. A wave of damp early morning air rolled into the room as Fordy opened it and she shivered. Wordlessly they walked over to Dapple, who gave a low greeting to Fordy.

Before untying his horse he took Anna in his arms. He felt the cool smooth soft silkiness of her shawl, which slid over her body as he pulled her toward him. She reached up to meet his lips and they kissed.

"You know I'll be here in two weeks. I won't let you down," he told her firmly.

She nodded and gave a weak smile, standing back while he mounted Dapple. Swinging the horse round he reached out, took her hand and kissed it. "Don't worry, we'll be fine," he said, with more confidence than he felt. Reluctantly he left her, alone and cold.

CHAPTER 11

The day of the journey to Yarm began with an unusual event for that spring; the sun broke out. Preparing Dapple for the journey, Fordy's spirits lifted. Having the sun on his back, the prospect of buying horses and the company of Abe and Chalky for the next three days was enough to cheer any lovesick fool. Knowing he'd see Anna again in a week contributed greatly to his feelings of wellbeing.

"Got everything?" asked Ben.

"I'm sure I have," replied Fordy, feeling the wallet inside his jerkin. "Money's in here, couple of lead reins in the bag."

"Now be careful, lad, don't be getting carried away with thee' sen. We can't afford o'er much for these fillies, there's…"

"Alright, Dad, I know, I can handle it, I usually do, don't I? Prices are gonna be…"

"Fordy, here's your pie," Mary Ann bustled out of the kitchen, "it's cooled down. I've packed it tightly for you."

Fordy took it from her and placed it carefully in his saddlebag.

"You're looking a bit happier today," she commented.

"You'd look jolly if you were gadding 'bout countryside like him," Ben said.

* * *

Fordy had arranged to meet the brothers at St. Anne's Cross on Leeming Lane. His way there took him past Kings Pasture House. In broad daylight the entrance gates and the secluded house were alien to him. He scanned the trees that enclosed the driveway; maybe he could catch a glimpse of Anna walking with Jasper through the grounds. Turning right down Bowbridge Lane he skirted round the boundary of Kings Pasture House and when he reached the part of the road that sat opposite the stables, he pulled Dapple up, and listened. Silence, nothing to give away the activities that went on here. All the big houses were the same, screened from view by layers of trees and shrubs to keep common folk at a distance and maintain the privacy of the gentry. In this case, the high hedges and walls hid illegal trading, not the social gatherings of the idle rich. Fordy gave up peering through the trees, he kicked Dapple on, and hurried down the road to his meeting.

* * *

"Bloody hell, Fordy, why are you always late?" bellowed Chalky, as Fordy came over the rise of the road towards Leeming Lane.

"I'm not late, it's you two that's always early," he called back, well aware that he should have got here a good while ago. The mood was set for a happy jovial journey.

Their ride took them over part of the route that Fordy had taken with John Burgess a month earlier. They crossed the Swale at Catterick, heading north before turning towards the east and over open country to Low Worsall. The Ship Inn at Low Worsall, a couple of miles from Yarm, would be their base for the next two nights. With plenty of stabling they could do their dealing in town and return to Low Worsall for the night before setting out on the journey home. Most importantly it offered clean rooms at good rates, unlike the hostelries in town which had a reputation for high prices and filthy accommodation. For centuries the bridge at the northerly end of Yarm was the last crossing point over the Tees before the coast. A new bridge at Stockton, downstream, had been built over forty years ago but many travellers still passed through Yarm on their journey northwards. Some inns offering beds assumed that most of these customers would only pass through the town once so saw no reason to offer quality accommodation while others exploited the lack of competition in the small community.

As regular visitors to Yarm Fair, Abe and Chalky knew where to find the best beds and always stayed at the Ship Inn. The low-ceilinged tap room was similar to Worlds End but the locals were a rougher crowd than frequented the No Mans Moor hostelry. Although ten miles from the sea, the River Tees was tidal up to Low Worsall so seafarers and those associated with the small inland port made up the majority of customers. The variety of accents and skin colours had been quite a shock for Fordy the previous year and, though still something of a novelty, he was better prepared for the vivid mix of cultures this time.

Pulling up outside the inn, the trio were greeted warmly by the landlord. Their horses were taken and stabled, before they settled themselves down at the bar. It soon became clear to Fordy that Abe and Chalky were set for a drinking session. Their capacity for ale knew no limit and, although well healed from the punches of Tom Dennison, the long ride had re-awoken an ache in his ribs. Making his apologies, he left both of his companions supping the local beer.

He was last out of bed the following morning and, at the breakfast table, it became clear that Abe hadn't made it to their room the previous night. Fordy was at a disadvantage being half asleep and something of a stranger so he sat quietly as the mixed clientele exchanged banter and jokes that had their origins in past encounters and shared events.

"What happened to Abe last night?" Fordy asked Chalky while they waited for their horses to be brought out.

"A wench took a fancy to him, she took him outside and he never came back. Didn't see 'im again till he appeared for breakfast."

"I hadn't realised he was one for the ladies," replied Fordy.

"I don't think he did either… not till last night," answered Chalky, "but the women round here know no shame. They'll not take no for an answer once they have their eye on you."

"You didn't find yourself a companion?" asked Fordy, nudging Chalky's arm.

"Er, no," spluttered Chalky, hesitating for a moment. "I like my ale… you know," he mumbled.

Fordy looked closely at him and wondered why Chalky always flushed and squirmed when it was suggested he find a girl. To his knowledge Chalky had never had a lass and it had occurred to Fordy several times that he never commented on a bonny face or a shapely waist. Perhaps he was frightened of women or had never found one that took his fancy.

"We're not all like you, you know. Some of us can keep our hands off the ladies," Chalky bounced back, appearing to have passed over the awkwardness. "You want to be careful up in town, Yarm's full of whores."

"I remember from last year," replied Fordy, with a grin.

* * *

Leaving Low Worsall, they set off at a slow pace. The immediate countryside was flat and open and, as they headed in an easterly direction, it was impossible to see any sign of the nearby town. Although Fordy had visited the fair last year he recollected little about the lay of the land but remembered that the town sat on a horseshoe-shaped piece of land which was surrounded by the meandering Tees on three sides. Approaching from the south, Fordy and the two brothers passed close by the river. Fordy looked down onto the dark wide stretch of water; it reminded him of the Swale over at Catterick until he saw a couple of small sailing boats travelling down it. Leaving the riverbank they swung north up into the town, passing two large fishponds on their left and a grand stone house to their right. Fordy could hear the noise of the crowds in the town and, as they neared the high street, the smell of rotting meat wafted up his nose.

"I'd forgotten how much this place stank," he called to the brothers.

"Aye," replied Abe, "I bet they throw their rubbish into the river. I expect you don't notice the stench after a few days."

Although tightly constrained by the Tees, the high street was a long straight road flanked with wide cobbled areas at each side. Down either side sat a mixture of properties; at first elegant Georgian houses home to professional people then smaller establishments housing shops and tradesmen. A square symmetrical red brick toll booth sat in the centre next to the road, with a weathervane perched on top of the pan tiled roof. There was an abundance of taverns, public houses and hostelries. The side roads that led down to the river were the sites of less refined establishments.

Entering the town just after nine o'clock the main street was already packed and they jostled their way up to the wide cobbled part of the marketplace where the horses were bought and sold. At this point Fordy bid farewell to the brothers, arranging to meet up at the Ketton Ox in a couple of hours.

The previous year Chalky and Abe had directed Fordy towards a breeder known for producing the type of animal Fordy was looking for and, once Fordy spotted the man he greeted him with a firm handshake.

"Mr Byers, good to see you," said Fordy.

Stan Byers was a small wiry man dressed in a loud tweed jacket. He sported a chunky gold watchchain across his waistcoat, which he constantly played with. His manner was assured as became a man whose reputation for horse breeding was known across the north of England and up into the border country.

"Mr Robson, how's that young filly I sold you?" He grasped Fordy's hand and smiled showing blackened teeth. Despite his appearance Stan Byers was one of the few breeders with an honest reputation.

"She's doing well; I have her with a neighbouring farmer at the moment, getting broken. I saw her last week and I have to say she's a fine creature."

"Aye, I'm not surprised, her dam's a beautiful mare. Are you looking for more like her?"

"I am; what have you got?"

Byers had several young horses tied to his cart where two lads were sat awaiting orders. They jumped off it ready to untie any horse that Fordy wanted to inspect closer.

Each filly was led up and down the cobbles so Fordy could watch the animals move. He ran his hands over every part of the two horses he had picked out and, after almost two hours negotiating, he spat on his palm and offered it to Byers.

"You have a good eye, Robson, you've taken my two best 'osses," laughed Byers.

"Will you be along next year to take my best again?"

"That's my intention. You'll come for a drink with me?" asked Fordy.

"I will, lad, let me have a quick word with me boys."

Fordy moved away from Byers' pitch and watched him speak to his sons. Seeing the family group together Fordy was struck by two thoughts. It must be grand to have a couple of youngsters to follow in your footsteps, and Byers' wife must be considerably younger than him. A smile rose on Fordy's lips.

Fordy bought Stan Byers a drink in the George and Dragon to seal the deal, but he was soon left alone; one of Stan's lads had called his father back; another customer was waiting.

As Fordy watched Stan Byers walk away he noticed his bandy legs, confirmation of a lifetime spent on horseback. He looked down at the brown liquid left in his glass. Swirling it round, he threw his head back and swallowed the lot. The temptation to have another one was strong but his next task loomed large. Fordy felt in his inside pocket for the sealed note John had given him for Jim Adams two days ago. Better get this over with, he thought.

Walking down the street towards the Ketton Ox he passed stalls selling all manner of goods; cheap jewellery, confectionery, hats and shawls. He hesitated at a brightly adorned table covered in ribbons and lace with bonnets hanging down from wooden frames at either end. He felt conspicuous as he inspected the goods that were on display to entice young women to spend their coppers. On his right were three giggling girls trying on straw hats.

"Hello there, dearie, looking for something for your sweetheart?" smarmed the large woman behind the stall. The three girls looked up at Fordy and burst out laughing, nudging each other.

"Don't be shy now dear, what's her colouring?" persisted the stallholder. "Is she dark or fair?"

"Fair, well, maybe dark…" mumbled Fordy. The three girls were almost in hysterics watching Fordy's discomfort. He would have bolted but was hemmed in by the passing crowd behind him.

"Here, dearie, a blue ribbon for her hair, she'll not be able to wear it when she's working, but it'll look pretty when you're out courting." The woman held out her grubby hand, the silk ribbon rolled over her fingers.

Fordy looked at her and glanced over at the girls who had momentarily gone quiet as they watched Fordy trying to decide whether to make the purchase.

"Look, it's beautiful silk, I do have to say, and it's only tuppence," bragged the woman.

Fordy coughed. "It's not worth that," he said, trying to back away.

"Well, a penny then," she snapped back, shoving the ribbon into a bag, thrusting it at him and holding out her hand for the copper. The girls started to snigger again.

There was only one way to end this; he stuck his hand into his coat pocket and brought out a penny, he laid it down on the stall and took the bag out of her hand without raising his eyes to the woman. He turned on his toes and pushed his way from the stall, hearing the woman berating the girls, insisting they'd better buy the hats as they'd had them on their heads for so long.

Fordy let out a long slow breath. Haggling over livestock was easier than dealing with that woman. Still, he'd survived.

He touched the bag in his pocket and smiled to himself as he pictured Anna opening his small gift.

On his right he saw the Ketton Ox, standing four storeys high. The cobbles in front of the tavern were covered with trestle tables and benches, all crammed with drinkers. Yarm reminded him of Bedale, with its wide-open main street, but the mix of folk here made Fordy feel like a foreigner. Then there was the embarrassing abundance of prostitutes who plied their trade around most of the public houses; he assumed the inn owners were complicit in their trade and that there was plenty of demand for their services.

He pushed his way through to the front door of the Ox and entered a hot and noisy room.

"You're a good-looking boy," said a husky voice. Fordy felt a firm hand grip his right buttock. "Fancy an older woman to show you the ropes?"

Fordy turned to see a woman daubed in makeup. Her age was indeterminable but she had a lively smile and a twinkle in her eye.

"Betty, leave the lad alone," called out the barman. "You want a drink, sir?" he asked Fordy, who pulled himself away from the overly affectionate Betty and leant against the bar.

"I'm here to see the Boss," said Fordy, in a low voice. The barman shot him a quick glance.

"Betty, make y'self useful," he nodded over to the woman. "Take this young fella down the back."

"You sure?" she asked, glaring sharply at Fordy.

"Yes, and be quick about it," answered the barman, giving Fordy a smile and a nod.

Progress was slow through the drinkers as she pushed her way to a door at the back. Fordy followed her through it, leaving the noise of the public bar behind. They entered a large open area. There were glass panes in the roof, allowing light in, creating an unnatural airy feel, but the stench of poultry and blood was rank.

They were in the notorious Ketton Ox cockpit. It was deserted apart from a handful of men tidying the place up. A couple were collecting empty bottles and tankards whilst another was raking the sand in the pit, in readiness for the next mains.

This was cockfighting on an industrial scale, a far cry from Jack Simms's pit at Newton.

"You like a bit o'cocking, lad?" Betty asked suggestively.

"Aye, I do, if I'm honest," he answered without looking at her as he followed her further back down the premises towards another door. This one was locked but opened to a rapid number of knocks from Betty.

"I've brought a young fella down to see t'Boss," she said and turned to Fordy. "My offer still stands, lad. When you're finished here come and find me up top. You'll find my rates fair," she chuckled and squeezed Fordy's buttocks again, before retracing her steps.

"Betty got her eye on you?" sniggered the doorman. "She likes 'em young."

"I'm not here for that sort of business; I'm here to see Mr Adams."

"And what makes you think Mr Adams is here?"

"I have a message from John Burgess, the miller at Bedale," said Fordy, attempting confidence. "He said I was to say that the cow had calved." John had told him this was the phrase he had to use to get access to Adams.

"Wait there. I'll see," said the doorman, bolting back the door.

Several minutes passed before the door reopened.

"Come on, follow me," said the doorman, making sure he rebolted the door after Fordy went through.

Again the atmosphere changed, this room was warm and dark. A few men were sat drinking, they looked up with suspicion as Fordy and his guide walked in.

"It's alright, lads, this fella's a friend. What's your name, lad?" asked the doorman.

"Robson," answered Fordy, still unsure of himself.

"Alright, lad, here, take some ale or brandy if you prefer," said the man.

"Ale will be grand." Fordy didn't feel like drinking but was sure it was necessary to maintain his credibility.

One of the seated men invited him to sit and join in a game of cards but Fordy declined, and, thankfully, the man took no offence. The room was filled with the smell of rich tobacco smoke and, although none of the men were well-dressed, the spoils of their trade gave them the air of wealthy folk.

His wait was short; a voice called his name and Fordy stood up. "You can come in now," he was told.

Fordy swallowed hard. Leaving his half-drunk glass on the bench, he walked into a small well-furnished room where three men were stood looking out of a large window. They turned and the smallest man moved forward. It was Adams.

"Ah, Robson, good to see you again. You've been offered refreshment, I hope?" said Adams holding out his hand in greeting.

"I have, sir," said Fordy, taking Adams's hand. "I have this note for you, from Burgess."

Adams took the crumpled envelope from Fordy. "I've been waiting for this. You must be an honest lad for Burgess to have entrusted you with this." Adams gave a gruff laugh.

"Well, I like to think so." Fordy smiled back, the irony not wasted on him or the other men in the room.

"You here for the horse trade?" asked one of the other men in the room.

"Yes, I've bought two fillies off Stan Byers," answered Fordy, with a little more confidence.

"You'll have paid handsomely for 'em but they'll be good stock," replied the man.

Fordy could see out of the window; there was a boat yard with the river at the far end.

"This'll be different country to what you're used to up Bedale way," said the man, looking out of the window with Fordy.

"Which river is this?" asked Fordy, feigning ignorance.

"It's the Tees, from here it twists its way north out to sea," said Adams from behind him. Fordy turned to reply and saw that the note he had delivered was nowhere to be seen.

"Well, I'll be off," he said, suddenly feeling unwelcome.

"You can get out at the side if you want to avoid the Ox," answered Adams, stepping forward to take Fordy's hand. "Thanks, Robson, we might bump into you again one day. Give my regards to Burgess," he said with the sinister smile that Fordy remembered from his first encounter with him at Saltburn.

"I will," said Fordy, giving him a nod despite himself.

He was shown through the door by one of Adams's associates. "Go right, you'll come out in the market," he said and slammed the door shut.

Fordy was left standing. Looking up he saw a shabby sign announcing he was in Silver Street. He took a few steps towards the main street but hesitated then turned to head back towards the river.

He walked down to the water's edge and watched the Tees flow past. Jetties and piers jutted into the tidal river where sailing craft of all shapes and sizes were tied up. Small workshops and warehouses lined the road that ran along the side of the wide river. Fordy knew nothing about life on the water but he recognised the commerce around him. In Bedale business of any consequence was limited to market day but in Yarm it appeared that every day was an opportunity.

Down here, away from the high street, the atmosphere was different. Men shouted and cursed at each other as they worked. Many were unloading boats, some toiled at their work in open sheds. Joiners, sail makers, blacksmiths, all crammed close to service the demands of the river and its traffic.

The stench was overwhelming, Fordy wasn't sure what caused it. He was accustomed to the foulest of air, but this was different and guessed it may be rotting fish.

Behind him was a building site, the cause of much of the noise that had initially attracted his attention. A scream went up. As he turned he saw several men gathered together and he ran over to them.

"Young lad here has fallen off the scaffold," one of the men told Fordy. Together they watched the boy being lifted to his feet by a couple of his workmates.

"He'll be alright, he landed on these bags of rags we have here. That's what they're for, to break a fall," added the fellow. Looking up at Fordy, recognition registered on the man's face, "Are you the fella that's just come out of yon door?" he asked, nodding towards the wall on the other side of Silver Street.

"Yes, why?"

"I was watching you from up on the wall, only one sort of man comes out of that door."

"What sort's that?" asked Fordy, with a laugh.

"Them that's up to no good," the man replied, joining in with Fordy's good humour.

"I had a message to deliver, that's all. I'm at the fair to buy horses."

"You want to be careful; no good comes of getting too friendly with Adams."

"I'm not his friend, like I said I was doing a favour for

somebody. What are you building here?" he asked, both genuinely curious and keen to change the subject.

"It's a shoddy mill," said the man. "If you know what that is."

"I've no idea," admitted Fordy, watching the young lad who had fallen off the scaffolding climb back up a ladder to his work.

"Its where old woollen garments are bashed to pieces, then the fibres are spun back together to make cloth. It's a new invention, brought up from Bradford, that's where we're from," said the man, happier gossiping than working. "Have you come far?"

"About thirty miles, I bought a couple of fillies earlier. I'm meeting up with my friends soon," said Fordy, in an attempt to move away.

The man persisted. "But you had a bit of business in there," he said, nodding towards the doorway again.

"If you're not from these parts, how do you know so much about what goes on in there?" asked Fordy.

"Been here three months, working on this mill. I've seen all sorts of folk come out of yon door. Gentlemen wi' silver canes and top hats, tradesmen, farmers and the unlucky ones who've had a bit o' rough treatment before being bundled out. You don't want to be mixed up with that bunch."

"You're probably right, but tell me about this river, I've never seen businesses clustered round a waterway before."

"The place that's takin' the bulk of the business is o'er at Stockton, it's four miles nearer the sea. But the river's bad to navigate, it silts up and twists and turns too much. Six years ago they 'ad a go at shortening it by cutting through one of the bends."

Fordy listened closely to the man, "I've never heard of such a thing," he said.

"That's not the 'arf of it. There's talk of canals and railways bein' built to bring coal to the coast from t'mine fields away up in County Durham."

"How do y' know all this?" asked Fordy.

"It's the talk of the town; all t'moneyed men keep having meetings about how t'get t'coal moved easier. Seems everybody wants coal these days, down in London to keep their 'ouses warm or them new-fangled steam engines; they burn coal faster than t'miners can dig it."

Fordy looked out across the river. On the other side were open fields where cattle and sheep grazed. The contrast between the two riverbanks emphasised the difference between his rural life and the industry that existed up here.

"I'd better be off, let you get on with your work," said Fordy.

They shook hands without exchanging names and Fordy walked slowly back up Silver Street.

In the high street he found Abe stood alone outside the Ketton Ox with a beaker of ale in his hand.

"Where've you been?" asked Abe. "You and Chalky have abandoned me."

"Walking by the river, got talking to a chap down there. By God, there's some trade goes on here. I could quite fancy it, moving stuff on the river and out to sea, a better idea than lugging pack horses around."

"You weren't so keen on Yarm last year, if I remember rightly," said Abe.

"It was my first time away from home, I'm getting used to it now," retorted Fordy. "Where's Chalky gone to?"

"Dunno, said he 'ad to see someone, wouldn't tell me who," answered Abe, taking a long swig of his drink. "You want one?" he asked, raising up his tankard.

"Aye," said Fordy, eyeing the crowds in the hope of seeing Chalky.

"I'll go in and get a round, hopefully Chalky will be back when I return."

Fordy nodded with a chuckle, moving over to a bench that had become vacant. He sat there for a few minutes taking in the happy atmosphere and tried to imagine what it would be like living in such a place. Would it seem exciting for a while before he began to crave the solitude of the Worlds End and his occasional trips to Bedale? What would Anna make of somewhere like this?

"Fordy," shouted a familiar voice. It was Chalky. "How did your business go?" he asked as he neared Fordy.

"Well, I secured two good animals. Abe's gone in to get drinks, I grabbed this table and bench a moment ago. Sit down quick before someone else takes advantage of it," Fordy told him, glancing up at Chalky's companion.

"I bumped into Giles, down the street," said Chalky, extending his arm towards Giles Redworth, who had hung back while Chalky greeted Fordy.

Fordy involuntarily jumped up out of courtesy, he hadn't realised it was Redworth who was with Chalky.

"Hello," said Giles heartily, offering his hand, which Fordy took.

"Please, take a seat," said Fordy, "if you'd like to join us."

"I would indeed," answered Giles. "It was a stroke of luck I spotted Chalky. I'm on my way to the cockfighting in the Ox. Chalky said he was heading there too, so I thought I'd join him."

Fordy observed the affable fellow who, on Fordy's short acquaintance, always seemed to be happy. His smile contrasted with the cold one that Adams had raised just a few minutes ago at the back of the Ketton Ox; Giles's eyes seemed to glisten with good humour. Maybe that was because of his secure position in life. There was no doubt

Giles was a gentleman, his polite clipped speech and, of course, his clothes. On their previous meeting in the dimly lit cockpit he hadn't really noticed the clothing but here in the daylight Fordy couldn't help but see the fine cut of his coat and breeches. Although modestly dressed as if for the hunting field, the cut and fit of each garment was impeccable, even causing Fordy to take notice of them. His white muslin shirt alone made him stand out from the crowd; most people put up with dirty grey linen on a daily basis.

"Look out, here comes Abe," said Chalky, shuffling up on the bench to make space for his brother and his handful of drinks.

"You found a seat," commented Abe, as he placed three tankards onto the table. "It's chaos in there, thought I was never gonna get served." Taking his seat he saw Giles. "Hello, Mr Redworth, what are you doin' here?"

"Hello, Abe, thought I'd join you chaps for a few mains," said Giles.

"I'd 'ave got you a drink if I'd know you were 'ere," said Abe, with his drink already at his lips.

"Not to worry, Abe, I've come prepared," he replied, taking a silver hipflask from his breast pocket.

Fordy realised that both Abe and Chalky knew Redworth well, they did all the blacksmithing work for the Redworths and he felt a little awkward in this small group. He also noticed that Abe addressed Redworth as 'mister' but Chalky was on first name terms. It wasn't any of his business but it did strike Fordy as a little odd. He sat there silently as the other three chatted about this and that, quickly finishing his drink.

"Are we going into the Ox for a couple of mains now?" asked Abe.

"I think I'll give it a miss. I've to go and see Stan again," said Fordy.

"I can't believe this. You're turning down a bit of cockfighting?" asked Chalky. "What's up wi' ye?"

Fordy had no desire to re-enter the Ketton Ox for a variety of reasons.

"If you must know I 'ad to deliver a message, in there," he said, nodding over to the Ox. "John Burgess asked me to give a note to a bloke called Adams. I 'ave no wish to see him again."

"Adams is in there?" asked Chalky urgently.

Fordy nodded and saw Chalky look at Giles with a frown.

"Jim Adams?" whispered Giles.

"Yes, scoundrel that he is," answered Fordy, realising this news meant something to both Chalky and Giles Redworth. "You know 'im?"

"Not socially," replied Giles, taking a gulp of liquid from his flask.

There were a few moments of uncomfortable silence.

"What's the matter with you all, who is this Adams fella?" asked Abe, loudly, getting up from the bench.

"Shush," said Fordy. "He runs the smuggling game round here. He's a rogue, I have no intention of going back in there."

"Well, he's nowt to do wi' me, I'm off in for a bit of sport. Anybody coming?" asked Abe, straightening himself up and checking his pockets.

Fordy looked at Chalky and Giles's stunned faces. "I've changed my mind as well," stuttered Chalky.

"I have an idea, I believe there's an archery competition going on over the river. Next to the church in Eglescliffe, on the butts. It shouldn't take more than five minutes to walk there," said Giles, already getting up from his seat. "How about it, Chalky?"

"I'm game. How about you, Fordy?" asked Chalky.

"How do you know about the archery?" replied Fordy.

"I'm staying up there, next to the archery field, at the Hall," said Giles, colouring up.

"Oh," said Fordy.

"Friends of my parents," said Giles, lamely.

"I'll give it a miss, thanks. I've a bit more business to attend to in town," said Fordy.

"Well, I'm going in to chance my arm in the Ox, while you lot dither about out here," said Abe, leaving the small group.

"Me and Giles'll go over the bridge and have a look at the archery up there," said Chalky, shuffling away from Fordy.

"I'll meet you back here at five," answered Fordy, pointing down to the town clock.

"Good to see you again, Fordy," said Giles Redworth, bouncing back from his moment of apparent awkwardness in his usual cheerful way, already making to go with Chalky.

Fordy offered a small nod of the head and took his leave. He made his way up the street towards the main bridge that crossed the Tees. On the bridge he stopped and looked down at the river and the various crafts and people moving around.

What was Giles Redworth up to, Fordy wondered. He comes here and stays with the wealthy family that own Eglescliffe Hall then spends his afternoon with Chalky? He dismissed this odd behaviour as he reflected on his own life. The confidence he had felt about his own ambitions at Worlds End was trickling away. Seeing Yarm and the possibilities here, he began to doubt himself. But it wasn't just Yarm that was unsettling him. Could he make a life for himself with Anna here?

There would be a demand for good strong horses in County Durham. They'd need thousands to pull the barges and wagons once the canals and railways were built. Was there an opportunity here for him? Did he and his father have the capital to start a business here, thirty miles from Worlds End. Would he have the courage to suggest this to his father?

He could dream of living in one of the fine town houses with Anna but achieving it… Navigating his future felt as precarious as one of the small boats below, in the river that had just collided with the bank.

* * *

That night back at the Ship in Worsall, Fordy spent a restless night and was only too aware that Abe had not followed him and Chalky up to their room. At breakfast Fordy was too wrapped up in his own thoughts to join Chalky in teasing Abe about his absence from the bedroom.

As the three men rode home, Fordy had little to say. The ride was slow, Fordy had his two fillies to lead and Abe and Chalky had three further horses to contend with.

It was late evening when Fordy finally arrived in the yard at Worlds End. His father and a few of the drinker's came out to greet him.

"We've come to look at your new horses," said Ben, holding up the glowing lantern, "How many did you get?"

"Two fillies, I'm taking them over to the stable," answered Fordy wearily. The group followed him. Hands were run over flanks, legs and necks and their mouths were inspected with approving nods and comments.

"They must have cost you a bob or two," said a voice at the back. There were mumbles of agreement.

Fordy stepped aside as the men considered his horses. He wasn't sure if the uninvited comments were welcome. The security of belonging to this community was reassuring in these troubled times but it was restrictive too. He imagined the interest that Anna would spark, should he bring her back to Worlds End.

It was acceptable to run an enquiring hand over a horse and give an open opinion. But what would be the response of their neighbours if he brought Anna home? Would they shy away, gossiping amongst themselves? Or could she put them at ease, their social differences forgotten?

He'd come home with two strong horses but he'd also brought back more doubts about his future.

CHAPTER 12

Fordy kept his new horses stabled for three days. Their initial nervousness dwindled as he spent time with them and he decided they were ready to be let out into the small paddock at the back of Worlds End.

Tenderly slipping an old soft halter onto the larger horse, he led her out through the field gate and quietly unclipped the lead rein. She stood, almost startled, and stared at Fordy. He then took the second one out in the same manner and gently released her. For a few magical moments they stood together, perfectly still, looking straight at him. Fordy was only an arm's length away but he resisted the temptation to touch them again. Then a crow called out from a nearby tree, taking the horses' attention, and the spell broke. They glanced up, swung away from Fordy and trotted off. Contentment bubbled through him; they were good strong horses, his choice was sound.

Today was to be his first chance to see John Burgess since Yarm; he planned to combine a visit to the mill with a request he had received to look at a horse that was for sale in Aiskew. When Mary Ann heard of his plans for the morning she asked him to drop by the Philpots with provisions. He set off mid-morning in good spirits with a basket of food secured behind him.

In the yard at Aiskew Mill a dozen labourers stood round a large table, taking refreshment. Fordy shouted a greeting to them as he dismounted Dapple. He could see John standing in the beck that fed the mill and walked over to him.

"We're trying to shore up the bank, all this bloody rain's ripping the soil out here," said John. Fordy leant over and saw the damage that the excessive water was doing. "We've got ten loads of gravel coming in from Catterick Quarry this morning, that's why I've got this gang on," he said, gesturing over at the group of men. "Are you wanting a word?"

Fordy nodded, "I'm on my way down to Ted Stapleton's. He wants a bottle of brandy, and he has a gelding to sell, so I thought I'd take a look at it."

"If it's that black thing with a fleck in his eye I'd warn you to give it a miss. I was watching him take it up the road t'other day; I reckon the 'orse is half blind… or half mad."

"Thanks for that, I thought he seemed o'er keen to get rid of it," nodded Fordy.

The two men walked out of earshot of the others. "How was Yarm?" asked John.

"Busy, never seen so many folks. I delivered your letter and got myself a couple of fillies."

"Did you see Adams?"

Fordy nodded.

"Did he have anything to say?" asked John.

"No, he was pleasant enough, but said nothing of consequence. After I'd delivered your letter I took a walk down by the riverside. Have you ever been into Yarm, or Stockton, come to that?" asked Fordy.

"Never." John shook his head.

"There's that much trade and activity there. Do you know about the mining up in County Durham and the

144

demand for coal? Did you know there's talk of canals and railways being built there?"

"Aye, I'd heard tell of it. But it won't affect us out 'ere. What's your interest?"

"Seems to be so many opportunities. Different to round here, more exciting, quicker pace…more chances to make money."

"Don't tell me you'd give up Worlds End and your 'orses to dig for coal?"

"No, I'm not a miner, nor ever likely to be one. But if there's to be canals and rail tracks, the demand for horses would be endless."

"You have a point but your father'd miss you."

"I know," replied Fordy. "It's just an idea, although…"

"Look out, our next load of stone's here," said John, walking back to the stream as a cart laden with gravel approached.

"I'll be away," Fordy said, watching John jump back into the running water.

Before leaving the mill yard Fordy stopped to exchange a word with Matt, Burgess's foreman, then he crossed the mill race onto Blind Lane which ran along the back of Aiskew. Coming out onto the main road he hesitated and checked who was around; he was still cautious after being jumped on by Dennison.

The village of Aiskew was separated from Bedale by Bedale Beck and, despite its proximity to the town, it had its own character. Apart from the usual shopkeepers and tradesmen, it had an unusually large number of wool combers. The laborious filthy process took place in dozens of small workshops behind the properties that lined the main road. Fleeces were warmed and combed to separate the long woollen strands from the shorter staple. The smell created from the warmed fleeces as the lanolin melted was repugnant; cottagers employed in this trade tended to stick together.

The air was heavy with that unpleasant smell of warm wool as Fordy went into Stapleton's yard. It was a quick exchange of goods. Fordy cast a sharp eye over the horse that was for sale, seeing that Burgess's words were true; Stapleton's horse was a screw. Making his excuses, he headed along the road for the Philpots' holding.

Pulling up outside their house Fordy noticed the place looked neglected. Philpot's once tidy flower bed was overgrown with nettles and the gate that led to Paul's wool combing yard was hanging off one of its hinges and tied up with string. Where there should have been the noise of a busy industry there was only the sobbing of a small child who sat on a stone at the side of the house.

Fordy shuffled forward on Dapple with unease. "Hello," he called to the child. She looked up at Fordy, screamed and ran off, disappearing round the back of the house. Fordy stayed on his horse, hoping he could avoid dismounting. He had no wish to enter the Philpots' house or talk to Mrs Philpot about her troubles. Dapple paddled with impatience and Fordy looked around in the hope a Philpot child might appear.

"'Ello," called a voice and a young lad came running out of Philpot's yard.

"Are you a Philpot?" asked Fordy.

"Aye, mister," said the lad.

"I've a basket for your mother, will you take it?"

"Aye."

"I'm in a bit of a rush," said Fordy, untying the basket behind him. "Tell her it's from Worlds End, and that I'm sorry I don't have time to stop."

"Aye," said the boy, taking the wicker hamper from Fordy. "Thank y' sir, I'll tell 'er."

Fordy gave a nod and a quick smile. Then, on a whim, rather than turning to go home, he took the lane that headed north. His business had been conducted much quicker that he'd expected so he had time to take a detour past Kings Pasture House. He'd be seeing Anna in two days but the desire to be near her at this moment was stronger than reason.

Heading towards Leeming Lane, the busy north-south highway, he could hear the sound of the stagecoach horns being blown. There was an important staging point at Leeming Bar, a mile to the east of Aiskew. The coachmen always blew several warning blasts as they approached, alerting the ostlers to be ready to change horses and any would-be passengers who were waiting to board the coach. At times Leeming Lane could be a dangerous place with coaches racing to meet their tight deadlines; passengers could expect to travel from York to Newcastle in as little as four hours in the summer months when the ground was good.

Once on the wide highway he kept to the side of the road. The Northern Flyer noisily shot past Fordy, heading north with whoops of warning from the horn blower. Within seconds the coach and four were gone, leaving behind a cloud of fine particles of soil and momentary silence.

Already in the distance another horn could be heard from the north this time. Fordy urged Dapple into a canter, keen to avoid another covering of dust. He got to the turning at St Anne's Cross just in time to get off the main road before the next coach flew by. He turned to see it was the Express, headed for London.

What was there to stop Anna's father putting his daughter on such a coach and sending her away?

It was a fast-moving world, here on this important highway. Time and distance were no barrier to travel. He'd heard tales of London and Edinburgh but he couldn't begin to imagine what they were really like and had no desire to find out for himself. The hustle and bustle of Yarm had been enough of a contrast to him after the slower pace of Worlds End. To be trapped in tight streets and never see a blade of grass was unthinkable. Not to mention the strange folks who lived in the cities. What would he find to talk to them about?

Leaving the noisy highway behind, he was soon alongside Stillerton's grounds, circling the perimeter hedge of Kings Pasture. He quickly moved past the stables and went round to the main entrance where he stopped. The metal gates were open. He looked up the drive; to the left, a wooded area ran alongside it. Dismounting, he led Dapple through the gateway, into the trees and tied the horse behind some large bushes.

There was no sense in what he was doing but his curiosity and thoughts of Anna had the better of him. Creeping through the trees and thick overgrowth, the big house came into view. He crouched behind a large bush and watched. There was a carriage pulled up outside the house. He gasped when he saw Anna cradling Jasper in her arms. She was speaking to a tall, older man, Fordy could hear his voice but he was too far away to make out what he was saying. Fordy guessed it was Anna's father.

A coachman was sitting up top and another man was carrying boxes into the carriage. He had been there a few minutes, silently watching the private domestic scene, when there was a noise behind him, like a branch breaking. He held his breath to hear better and turned. He heard the sound of rustling leaves and saw movement a few yards away. He straightened up and took cover behind a wide tree. Peeping round he saw Picard, one of the men who helped out with the contraband at the stables. He was holding a bludgeon and despite his bulk trying to move quietly through the trees.

Fordy ducked to the right of Picard, knowing he was the quicker and nimbler of the two of them; with luck he should be able to get back to Dapple without being caught. Keeping his eyes on Picard, he took a step but his foot caught in the twisted briars; as he tripped backwards Picard ran at him and grabbed him by the throat.

"What you doin', Robson?" Picard growled in his heavily accented voice.

Fordy had no chance against the bulk of this man. He grunted but didn't struggle.

"You're coming with me," said Picard, as he started to drag Fordy through the wood. But Fordy's downfall was also Picard's, as the briars clung onto his breeches. Still holding onto Fordy, he lost his balance. Fordy saw his chance and threw his weight against the teetering Picard who tumbled backwards over a fallen tree, landing on his back with his arms and legs in the air.

Fordy regained his balance, gasping for breath and saw the great dolt was stuck. Picard started to roar. Fordy glanced back at the group around the carriage; one of the footmen was running over to see where the noise was coming from. Fordy turned on his heel and picked his way back to Dapple as quickly and quietly as he could. He saw his horse standing with its ears pricked, alerted by the noises in the trees. Without hesitation he threw himself onto Dapple and fled out onto the open road.

He didn't think he was being pursued but he kept Dapple at a canter all the way down Hollow Moor Road. Checking behind again, he saw an empty road and slowed the horse to a walk. Fordy laughed with nervous energy and slapped Dapple on the neck, "By God, they'd 'ave 'ad us there," he told the horse, "but it's our secret, old lad, Father would explode if we told him."

Once the exhilaration of the escape wore off, Fordy again began to worry. Seeing Anna with her father reinforced the gulf between them. How much did she modify her behaviour when they met at night? Surely the drawing room of a grand house would suit her situation better than a ramshackle old gardener's shed and wandering through an overgrown orchard with him.

* * *

No matter how many times he thought about the impossible situation with Anna he could not give her up. Two days after being caught in the wood by Picard he was back on the road to Kings Pasture House. He had the crumpled paper bag containing the ribbon in his jacket pocket.

The garden gates were left ajar and Dapple sauntered through them, content to lead the way.

She was waiting for him, next to the tree where he always tied the horse. The sharp wind that had persisted all day swirled through the orchard and gusted over the pair of them. Anna's hair flew up and she pulled her shawl closer,

"Let's get inside," she said, quickly kissing him. "It's too cold to linger out here."

Inside the fire glowed with red embers, Fordy realising she must have been here several hours warming the room.

"Where does everyone think you go when you come here, do they not miss you at mealtimes?" he asked.

"Not really, there's only Mrs Dinsdale and sometimes that awful man of Father's skulks around. Have you come across him? He's called Picard."

"Yes, I have." Fordy swallowed hard. "He's usually down at the stables when they're handling goods. He's a nasty piece of work," he said, cautiously, hoping the subject of an intruder in the woods wasn't going to be raised.

"Whenever Father comes home, Picard comes up to the house and they have secretive meetings in his study." She curled up her nose, "Horrible man, Picard I mean, not Father, but then… "

"Has your father been home recently?" he asked, already knowing the answer.

"Just this week, he came to collect some of Mama's belongings. He had no right to do that, they are my things, or will be when I'm twenty-five, but I can't stop him…" Her voice dwindled and Fordy couldn't find any words to comfort her. He was interested to hear about this man who kept his daughter in solitude, but fearful of upsetting her.

"Let's forget about them. Tell me about your trip to Yarm, was it successful?" She lifted her head and smiled at Fordy.

"Very… I bought two fine fillies."

"What are they called?"

"They answer to Heather and Honey," he said absently. He stuck his hand in his coat pocket.

"'Ere, I bought you a present in Yarm." He put the crushed brown bag into her hands.

"I haven't been given a gift for ages, what is it?"

"Open it, you'll see." His confidence about the ribbon was low, he couldn't bear to watch her open it and see her disappointment. He turned away and went to help himself to a glass of wine.

"Blue ribbon," she said excitedly, moving straight to the mirror and tying it into her hair, "Thank you, Fordy, it's lovely, my favourite shade of blue."

He walked up behind her and encircled her waist with his arms. He kissed the back of her neck. Pushing his face into her soft curling hair, he breathed in deeply.

"Your perfume… what did you say it is?"

"Lily of the Valley," she said, involuntarily smelling the inside of her wrists.

"Where do you get it from?" he asked.

"It was Mama's favourite fragrance, she got it from London."

"And how do you get it now?"

She turned to face him, "Father collects it from London. The shop is called Floris. It's the most beautiful establishment in the world with all kinds of lovely things to buy; perfumes, lotions, hairbrushes, jewelled clips, the list is endless. You remind me now. I am almost at the end of my last bottle. I shall have to get Father to collect some for me, although I hope he doesn't owe them money."

This revelation bit at the heart of Fordy's dilemma. The unspoken gulf between them was confirmed with her choice of toiletries and where they were bought.

"That night we first met; your perfume overwhelmed me. You smelled so beautiful and…well… sort of fresh." He swallowed hard with embarrassment.

"It's lovely, I agree." She lifted her arm to his nose, encouraging him to breath in the aroma.

"Everything in here smells different," he admitted, "to what I am used to, at home."

"In what way?"

"The furniture for a start, I'm not sure what it is…"

"Does it matter?" she asked, kissing him. "Are you going to neglect this poor girl just because the polish we use is different to yours?"

Fordy didn't know if Mary Ann used polish but before he could say anything Anna's hands slid over Fordy's chest, round his back and into his trousers.

"You saucy wench, there were plenty like you in Yarm, eager for a tumble," he whispered in her ear.

"None that smell as good as me ..." Her fingers loosened his britches and she pulled out his shirt. Her kisses were hard, she pushed against him with her body.

Fordy responded, matching her urgency. He couldn't be bothered with undoing her dress and reached down for her skirt; lifting it, he ran his hands up her thighs.

* * *

Later, as they lay wrapped in each other's arms, Anna dozed but Fordy remained alert. In the flickering candlelight Fordy shivered and reached onto the floor to retrieve a blanket. Sitting up, he laid the cover over Anna then went to the dwindling fire. He quietly placed a few small logs on it and blew at the embers, encouraging the flames to come back to life. Mesmerised by the small flames licking over the dry crusty bark on the wood, he sat on the hearth rug for some time.

He heard her move and went to her. He stood watching her.

"What's the matter?" she asked, frowning.

"Nothing, it's you. You're so beautiful."

"Come and sit," she said, reaching out her arms, pulling him down and curling her body round him, stroking his back and running her fingers over his muscles.

His skin tingled under her delicate sensuous touch. This was very different to quick fumbles in the hay or rolls in the grass; he'd taken girls quickly and nonchalantly.

But no one had told him about this. No one ever said that to lay with a woman you loved was beyond every happiness you could imagine. He shivered again.

"What's the matter?" she asked, raising herself up to stare at his face. "You look as if your life is about to end." She smiled and reached up to kiss him. "Why so forlorn when we have discovered such happiness?"

"I was thinking how lovely you are, that's all," he replied.

"That's good to hear," she laughed gaily, pulling him closer.

CHAPTER 13

The third Saturday in June found Fordy and his father at a local farm sale in Finghall. The tenant was retiring and, as was the custom in the area, local farmers and business folk turned out in the hope of buying some second-hand tackle and to give their neighbour a good send off.

The day was overcast with a lazy wind that ebbed and flowed over the field. Ben and Fordy were after a couple of stone troughs. While they waited for the auctioneer to begin the sale, they bought a pint and a pasty at the bar. Taking their refreshments over to a bench they sat down and took their food and drink in silence. Fordy watched the familiar scene. All of the items that were to be sold had been laid out over the grass and on trestle tables. The sale would start with small items from the house, everything from linens and bedding through to kitchen utensils and furniture. Later came the tools and small equipment; spades, forks, skeps and scales; all essential for the day to day running of a small farm. At a specified time in the middle of the proceedings, the livestock would be paraded and sold. Fordy had noted there were three cows, seven heifers and thirty-seven ewes to go under the hammer. Lastly the big machines would be sold, including a plough, a turnip chopper and a couple of chain harrows.

"I fancy a look at 'is tack," said Fordy, wiping his mouth on his jacket sleeve after finishing his food.

"There'll be nowt worth 'aving," said Ben, shaking his head. "He'll be takin' any of the good stuff wi' 'im. He never 'as had a good name for looking after his equipment."

Despite Ben's words he followed Fordy over to the tables where the bridles, saddles and harnesses were displayed. He stood back as Fordy flicked his way through the various pieces of leather and metal. He dismissed most of it until he found three new saddlebags.

"Here, Dad," said Fordy quietly, "I might have a bid on these." He quickly put them down, covering them over with a box of old stirrups. No need to draw attention to them and give himself competition when the bidding started.

"Shall we walk over to those stone troughs we fancied?" muttered Ben. It was always best not to let anyone know what you were after at one of these sales, your close friends and neighbours were your rivals once the auction began.

Wandering over to the lines of equipment laid out over the ground Fordy looked around with a critical eye at the folks around him. How would Anna look at these people? What would she think of the rough assortment of country folk? There were a few educated farmers and their wives but overall this crowd was a bundle of rags. Dozens of children in hand-me-down clothes ran carelessly about, enjoying their freedom. Labouring men and their families, escaping from the drudgery of their daily lives, were happy to spend an hour or two in the open air, sharing a word with friends.

Fordy had never questioned the quality of his neighbours before. His father had taught him that everyman who worked for a living was due respect. Until now Fordy had also lived by that code but today it didn't seem quite so simple.

"Ben, Ben Robson, I've been looking for you," called a booming voice.

Everyone turned their heads to see His Grace the Duke of Malbury enter their midst, men stepped aside, doffing their caps, and the womenfolk gave little curtsies, whilst trying to quieten and restrain noisy children.

Ben walked forward and took his hat off before proffering his hand, which was firmly taken.

"Your Grace, how are you today?" asked Ben with a nod.

"Fine, fine, looks like there's a good turn out," said the Duke of Malbury.

"That's the way round here. Jack's never done anybody a bad turn and folks are always loyal," said Ben approvingly.

"Now, you cut to the chase don't you, Ben, with your talk of loyalty but I'll speak to you about that in a moment. It's young Fordy I want a word with," said the imposing Duke, who had made an attempt to dress down in a cord jacket and black breeches.

At his side stood Peterson, his agent, who was clutching a leather satchel in one hand and a wedge of papers in the other. His mouth tightly nipped, he danced around behind the Duke.

Fordy stepped forward, removing his cap and giving a nod. The Duke took his hand with enthusiasm.

"I wanted to give you first refusal, Fordy. There's fifty acres coming up next door to you at Worlds End, old Billy Smith has let us know he wants to give up High Field Farm. I know we said you could have forty acres over near Catterick next year but this is nearer for you. What do you think, lad? Would it suit?" asked His Grace. His lackey behind him appeared to get more agitated and started muttering.

"This is a surprise sir; did you know about this, Dad?" he asked, turning to his father.

Ben shook his head.

"Of course I'm interested, we're about bursting with 'orses," said Fordy, looking back at the Duke.

"So, it's a yes, is it?" asked His Grace, slapping Fordy on his back.

"What do you think, Dad?" asked Fordy.

"I'd snap the man's hand off before he changes his mind," nodded Ben.

"You'd better say yes quickly because my man here thinks I shouldn't be offering it to you. He has another tenant in mind, don't you, Peterson?" said His Grace sharply to his agent.

Peterson flushed and continued to mutter.

"Take this note," said His Grace, giving Fordy a folded piece of paper. "I'm away again tomorrow, up to London. You need to meet with Peterson at my solicitor's in Bedale next week."

"Yes, sir," said Fordy, taken aback by the speed of the man and the transaction, clutching the paper tightly in his fist.

"You understand, Peterson?" said His Grace, turning to his agent. "This is to be completed next week; young Robson is to take over High Field Farm on Michaelmas Day."

"Yes, Your Grace," mumbled the sullen faced Peterson.

"Excellent," said His Grace. "I think if you go and see Billy Smith, he'll give you the spot at the end of July; he's keen to be away. I know by rights, Michaelmas Day is the quarter day."

"I'll go and 'ave a word wi'him," nodded Fordy.

His Grace turned to his man, "Now, off you go, Peterson, I want a private word with Ben."

Unable to do other than obey, the dark-suited agent slid away across the field.

"Now, Ben, I need some honest words from you, my old friend." His Grace threw his arm round Ben's shoulder, leading him away from the prying ears. Fordy made to leave them.

"I want you in on this, Fordy," said His Grace, beckoning with his arm. "Come closer."

"Sir?" asked Fordy, moving towards the two older men.

Taking a secluded corner beside a hedge, well clear of folk, the Duke lowered his usually loud voice. "I've been away far too long, there're a number of matters that need my urgent attention, and one of them is the Philpots. You are no doubt aware of the situation?"

Both men nodded.

"I can't be seen to get involved with it but I don't like this business. I won't be on the bench for their case but I'm making enquiries to find out which of my fellow magistrates will be presiding. I know the law intend to make an example of them down at York. Now that I'm back in England I'll do everything I can to influence the outcome but my immediate concern is the family. Do you know where the lad is?"

"Aye, sir," said Fordy, "we got him away with the drovers, about a week after his father was arrested."

"Excellent," he snorted, digging into his pocket. "Here, take this, give it to Mrs Philpot. I want no trace of this coming back to me. I've too many irons in the fire at the present time." He pushed a leather purse into Ben's hand, who took it silently and slid it in his jacket pocket.

"You always were a soft touch, Charlie," said Ben, taking the liberty of addressing the Duke by his childhood name. "Aye, you and me both, Ben," replied His Grace, giving Ben's shoulders a hearty squeeze.

"I'd best be away; I have other matters to attend to today. As I mentioned, business takes me away again but I should be back in July. When I return, I shall be here all summer; I know I have neglected my Yorkshire estates," said the Duke, taking Ben and Fordy's hands again. "We'll share a few nights over some of your ale, Ben, when I get back," he added, before striding off.

"He's like a whirlwind," observed Fordy.

"Aye, he is. He means well but he'd do better to spend more time here on his Yorkshire affairs, not leave the detail to the likes of Peterson. Men like him are over fond o' lining their own pockets."

"What is Peterson up to, do you know?"

"While the Duke is away he has a free hand. I suspect he was wanting to put a tenant in High Field Farm who would pay him for the favour. But it's not just Peterson, there's plenty of men around the Duke who spend their time lining their own purses."

"John Burgess told me that the only thing keeping him safe against Adams was the influence of the Duke of Malbury."

"That'll be true enough. But like I said, His Grace doesn't spend enough time here to make his authority felt."

Ben's words echoed ominously in Fordy's ears. Without the Duke of Malbury present Adams may well think he had a free hand, just as Peterson did. Both of them bullying and manipulating folk with the sole intention of making money for themselves.

Fordy and his father wandered back to the crowded area, exchanging a few words here and there with neighbours and friends but no one was bold enough or rude enough to comment on their long conversation with the Duke.

The auction had begun, household goods had been sold and a start had been made on the small tools. Shovels, axes, brushes and nails were going under the hammer; most of it had seen better days, but still, nothing went unsold. Fordy watched the retiring farmer and his wife standing beside the auctioneer, who would occasionally ask the farmer a question about an item that was about to be sold. The retiring farmer stood tall and proud but his wife had a handkerchief in her hand and was dabbing at her eyes, collecting the tears that she seemed to be shedding continuously. It was a day of mixed emotions for the couple, sad to leave their old way of life and to see their possessions dispersed through the neighbourhood. Letting go of an old spade with its peculiar, twisted shaft or a milking stool that had been repaired last Christmas eve was a wrench but as much as the past would pull at their sentiments, they would hope for brisk bidding. Higher prices meant a more secure retirement.

Fordy knew the old couple and as he observed their dignified behaviour he considered the implications of getting old for the first time in his life. Making arrangements for the few years at the end of your life when hard labour was beyond you was a troublesome matter. Most folk relied on their family, hoping their children or grandchildren would look after them. In this case, the retiring tenants had one daughter who lived up at Leyburn; Ben had told Fordy that they were going to rent a small cottage near to her. It was assumed they'd managed to put a bit by over the years and, along with the proceeds from today's sale, they would have enough money to see out their days in reasonable comfort.

There was no doubt in Fordy's mind that he would look after his father and Mary Ann when the time came. But today, his thoughts moved on; would he have a brood of children to care for him? Could he provide a comfortable old age for himself and a wife? Would he even live to enjoy an old age? Life was precarious, many folk never saw fifty, and providing for an old infirm relative wasn't a problem everyone had to overcome.

Looming in his thoughts was Anna: who would she be sharing her twilight years with? As much as he desired her now the prospect of sharing their lives together was too much of a leap for his imagination. If such a thing were to happen, what would their lives be like? He was a working man and she was… she was a lady, used to the refinements in life that he would never be able to offer her. She wouldn't expect to spend her old age eking out a few pennies to last the week or searching for firewood to keep them warm through a bitter winter. His thoughts were interrupted by his father nudging his arm.

"Things are not going well for that fella o'er there, he seems to have 'is 'eart set on them buckets but yon woman is going to have the better of him," whispered Ben, with a chortle.

Fordy had been oblivious to the ongoing sale, he gave his father a nod, implying he was well aware of the situation and watched the two prospective buyers go head-to-head for half a dozen buckets, which had all seen better days.

Today came with its complications for the buyers too. Many would go the extra penny or two to help send off their retiring neighbour but no one would want to be robbed. Then others got carried away in the heat of the moment and found they had paid over the odds for an item. Sometimes there was friction when strangers appeared and outbid a local. Folks had no business coming into a community and creaming off the best tackle but there little anyone could do other than walk away and ignore the trespassers.

The auctioneer ruled the day; once the hammer was brought down, the matter was closed although there'd be plenty of bartering going on amongst the crowd throughout the afternoon. It was a chance to do a bit of extra trade and many a deal would occur with a wink and a quick handshake away from the eye of the auctioneer.

When the stone troughs were called out, Ben stood back as the bidding began, allowing Fordy to make the decision on how far to go. He secured them for a couple of guineas then waited for the saddlebags to go under the hammer. On this occasion Fordy was unlucky and watched as two men bid each other up higher than the items would have cost new. With no further interest in the sale and satisfied with their day's endeavours, they headed back to Worlds End.

That night Fordy lay awake into the small hours. He was in a hole with no idea of how to get out of it. He'd put on a good show over tea for his father and Mary Ann, sharing in their delight over the offer of High Field Farm. They had run on excitedly with their thoughts and ideas.

"We'll make a start on the fencing and gates," Ben had said. "If Billy's moving off at the end of July we can get some horses onto that pasture for a few months."

"There might be chance of a late crop of hay too," added Fordy, "I'll go over and see Billy next week and 'ave a look over his fields."

"What sort of a state do you think the house will be in?" asked Mary Ann.

"I think we'll have our work cut out, pulling it round," said Ben.

"It'll be to scrub from top to bottom, there'll be years of muck in that house," she speculated.

"There's no 'urry, you're in no rush to move into the house, are you, Fordy?"

Fordy's thoughts had been drifting during the conversation. Anna troubled him the most but the restlessness he had begun to feel made it impossible to make any sense of the conflicts in his life. Fordy owed his father his allegiance but, just as their long-term business plans were coming to fruition, his eyes had been opened to new possibilities. Life had seemed so simple just a few weeks ago.

"Fordy… I asked you about the house," repeated his father.

"Which house?"

"High Field, I said you'd be in no rush to move up there," answered Ben.

"No," Fordy shook his head. "No rush at all."

* * *

On his way to see Anna for his weekly visit, Fordy was preoccupied with how to tell her about High Field Farm.

He didn't want to give her the impression that he thought that she would want to live there with him but he hoped she would be enthusiastic about his lucky break. Conversely, she might believe that this progression in his life would put another barrier between them. Worst of all he was finding it difficult getting much enthusiasm up for the whole enterprise now that he was distracted by other business possibilities.

Settling himself beside her on the couch in her garden hideaway he broke his news in a blunt manner despite rehearsing its delivery several times in his head.

"I've been offered a farm next door," he said.

"What does that mean?" she asked.

"I've the chance of taking it over, it's only fifty acres but we sorely need it for the 'orses. We saw the Duke on Saturday, up at the farm sale, he said I could have it, if I wanted it."

"Which duke?"

"Malbury, he lives up at the castle."

"I know where the Duke of Malbury lives. Do you know him?" she asked sharply.

"Well… yes…sort of. My dad and him are on friendly terms. Why?"

"You never said."

"Round here everybody knows everybody else, from the gentry down to the wool comber's apprentice."

"I still find it hard to believe you were with him on Saturday and he casually offered you a farm," she said.

"There was nothing casual about it. Originally he had said I could have some land over at Catterick but this place 'as come up unexpectedly and the Duke thought it would suit us better. Do you see?"

"Is the Duke of Malbury familiar with all of your business dealings?"

"I don't think so, it's just that he… er… takes an interest." Fordy stuttered his words. Explaining their relationship with the Duke of Malbury was challenging for him. No one locally would question the arrangement. Plenty of businessmen dealt with His Grace in one way or another, like John Burgess. Not that Fordy would confess to knowing it. Business was private, it didn't matter who was involved.

"Have you told him about me, that you visit Kings Pasture every week and take advantage of Stillerton's daughter?" she bit back at him.

"What's the matter with you? Of course I haven't told him. I've told no one, I wouldn't…" Fordy tailed off.

"I thought I was getting to know you but now you tell me of your friendship with the highest-ranking gentleman in the district. Even my father is only on nodding terms with the Duke of Malbury."

"That's because your father is a greedy foolish…" Fordy stopped, realising his mistake. In grim silence she began to pace the room. Fordy reached for his glass of wine, waiting for her to speak. He could hear her breathing heavily behind him; he resisted the urge to go to her. Kind words weren't going to alter the facts.

"I see it now," she said eventually, coming back to the sofa but choosing not to sit. "Up here a man is given credit for his honesty, his trustworthiness. It doesn't matter if you have twenty thousand a year if you are a scoundrel, you don't get respect or courtesy from your neighbours…" she hesitated … and you don't even get a nod, if you're a buffoon who's spent all his money, like my father," she added with bitterness in her voice.

"Yes, that's how it is," replied Fordy. He hadn't expected this reaction. He had hoped she would be excited for him, but she seemed more concerned about his family connections. Anna's view of the world was at odds with his and that challenged his beliefs. Although he wasn't sure it was good to keep questioning the structure of his life as it unsettled him too much.

She stood in silence for a few moments longer. Fordy daren't ask what she was thinking, fearful that her answer may be contrary to his feelings for her. Finally she broke her reverie.

"I have an idea, let me draw you and, whilst you sit you can tell me your news," she suggested.

He would much rather have talked about his farm and his horses without this fancy rigmarole of sitting for a drawing. But the night had got off to an uneasy start; he would do as she asked.

"Shall we go outside? You could sit on the mounting block," she added.

So they decamped to the garden where he perched himself on the steps. At first Jasper sat beside him but soon forsook Fordy in favour of scenting rabbits.

"Where did you learn to draw?" asked Fordy, whilst Anna began to adjust her easel and paper.

"I had an Italian governess for ten years who encouraged me," said Anna.

"So, you'll speak Italian as well then?" asked Fordy.

"Yes, I'm fluent or I was. There's not much call for it up here," Anna shrugged and fell silent, concentrating on her work.

Fordy sat on the hard stones, unsure of whether he should talk. He watched her, fascinated; she was suddenly serious, absorbed in her task.

"There now, I'm set up," she said taking up her pencil, "you can tell me all about High Field Farm."

While Anna set about creating a likeness of Fordy, he explained to her in further detail of how he had come to be offered the farm.

"Do you have some reservations about it?" asked Anna, her eyes on her drawing, not Fordy.

"I do," he answered before he could stop himself. "Why do you ask?"

"I sensed it from your tone. What's bothering you?" she asked, stopping her drawing.

"When I went to Yarm I saw a different world. Lots of different business opportunities…" he tailed off. What was he doing talking about trade to a woman of quality?

"And?"

"Are you truly interested?"

"Of course, tell me."

"It's the mines and the coal, you won't…"

"I know all about that. It's all my father talks about when he comes to see me. He wants to put some money up for a new railway but it would have to be my money and I won't agree to it. He tells me that all his friends in Durham are scrambling to invest in these schemes. He's been to several meetings but no one can agree on the way forward. He's wasting his time though; I'll not sign over my inheritance." She glanced up at him for a response.

Fordy didn't answer; she returned to her drawing.

Was he the only person in the world who had been ignorant of what was happening further north? Had he been so wrapped up in his little world of trading tea, breeding horses, and chasing women that he had failed to take notice of the world around him?

Eventually he spoke. "It's the demand for 'orses. They'll need thousands of 'em for pulling wagons and barges."

"What's stopping you?"

"I don't really know. The person I need to speak to is my father but I am fearful of upsetting him. We have planned for extra land and increasing the numbers of 'orses but it's Cleveland Bays we had in mind. They're versatile and suit folk in these parts. That's where we thought the market was… but compared to the chances up north… we're of no consequence out here."

"And it appeals to you? Breeding animals to work on the rail tracks and waterways?" she asked plainly.

"Aye, it does, I liked the bustling activity up there. I know it sounds stupid…" He dropped his gaze to his lap.

"I think it sounds exciting. Just because you think you have found a new venture doesn't mean you have to turn your back on your father. If, as you say, the Duke of Malbury has your best interests at heart, he may know of a place you could take in Durham. You'd still need your land out here, somewhere to keep your young stock."

"I hadn't thought of that. I've been getting so twisted up with this restlessness my mind's all over the place."

He watched Anna as she drew. This was no infatuation. He knew he had met his equal. He had never expected to meet a female with a logical head for business. More puzzling was the fact that she grasped the concept of trade. With her background and breeding he had assumed her head would be full of the latest fashions and dance steps.

Maybe she was right, perhaps life wasn't as complicated and difficult as he had begun to believe it to be.

"Have you finished drawing?" he asked. "My backside is numb; these slabs are damned cold."

"I'll finish it off tomorrow, when the light's better but come and look at what I've done so far, if you care to."

He jumped off the blocks and bent forward, squeezing at his buttocks to bring them back to life.

"You've put that wretched dog in as well," he laughed, looking over her shoulder at her drawing.

"I had to; without Jasper I may well have never met you, my darling."

"True enough. Is it a fair likeness?" he asked.

"You must know your own face; don't you look in a mirror?"

"Not if I can help it," he replied, as he inspected the drawing. "It's well drawn, you have an eye for detail but I'm not sure I'm the best person to comment, although you have certainly captured Jasper well enough."

"Let me sign it," she said, bending down to the corner. She wrote, 'Fordy and Jasper in KPH garden. June 1816. AJS.'

"What are the initials for? asked Fordy.

"Annabelle Jane Stillerton."

"I didn't know your full name. There's so much we don't know about each other." He bent to kiss her.

"That's true. What other secrets are you keeping from me, Fordy Robson? Have you another girl in town? Are you going to disappear from my life as quickly as you came into it?"

Fordy stepped back. "I've just shared with you my ideas about my business and my horses and you now accuse me of having another woman."

"I'm sorry, I shouldn't have said that. I feel so trapped, like a pawn in a game of chess. My father could take me from here without a moment's notice. We have a few brief hours together once a week, then you go off back to your real life, leaving me here, alone."

"You see my problems so clearly and suggest simple answers but you are as anxious about your situation as I am about mine," he said, taking her hands.

"And do you have an easy solution to my worries?" she asked.

"No. What do you think we should do? I could never enter your world; I haven't the money or the upbringing to even contemplate it," he said.

They had come to the heart of the matter now. As much as he would have preferred to put this off, he continued. "You couldn't possibly cope with the life I lead. We'd have no fine house or furnishings. Our days would be long and all of our rewards won through hard work and toil. I haven't the means to give you the life of a lady."

"I know," she answered.

"No doubt you have come to the same conclusion as me," he said, the words choking in his throat.

"What is that?" she asked.

"Your father will decide to take you away from here. One day I shall come to see you and you will be gone. If you were to be taken away by your father it would break my heart but I think that's what will happen."

"Don't say that, I couldn't bear it," she sobbed.

"As harsh as it sounds now, it maybe wouldn't be so bad after a few months, you would return to your own world, find a man who was kind to you, marry him and have lots of bairns. You'll live in a grand house and your few months of ranging round this garden with a local ruffian will be a memory. Who knows, in a few years' time you may visit Kings Pasture House with your husband and children, perhaps you'll see me on a horse as you drive past in your carriage and discreetly give me a nod and a wave."

"Is that what you wish for me?"

"No," he said flatly. "It would destroy me to think of you in another man's arms."

"There's always my money," she said, quietly.

"You said you don't get it until you are twenty-five, that's four years away."

"That's true but it also becomes available to me when I marry."

Fordy wasn't sure how to take this news or what she meant by telling him. Could she be suggesting they should marry and use her money? He turned away from her, trying to think of how to answer her.

"My legacy could be valuable to me if I should marry the right man but it also makes me vulnerable to my father's wishes," she added.

"In what way?" said Fordy.

"He could assert his authority over me and force me to marry someone, if it suited him," she replied.

"What do you mean, 'if it suited him'?" asked Fordy.

"My mother's will stipulates an amount for my dowry but once that is paid there is no reason why my father couldn't extract some of my legacy from my estate should he find a suitable husband for me who would agree to such an arrangement," she explained.

"Your situation is precarious," muttered Fordy. He had already realised that Anna could be exploited by her father but talking about it with her was difficult. He was out of his depth; buying and selling livestock and even negotiating the letting of a farm was one thing but to be discussing dowries, legacies and wills was beyond him.

"I don't know what to say," he said, taking her in his arms. He couldn't possibly think that she would consider him a suitable husband. But then why had she mentioned her legacy and explained it to him if not to suggest they marry? If this had been any ordinary girl that he'd fallen in love with who was having troubles with her father he'd ask her to marry him. Of course an ordinary girl wouldn't have the problems with her inheritance that Anna was facing.

She sank into his arms; his overwhelming desire to protect her made him hold her even closer.

Fordy fumbled out some words he hoped might encourage her to give him some more solid clue as to what he could do to help her. "But you have four years of this, until you are twenty-five, there is no escape unless you can find a sympathetic man to marry…"

"That's what happened in Italy but once Father found out that I had formed an attachment, he brought me back here."

Fordy needed time to think. Should he speak to someone about this? He rarely discussed his romantic encounters but this was different. He'd got himself tangled up in complex situation and knew there was no easy way out.

As he left Anna and rode home he felt more despondent than he had ever felt in his life. Always happy to take the road of least resistance Fordy knew he was being faced with issues that would ultimately require decisions to be made. He couldn't just slide along taking opportunities as they fell into his lap any longer. Everything was on its head.

He should be content with the opportunity of the new farm that the Duke of Malbury had offered and be throwing himself into making a living there, making reality the plans that he and his father had discussed over the years. Instead he was attracted to the possibilities of the industries to the north and he had fallen in love with a woman who was not only too good for him but brought with her a river of troubles that he couldn't hope to swim through.

CHAPTER 14

A week after Anna had told Fordy the details of her distressing situation Fordy received word from the Duke of Malbury's solicitors, Tallow and Tallow, that he was expected at their offices in Bedale at noon on 1st July to sign the rental agreement for High Field Farm.

On the day of the appointment he presented himself with some apprehension. Was he signing his life away to a commitment that was going to become a burden? Since Easter his life had become topsy-turvy; had he brought these events on himself or was life simply playing games with him? Was he being thrown up in the air and left to land through chance or had he allowed himself to be manoeuvred into a corner with his devil-may-care attitude to life? No doubt Mary Ann would tell him that there were evil spirits at work and he should take more care not to walk under ladders or let black cats cross his path. Whatever was the truth of the matter he felt less than comfortable as he entered Tallow and Tallow's.

He was taken upstairs and shown to his seat by a small timid clerk who quickly disappeared once he was seated. Sat on a hard, lumpy chair, amongst piles of books, ledgers and loose papers, waiting to be seen he began to regret his decision to forego a drink at the Oak.

His doubts about taking High Field Farm persisted, his situation made more difficult because he still hadn't found the courage to share these misgivings with his father. Despite Anna telling him about her inheritance Fordy couldn't begin to realistically imagine a life with her. Ideally, he needed a farmer's daughter, used to the long unpredictable hours of caring for livestock and the land; a lass who could run a household, cook and help outside when needed, not to mention rearing any children they might produce.

His mood ebbed as the minutes passed, his chair becoming intolerably uncomfortable and the unfamiliar cloying smell of fusty paperwork added to his unease. What was keeping Mr Tallow? He could hear low voices through the door that bore the solicitor's name. Suddenly the door flew open. Mr Tallow stood in the opening.

"Fordy, is it?" he asked.

"Yes, sir," answered Fordy.

"Come in, I've been going over the finer points of the tenancy with Peterson here," said Mr Tallow, showing Fordy into his office.

Peterson made a half-hearted attempt to stand, giving Fordy a curt nod.

"Take a seat, Fordy," said Mr Tallow. "Now, I know I act on behalf of His Grace, but he asked me to make sure the terms were favourable for you. I've had a copy written out and we can go through it together now."

Fordy hadn't been sure of what to expect at this meeting. "Alright," he agreed, looking across at Peterson, who sat silent and tight lipped.

Mr Tallow read through the details, commenting on any irregularities or special terms. He had a slow melodious voice and hesitated over words and phrases, glancing at Fordy to check that he understood what was being said.

The main matter for discussion was Billy Smith's departure from High Field Farm at the end of July rather than the usual practice of staying until quarter day in September. Rent would not be due for Fordy to pay until that quarter day, allowing him time to repair fixtures and fittings, many of which had fallen into disrepair.

Concluding the matter with signatures from each party, Peterson abruptly stood up, "If you'll excuse me gentlemen, I have other business to attend to."

Fordy and Mr Tallow quickly rose to their feet to shake Peterson's hand but the man was gone before either was upright.

"Take your seat," said Mr Tallow, pointing towards Fordy's chair. "Have a glass of port to celebrate your tenancy."

"Thank you, sir." Fordy was desperate to comment on Peterson's hostile manner but daren't for fear of causing offence.

"Now there's a fellow," said Mr Tallow, leaning back in his chair, savouring his drink.

Fordy shuffled uncomfortably and gave a small cough, waiting for Mr Tallow to expand on his views of Peterson. It occurred to Fordy that Mr Tallow would see most of what occurred in Bedale from this office with its window that looked down onto the high street, should he have time to stand at the window and watch. Fordy wondered if he had observed his escape from Tom Dennison several weeks ago.

"Is your father well?" asked Mr Tallow, after a long pause.

"Yes, sir, he is." Fordy watched the solicitor, who appeared more interested in his drink than any legal matters. He emptied his glass and placed it on the solicitor's desk. Should he get up to leave, was the meeting over?

"Another one? To help you on your way," suggested Mr Tallow, reaching forward for Fordy's glass, replenishing it from the decanter that sat on a small table beside the desk.

"Thank you," said Fordy, appreciating the signal from Mr Tallow that he wanted him to stay.

"Peterson doesn't think you should get High Field Farm," Mr Tallow confessed.

"I got that impression," answered Fordy.

"He thought it should go to a friend of his," said the solicitor, "and he said it's most irregular to give a place like High Field to a chap that isn't wed."

Fordy didn't answer, unsure of what to say.

"Our Mr Peterson has been running the Malbury Estate on his own terms. I've been telling His Grace this for years now and, finally, he is listening to me. Peterson has been taking backhanders for too long. I think he may be out of a job when His Grace returns this summer," he concluded, in his slow matter of a fact voice.

"Aye, my dad says there needs to be a firmer hand up at the castle."

"Does he now? What else does he say?"

"That His Grace should keep a sharper eye on his business dealings. That there's too many folk doing as they please, lining their own pockets, at the Duke's expense."

"Aye," said Mr Tallow, "your father's right."

Once again silence fell between the two men. Fordy feared he had said too much as he watched the solicitor turn to look out of the window.

"It's been good to meet you, Fordy," said Mr Tallow, rising from his seat and offering Fordy his hand across the desk. "I'll get this finalised, call in any day you are in town and pick up a copy. You usually come down on a market day, don't you?"

"I do." Fordy swallowed, "There won't be much you miss from this window... that goes on in the High Street."

"You are right," said the solicitor, raising his eyebrows, "not much at all."

Leaving the building Fordy was in no doubt that Mr Tallow had seen him fleeing from Jane's father. Those Dennisons were a damned nuisance, making him look a fool in the town. Standing at the solicitor's doorway for a moment, he could hear loud jovial voices from the Oak next door but decided against entering. He looked up at the church clock; it was after one. He decided to buy some pies, then go over to Abe and Chalky's blacksmiths shop to eat them.

Once outside the baker's shop, the smell of fresh baking got the better of Fordy and he pulled out a steak pasty. Standing in a doorway on the high street, he bit into the hot crusty pie; the pastry crumbled in his mouth but the steaming savoury meat filling burnt his tongue. He involuntarily spat it out but, unable to catch it, it splattered on the ground just as two well-dressed ladies passed him. They both glared at him.

"Disgusting behaviour," said the older one, pulling her companion away from Fordy.

He watched them march down the street and looked back at the pie still in his hand, his cheeks flushed. Knowing he should wait until he got to the smithy, he blew gently on it then took another tentative bite. There was nothing that tasted as solid or satisfying as a warm salty beef pie and, as it had cooled a little, he ate more of it and felt comforted. Finishing off with several more large mouthfuls, he could feel the gravy oozing down his chin. The pleasure of the pie was knocked when he saw the two genteel women return down the street. Before he could raise his hand to wipe away the juices that were on his face he heard the mature lady mutter something about uncouth wretch. He couldn't care less about the stuffy old matron and shot a glance at the younger one, hoping she might find his behaviour amusing, but she looked even more repulsed than her companion, her nose curled up and a look of contempt on her face, as they swished by.

Pulling his arm across his face to remove the remaining traces of his pie it occurred to him that it might have been Anna walking passed him as he gorged on the food. What would she make of his behaviour? He knew even Mary Ann would have given him a stern word about eating in the street. But what was a fella meant to do when he was hungry?

Taking your food at a leisurely refined pace was alright for those who had nothing better to do but for anyone who was busy and trying to make a bit o' money those niceties were a nonsense. Looking down the high street where the two haughty women had disappeared he momentarily hated them and all they represented. He consoled himself with the thought that he was honest and would never despise anyone who was trying to make a living… even if they did eat food in the street.

However, he decided to finish the pies off at the smithy and, licking his fingers clean, he set off for the blacksmith's shop.

"Fordy, is that you?" asked a familiar voice from behind.

His heart plummeted. He kept walking, pretending he hadn't heard.

"Fordy… please stop. I really want to talk to you."

There was no escaping. He turned to see Jane following him.

"Thank you… for stopping," she said, breathlessly.

"I've nowt to say to you," said Fordy. This was the first time he had laid eyes on her since her father had thrashed him. She looked somewhat dishevelled, her hair was longer and curlier, and there was no disguising her thickened waist.

"I can understand that but there is something I need to say to you. I never told me dad it's your bairn. He jumped to that conclusion on his own," she said, "I wanted to say I'm sorry before…"

"You'd 'ave been happy enough to land me with another man's brat but you're sorry your dad gave me a beltin'," he hesitated, watching her reaction. "Well, I'm glad to 'ave 'ad the beating, better that than being lumbered with you and your bastard child. Now bugger off."

Her face was defiant. "I'm not being dropped; Andy will stand by me."

"I thought he was all set to wed Elsie Smith and become a farmer. You gonna turn Andy into a butcher's boy along with your gormless brother?" Fordy flared at her.

"You've no call to say such nasty things when I'm apologising out of common decency, Fordy."

"You're crackers, Jane. I was never going to marry you. You're a lying little slut. The whole town's laughin' at you."

"I've told you before, Fordy, you'd do well to hold your tongue." Her face sharpened, to that familiar meanness Fordy knew so well. "We all know what you get up to at Kings Pasture House. You might think you're being clever evading the excise men but the truth of it is, nobody gives a damn about you and you petty dealing. Don't you think you'd have been caught by now if anyone cared?"

"And you wonder why I wanted to get away from you?" Fordy bit back. He knew he should walk away.

"All your pathetic contraband and the way you creep around with John Burgess. I know he's in trouble. He's in way above his head."

"Where do you get your grubby information from, Jane?" he snapped back. He could see she was getting agitated, already flustered when she stopped him, her face was now flushed red and her eyes had widened.

"You'd be surprised who I know. I know you were skulking around in the woods at Kings Pasture the other day." She threw the words at Fordy.

Fordy's heart skipped a beat, he stared at her vicious face and stepped forward. How much did she know? Was she aware of Anna and their meetings? How did she know about Picard finding him in the woods? He remembered Fred Higgins telling him he'd seen Jane up near Kings Pasture.

"The only person who saw me up at Kings Pasture was that filthy frog Picard. Is that your source of information?"

"Wouldn't you like to know?" she smirked at him, just a little too confidently.

"Has Picard filled your belly?"

Jane's hand went to her swollen stomach. Her mouth dropped open, her victorious smile now gave way to an expression of momentary defeat.

Had he hit home there? He turned and marched away from her.

Fordy hated confrontation, his heart was thudding in his chest, but he was glad he had faced her down. Striding towards his friend's smithy, he worked through what she had said. If she knew about Anna she would probably have said, he hoped that his secret was safer than hers was. But if Jane was pregnant with Picard's child why didn't he marry her? Why try to trick some other poor sod down the aisle?

In the blacksmiths yard he found Chalky shoeing a young colt, its owner waiting patiently for the work to be completed.

"I'll be done in a few minutes," Chalky called to Fordy.

The owner of the horse was unknown to Fordy so, feeling under no obligation to make conversation with the stranger, he went and sat on a low wall to eat his second pie. He watched Chalky work, quietly fitting a shoe to the horse. The day was cold for July but Chalky worked bare chested, his only protection a well-worn leather apron. Fordy had watched the brothers and their father shoe many a horse but today, as he sat and calmed himself from Jane's words, he noticed the bulky perfection of his friend's muscular torso.

Eventually Chalky was happy with the fit and he quickly hammered the metal onto the horse's hoof. Concluding his business with the customer, he went to Fordy and sat with him.

"Are you on your own today?" asked Fordy.

"Aye, Father and Abe are next door at the hall, helping with some gates," said Chalky. "We thought it would be quiet here this morning but it's been non-stop. I've had two thrown shoes, a coal scuttle to mend and I'm meant to be making a start on a weathervane."

"Here," said Fordy, "I bought some pies, want one?"

Chalky took one and bit a huge chunk out of it. "So," he said, his mouth full of food, "'ave you been and signed up for t'farm?"

"I 'ave," said Fordy, and he recounted his visit to Mr Tallow.

"Then, as I was coming over here, I got stopped by Jane," said Fordy. "She's a sly vixen. I asked her if Picard had rutted 'er."

"You mean that Frenchie up at Kings Pasture?"

Fordy nodded.

"You think Jane's been dallying with him?"

"She knows too much about my visits to Kings Pasture, and she knew I'd had a run in with Picard. T'other day, Fred Higgins told me he'd seen her scurrying around in the woods next to Kings Pasture."

"So why doesn't Picard marry her if he's fathered the bairn?" asked Chalky, reaching for another pie.

"No idea, maybe he has a wife and family tucked away," shrugged Fordy.

"Aren't there two foreigners up at Kings Pasture?" asked Chalky.

"Yes, the other one's called Rennie, quieter than Picard. They're employed to lug barrels and boxes, and both built like bulls. They reckon to be Flemish, but I'm sure they're deserters from Boney's army. Only a scoundrel like Stillerton would employ such dodgy bastards."

"He'll need to have a couple of thugs hanging around to protect all the contraband they have up at the stables. Not that I'm sticking up for any of 'em. But smuggling's a risky business… there's only you that treats it lightly," said Chalky, reaching for the last pastry.

"Maybe I have been lax in my ways," Fordy said thoughtfully. "Anybody can get caught… even me."

"What's brought this on? You're the last man to worry 'bout t'authorites."

"I feel like everything I do goes wrong these days, even the…"

"You're the luckiest bugger I've ever met, nowt flops for you."

Fordy shook his head. "You have no idea, Chalky, if I had nine lives, I think I've used 'em all up."

"What's gone wrong?"

"If I tell you, you'll keep it to y'self?" asked Fordy. He had never shared his concerns with anyone other than his father before.

"Course."

"I've put up a bit o'money on a venture with John Burgess. At first I thought there was no risk but now John's getting worried. It's with Jim Adams, you know, the bloke who runs the smuggling…"

"Don't tell me you've got tied up with Adams?" interrupted Chalky with a groan. "I know you delivered a message to him at Yarm but I didn't think you had any connections with 'im."

"It's through John. I wouldn't have done it on my own. Adams is looking for more money now, some big backer has pulled out and he's putting pressure on John."

"I wish you'd told me of your intention to jump in with Adams. A friend of mine has got tangled up with him and is finding it difficult to escape. Adams is a rogue and he'll exploit anybody's weaknesses…" Chalky tailed off and for a few moments both men were quiet.

"What is this venture that you've got involved with?" Chalky asked, breaking the silence.

"A ship load of silks, spices, stuff from the east. I don't know any more than that. I don't even understand it if I'm honest. It just seemed like an easy way to make some money."

"Is that what's been bothering you these past few weeks?"

"How do you mean?" Fordy snapped back.

"You've changed. You hardly bother with the cockfighting, once you've sold your goods, you go home… and… well, you seem quieter somehow. We don't share the banter like we used to do."

"Everything's on its head for me." Fordy got up, his agitation made him fidgety. "You'll think I'm a dunce… but… I'm not sure about takin' High Field Farm," moaned Fordy throwing his hands in the air. He paced the area for a few seconds before sitting back heavily on the wall.

"You're kidding me, it's all you and y'father 'ave worked for. Building up a good strong herd o' bays and getting more pasture. What in God's name has happened?" exclaimed Chalky.

"I feel trapped. I was fair taken with Yarm and what I heard there. All that talk of mines opening, canals being dug and rail tracks laid out to carry the coal."

"What sparks your interest?" Chalky's tone was a little more enthusiastic now.

"It's still 'osses. The demand for 'em will be endless."

"I don't see your problem, what's to stop you getting into this business? All you need are a few contacts," encouraged Chalky.

"You think my father would listen? I might have to live up there. He's not getting any younger, he has Worlds End to run. I'd always thought I'd be here to help out. Not that I see myself as a landlord but…" he tailed off.

"There's summat else, isn't there?"

"Aye," said Fordy. The temptation to share his worries about Anna was overwhelming. He put his head in his hands, staring at the floor.

"It'll be no surprise to you that I've met a lass…"

Chalky threw his head back, laughing loudly. "More woman trouble, what a relief. I thowt it was gonna be something serious."

"It is serious, Chalky, honestly, it's a bloody nightmare. She's…"

"Hello there," came a shout. "Anyone here… my horse has thrown a shoe?"

Round the corner came a well-dressed gentleman leading his horse.

"Ah, it's you, Chalky, I hoped I'd find you here, you're just the man to help me out," said the newcomer.

Chalky jumped up. "Oh, hello, Giles. This is a surprise… let me have a look at your horse, see if I can help. Which leg?"

Fordy recognised Giles Redworth who he had last seen at Yarm with Chalky. Fordy watched Giles indicate the front left hoof and Chalky stroked his hand over the horse's nose, across its neck and tenderly down. Gently applying pressure on the animal's hock, he lifted its leg and inspected the foot.

"Any chance you found the shoe?" asked Chalky.

"I did," Giles announced triumphantly, pulling it out of his saddlebag. "How are you, Chalky? It seems an age since I saw you," he added, whilst reaching out to touch Chalky's naked back.

Fordy didn't think Giles knew he was sat here; feeling embarrassed he coughed and jumped up before Giles's hand made contact with Chalky's flesh. Fordy could see he had startled Redworth who quickly stepped back from Chalky and looked up to see who was also present.

"Hello, Mr Redworth," said Fordy, hastily.

"Ah… it's you, Fordy, you gave me quite a fright sculking there in the shadows," he said, shakily.

"That wasn't my intention, sir. I was just taking a bite to eat with Chalky, here," said Fordy, feeling he had to give a reason for being in his friend's workshop.

"Quite, sounds like a jolly good idea," replied Redworth, his usual jovial tone had returned. "How are those horses you bought over at Yarm?"

"They seem to be good strong animals," said Fordy. He glanced at Chalky who appeared to be unaware of the few moments of awkwardness and was still inspecting the horse's hoof.

Fordy struggled to say anymore. There was something not right here but Chalky seemed relaxed enough and Giles Redworth was as friendly as usual. It didn't seem that either of them were ill at ease with each other but he suddenly felt he shouldn't be here.

"I'll be away, Chalky; let you get on." Fordy said, aware that the time for further revelations about Anna had gone.

"Right-oh, we'll finish that business another time," said Chalky, giving Fordy a reassuring smile before turning back to Giles and his horse.

"Good day, sir," nodded Fordy, involuntarily pulling his hat from his head.

"Good day to you too, Fordy. Jolly nice to bump into you again," said Giles with one of his beaming smiles, returning Fordy's dip of the head.

Leaving Chalky to his work, Fordy went and collected Dapple. His mood was bolstered by Chalky's reaction to his idea about selling horses into the new industry in Durham, pleased he had been as encouraging as Anna. He had wondered if she'd fully understood what he was talking about. But if Chalky thought the same, perhaps it was time to talk to his father. Was he worrying over nothing? Could his concerns over Anna be overcome at the same time?

In amongst his worries he wondered what was Chalky up to? What was the nature of the connection between him and Giles Redworth? Did they share an interest in cockfighting or was there something else that seemed to draw them together? There was no doubt Redworth appeared to be a pleasant gentleman but Chalky was hardly his equal... Fordy tried to dismiss it, it wasn't any of his business.

Then there was that other matter Chalky had referred to concerning Jim Adams. He knew all of Chalky's friends, they were the same as his and he knew of no other chaps who had got involved with the smuggling. Who could it be that was feeling pressure from Adams? Fordy felt he needed to know, it may affect his own situation, but these matters tended to be sensitive and not readily disclosed. He resolved to attempt to speak to Chalky soon about it.

Feeling a little more settled about the prospect of taking on High Field Farm he decided to call in on Billy Smith on his way home. He found Billy mucking out a low shed that had housed young calves over the winter. The growing animals were now out grazing in one of his grass pastures.

"Now then, Fordy," Bill greeted him, putting down his gripe and meeting Fordy with a handshake. "I've been expecting you to call. I'm just tryin' to tidy the place up a bit."

"Aye, well I didn't want to come before I saw Mr Tallow. Everything is signed now, so I thought it was a good time to see what you and I can arrange."

"You'll be wanting the spot for 'osses?"

"That's my intention, I'll probably keep a couple of sows, like you, but I'll not be bothering with any cows."

"I don't blame you, lad, them bloody awd cows 'ave buggered my hands," said Billy, lifting up his knobbly twisted hands. It was a common enough sight; years of milking invariably left a man or woman with swollen useless fingers.

Looking round Fordy reaffirmed what he already knew; the place was suffering from neglect. You couldn't hold it against the Billy, though. He was well into his sixties with no son to follow on, why would he spend time and money on his landlord's assets?

"I should have given up this spot years ago, but you know what it's like, you get attached to a place," he said, looking up at Fordy, searching his face. "Well, maybe you don't know, you're not old enough to be sentimental. This place needs the vigour of a young man to bring it back to life."

"You'll not miss it?" asked Fordy, with a sense of relief.

"I will not," was the emphatic reply. "Come on, let's have a mug of tea."

Sat in the kitchen Fordy could see the house was as neglected as the buildings; Billy's wife had been dead fifteen years, and it showed.

"My sister comes in as often as she can but her 'ip plays up and she can't manage the walk up 'ere. She's been at me to give the place up. 'Ere lad, get that down you," he said, passing over a large steaming mug of tea. Fordy knew it would be good; Billy was one of his best customers.

"Like I said," Billy continued "this spot'll tek a bit o' pulling round but you've got time on your side."

Fordy glanced round the low-ceilinged kitchen. Regardless of the dirt, it was dark and cramped. Did he seriously believe that Anna would come and live here and be happy?

"Are you looking to tek a wife?" asked Billy, breaking into his thoughts. "Tha'll need a warm bedfella' up here on a winter's night. Wind fair rattles down t'valley. And tha'll need a wench t'cook and clean and 'ave your bairns," he chortled.

Fordy gave a low laugh, "You're right Billy, I will."

If only it was that simple.

CHAPTER 15

"It turned out better than I expected but it was clear Peterson, the Duke's agent, didn't want me to have High Field Farm," Fordy told Anna on his next visit. "Tallow, the solicitor, is a rum fella, seems he 'as everybody's measure."

"In what way?" asked Anna.

"He knows that Peterson is peeling money off the Duke at every chance. He says he's been warning His Grace of Peterson's dishonesty for years. I think there might be a bit of a shake up there, if only the Duke would get back to Yorkshire and see to his affairs. Tallow's a sharp fella; he misses nowt from that high window of his. I'm sure he saw me racing down…" he stopped himself.

"Racing down where?"

"Nothing… just a bit o' high jinks with the lads. Anyway, back to High Field, Billy Smith is glad to be away and…"

"Have you spoken to your father about expanding your business?" she cut in.

"No," Fordy said and turned away. She had that knack of slicing to the quick.

"Why not? You can't make any progress till you do," she persisted.

"I thought you'd be happy for me, now I've got High Field Farm secured and I've been to see Billy."

"Of course I am but your task is only half done. The crux of the matter is talking to your father," she answered. "And there's another matter that you need to consider."

"What's that?" he asked, turning to look at her.

"When are you taking me to see your new farm? I can't wait," she said excitedly, picking up the dog, "and neither can Jasper."

He watched her dance around the room with her pet without replying to her question. Moving over to the small window he looked out of the dirty glass on a cluster of trees stunted by ivy.

She went to him. "What's the matter?"

He feared a trip over to High Field might lead to her father discovering her activities. But just as alarming would be her disappointment when she saw the dilapidated state of the place, especially the house.

"I can't take you yet, Billy hasn't moved out, anyway, enough talk of farms, I have a problem that I need you to help me with," he said, pulling her towards him and wrapping his arms round her. He hoped that over the next couple of weeks she might forget about visiting the place or he may prove successful in dissuading her.

* * *

Fordy got word that Billy had left High Field the third week in July. A local dealer had taken his remaining stock and Billy had no reason to stay on. Once Anna was aware that the farm was vacant her requests to see the farm and relentless questions were too much for Fordy. He gave in to her and a date and time was set for the visit.

* * *

So as July gave way to August Fordy rode over to collect Anna on the first day of the month. There had been a short break in the poor weather and many farmers were taking advantage of this. As he travelled to collect Anna the roads were busy with farmhands and horses, their main activity was making hay; Fordy could see most grass fields that he passed had already been mown. Haymaking needed many hands, men who were skilled with a scythe to cut the grass, then hordes of woman and children to toss and turn the wet grass, allowing it to dry in the sun. All they needed now was a dry week for the grass to turn into hay and the chance to get it safely stored into hay stooks, ready for the winter. On this brighter day, spirits were high; he could hear laughter from the fields and the greetings from the folk on the road were lively and joyous.

Fordy was glad to join in the jolly exchanges on his way to Anna's but was uneasy, still anxious about taking her to High Field Farm and guilty about deserting his own work at Worlds End and lying to his father. He had rushed his jobs that morning and made the feeble excuse about having arranged to meet up with a builder at High Field in order to get away in time.

Fordy had agreed to meet Anna at the entrance to the lane he used on his night-time visits. He'd suggested she try to make herself look drab, in an attempt to disguise herself. When she appeared out of the trees that led back to the house he was impressed by her old, dark, shabby dress and shawl.

"Is this really you, Anna? I can hardly recognise you," he exclaimed, jumping off Dapple and embracing her. His love for her and his pride in her steely determination suddenly bubbled up. "I do love you, lass," he said, hugging her closely to him.

"Are you trying to put me off visiting the farm with a declaration of love?" she laughed, pushing him away.

"No, you've ground me down with all y' nattering. I wouldn't dare refuse now. Best put your bonnet on before we get on Dapple."

He took Dapple over to the fence, remounted and leaned over to help Anna climb up the railings. The horse stood perfectly still as Anna transferred herself onto Dapple, behind Fordy. Settling herself to a comfortable position, she wrapped her arms around Fordy.

"A mounting block would have made that a lot easier but I'm secure now," she commented happily, kissing Fordy on the back of his neck.

"What an exciting adventure this is," she exclaimed. Her delight was at odds with Fordy's worries; this visit could be the end of things between them. However, the nearness of her and the feel of her body against him quelled his unease for a while.

Fordy clicked Dapple on, rubbing his hand over the horse's neck. He had a lot to be grateful for; a reliable horse, a bonny lass sat behind him and a new farm to call his own. If he dwelt on the good things in his life there was no need to worry. But there were always problems lurking in the background. He really must make an effort to speak to his father about his business ideas. There had been no news from John Burgess regarding Adams. The Duke of Malbury was still absent and the Philpots continued to be held in York Gaol. Then, of course, he returned to the problem of the future of him and Anna, although he suspected her disappointment with High Field Farm might solve that. He tried to prepare himself for the moment when she suddenly realised the reality of who he was and what life with him would really be like.

"Don't be expecting anything fancy, the place is a mess," he said to her.

"I'm aware of that, you must have told me that a hundred times," she insisted.

Their ride over was uneventful, although having her sat behind him on Dapple with her arms wrapped tightly around him had been distracting. With the warmth and touch of her body against his back, he fought to keep his mind on the road and his horse.

Approaching their destination, the road climbed steeply for a few hundred yards. High Field Farm was aptly named, it sat on a piece of high ground to the east of Worlds End.

Fordy turned Dapple in to the driveway and the ram shackled old house sat in front of them. "There you are," said Fordy, "what do you make of this?"

The mass of nettles and weeds that grew around the house had taken a hold; even in this cold summer such plants still thrived. The place looked even more neglected than on his previous visit, perhaps his eye was increasingly critical with Anna beside him.

Built of cobbles collected from the fields, High Field Farm had never been more than a cottage. An ugly gable end had been added on and was built with a mixture of stones and brick from the nearby brick yard but none of it was pleasing to the eye. The windows were small and irregular; on his last visit Fordy had noticed the wood was rotten in all of them and they needed replacing.

"I love it, it's wonderful," she exclaimed. "Keep going, I can't wait to see inside."

"One problem with this 'ouse is that this side faces north, so it always looks cold and dark. Round the other side it looks a bit more cheerful, that's where you'd grow a few vegetables…" he hesitated, realising his blunder at voicing the possibility of Anna making use of the garden. Thankfully, she let it pass.

"I'm telling you, you'll be sorely disappointed once you've seen it up close," Fordy mumbled, fearing she wasn't taking the slightest bit of notice of his warnings.

Dismounting and securing the horse's reins to the saddle, Fordy left Dapple grazing on the short grass, confident the animal wouldn't stray. Approaching the back door he noticed a few broken bricks laid on the ground and looked up to see where they had come from.

"Something's amiss up there," he said to Anna, stepping back to get a better view of the roof. "Look up at the old chimney, it's crumbling, that'll have to be sorted out quickly, it could damage the roof. I told you this spot was rough."

"It can be repaired, can't it? You must know a builder amongst all of your friends and neighbours."

"Aye, I do," he said with a prick of guilt, having used that excuse to his father earlier.

Fordy kicked at the stone where Billy had said he would leave the key. He bent to pick up the rusting old piece of metal. "Here, this should open the door," he said. "Not that there's much to lock up."

"May I?" she asked, taking the key.

"Of course," he answered, as she attempted to turn the lock in the old door. Unable to move it, Fordy took over and eventually turned the key but the door refused to open. It sat heavily on the ground; Fordy lifted it by its handle and shoved it forward.

"I think the hinges have dropped," he said, collecting his breath. "Another bloody job to do." Even if Anna wasn't daunted by the list of tasks, he was getting increasingly dispirited, knowing how long these fiddly jobs took, not to mention the damned expense.

Moving in through the half-opened door, they found themselves in a passage which ran the length of the house.

Fordy knew the kitchen was on the right and guided Anna into the low-ceilinged room. Billy had left a few pieces of furniture in the here, and on the kitchen table sat two plates and a couple of pot mugs. There was also a half-eaten joint of ham, already crawling with maggots, and a mouldy loaf of bread.

"How odd," said Anna, "to leave the remains of their last meal on table." She slid her palm over the back of one of the chairs. "The furniture is old but you can see it has been cherished at one time. Look, under the dust there's a well-polished surface. A bit of wax and some of these items will come back to life."

"Mmm, maybe, but it's the structure of the house that bothers me the most," said Fordy absently, inspecting a large crack than ran down from the ceiling to the top of the window that faced south.

"You're right, there is some work to be done in here," said Anna, walking around the room tapping at the dusty plaster, looking for loose cracked areas.

Fordy watched her move from the fireside to the window. It was strange to observe her in these unfamiliar surroundings. He had grown used to seeing her in the secluded garden and shed. The restrictions of that place had given Fordy a limited view of her, where he saw her as a tragic, enchanting creature. But here, in this ramshackle old house, she showed more of herself. Not the spoilt indulged creature he feared, her spirit and ability became apparent. She was a real person, not some sprite he had awoken from a flowerbed. He didn't want her trapped at Kings Pasture but whilst she was imprisoned there he could keep hold of the image he had created for her. Out here in the real world, he wasn't sure what to expect from her. He was right to question the complexity and depth of Anna's nature. But he had no yardstick by which to gauge her actions.

"Can we look upstairs?" she asked, halting his thoughts.

"I've not been up there yet; can you find the steps?" he answered quickly, forcing a cheerful tone. She disappeared out of the kitchen back into the passageway.

"Here," she called, "the stairs are behind this door."

He followed her and saw a narrow steep flight of steps. At the top they discovered a good-size bedroom. Another door in the opposite wall led straight into a second bedroom.

Quickly glancing round the first one, Anna rushed to the low window of the second room.

"This would be my choice of bedchamber, look at the view," she said, turning to Fordy and extending her hand, encouraging him to look out of the window. "I can't believe how far I can see, we can even see the Western Dales. Imagine the sight of the setting sun from up here."

"But it's north facing, it'll be freezing in here come winter," countered Fordy.

"Well, there's a big fireplace here that would keep the place warm," said Anna, going over to it, "and you'd have me to snuggle against," she added with a grin. Fordy ignored her remark. A flat piece of metal had been inserted over the recess where the grate sat. She tugged at it, and it easily fell towards her. Fordy went to help her, "What's this for?" she asked him.

"It's to stop the cold blowing down the chimney, not that it would make much difference in this draughty old place, this fireplace hasn't been touched for many a long year," said Fordy, lifting the metal shield away and leaning it against the wall.

"Look, Fordy," said Anna, kneeling at the hearth. "there's paper and twigs under this thick layer of dust. It's ready to be lit. I wonder who left it like this?" she said quietly.

"It wouldn't be Billy if the state of the rest of the house is anything to go by," said Fordy.

"I agree, this is something a woman would do, maybe his wife, or his sister." For several moments she stared at the dry knotted kindling that lay in the grate. "Do you feel that we are intruding on someone else's life in here?" she asked.

"Not really, why?"

She got up from the fireplace and went to him.

"Stand still for a moment and hold your breath," she whispered, taking his hand. "Can you hear them?"

"Hear who?"

"The voices from years gone by… listen."

He stood quietly with her for a few moments but could hear nothing other than a crow calling from outside. He let out a loud laugh. "What a load of nonsense."

"It isn't, can't you feel it? When a house is quiet, all the folks from its past can be heard, if you take a moment to stop and engage with them. Can you not hear the laugh of a child?" she paused. "Can't you detect the sound of someone climbing the stairs? Listen closely," she whispered, "outside there's a man shouting."

Fordy stilled his breathing to listen and the house creaked then he took a quick breath, "That's just the roof timber stretching in the warmth of the day," he said hoarsely, coughing to clear the phlegm that had suddenly risen in his throat. "I still say you're daft. You're as superstitious as Mary Ann. You sound like those idiots that reckon this miserable summer is a curse on us for defeating Napoleon and teaching those Frenchies a lesson." He pulled her roughly toward him and kissed her.

"I'm not kissing you if you refuse to indulge me." She pushed him away.

"Oh yes, you are, I've brought you here, now the least you can do is kiss me." He reached for her arm; she slid away from him and turned, moving to the corner of the room.

"It looks like you have me trapped. I should have known better than to allow a ruffian like you to entice me into an empty house," she said playfully.

"Yes, you should take more care over the company you keep," he pressed her against the wall and kissed her.

"I could resist and scream, you know," she said, biting gently at his neck.

"Holla as much as you like, there's no one to hear you," he whispered into her ear, kissing it. His slid her shawl off and ran his hand over her breasts.

No longer resisting him, he could hear her breathing deeply as she pulled him closer.

"I saw there's an old blanket in the other room, shall I get it?" he muttered.

"No, no," she answered urgently, pulling up the skirt of her dress. "Oh Fordy, I think I love you," she said quietly.

"I know," he said, loosening his trousers.

She pulled him towards herself and he lifted her up. "It's not the easiest position, is it?" she gently joked.

"No, but just as satisfying," he kissed her, "I think you are a witch, with all your talk of voices from the past and the way you have entrapped me…"

She groaned with pleasure as he took her weight and her body rested between him and the wall.

* * *

Downstairs, in the kitchen, Anna unpacked the small bundle she had brought with her. "I took this meat pasty from the pantry this morning," she said, handing Fordy a slice, "and a handful of raspberries I found in the garden. Here, take one."

"You've brought plenty of food," commented Fordy, "won't Mrs Dinsdale ask where it's all gone?"

"Hopefully she'll just put it down to my newfound appetite."

Fordy took the wedge of pie she offered him. He walked over to look at the range that sat in the open fireplace. "This'll need some attention, maybe even a new one, I think it's cracked, look here," he said, beckoning Anna over to inspect the rusting old stove.

She crouched down beside him and agreed with his assessment. "Where would you get help from to mend or replace it?" she asked.

"There's a bloke down at Bedale who'll give us a better idea of its condition," he said thoughtfully. "If we get this place cleaned up and sort out the cooking arrangements, it's maybe not so bleak as I first thought."

"I think it's charming. This kitchen window faces south," said Anna, walking towards it. The thickness of the walls allowed for a window seat and, although it was caked in dust, she sat down on it. "This will be a light airy place once it's freshened up with a coat of paint."

"You are sounding like Mary Ann again." Fordy took the seat beside her and kissed her.

"Do you think you could live here?" he asked.

"Yes…I could," she replied.

His mouth dried, could he utter the words that hammered in his head? Torn between his impulsive love for her and his usual steady decision making, he remained silent. Normally he would have wanted to court a lass for a good twelve months. Wasn't there a saying about summering and wintering 'em? But this situation wasn't normal… too many pressures. He knew he should be decisive but couldn't bring himself to do it.

"Me and the lads usually go to Richmond Races for the August Meet," he said, changing the subject.

Raising her eyes, she looked expectantly at him.

"I'd love to ask you to come with us but there'd be o'er many folk there. You might be recognised," he said, defeated before he could even get past the starting post.

"There's nothing I'd like better than to go with you but I think you are right. It would be foolhardy," she agreed, appearing as deflated as Fordy.

"Come on, let's be getting you back home," said Fordy.

The day had been an adventure but, now the pleasure was over, it was highlighting the gulf between them. Alone, in her company he was the happiest man on earth, he had never met anyone who he felt so at ease with. But if they allowed their real lives and problems into their conversations Fordy was knocked back by the difficulties they faced. The impossibility of their situation only served to heighten his sense of frustration and his desire for her. He wanted to take her to the races, he wanted to ask her to marry him but couldn't bring himself to do either of these.

His head spun with the problem. If he asked her and she turned him down, surely that would be the end of it all. He would rather continue not knowing than having the reality of rejection to cope with. On the other hand, if she accepted him he may well be condemning her to a life of manual work and hardship. She may feel she could cope with that now but over the years would she come to resent him and regret her decision? He feared the only life he could offer her wasn't good enough.

He wanted to spend the rest of his life with her but he knew he had no words to use to begin to express his love for her and his hopes for their future together.

* * *

It had been four days since Fordy had taken Anna to High Field Farm. He was looking over his horses in the stables before going to bed. Out here he was alone with the reassuring company of his animals and his troubling thoughts. In the confined space of their stalls the horses shuffled and moved, at peace with themselves. He could hear the steady rhythm of their breathing, giving this place its distinctive warmth and smell. He often lingered here, on an evening, reflecting on recent events. He had plenty to occupy his mind tonight: Anna and her reaction to the condition of the High Field. She had surprised him. Perhaps she had what it took to live with him and build a life together. If she could secure her inheritance, life would certainly be easier for them but he preferred to consider that they could make a success of it even if she was unable to get her money. There was no doubting that her father would obstruct any suggestion of marriage and he would probably use every lawful and unlawful tactic to deny her mother's legacy.

If they were to be wed it would have to be a hurried affair, before her father could be alerted to the situation. He knew folk got married quickly with a license. Usually because there was a bairn on the way. And often with an irate father standing over proceedings. Remembering that business with Jane a shiver ran over his shoulders.

It was a still cold night and he could hear his father and the drinkers in the tap room. From the intermittent shouts and laughter Fordy guessed a game of cards was going badly for someone. Before returning to the house he went to collect a bottle of brandy from his stores.

Across the yard, in the barn at the end nearest the house, there were a set of wooden steps that led up to the small storeroom where he kept his contraband. This small room was above the archway that led into their cobbled yard at the back of the house. Originally it had been accessible from both the house and the outbuildings but Ben and Fordy had sealed the bedroom access when they started to use it as a store for his goods.

The room was windowless and dark. Fordy lit a candle before looking for the particular bottle he needed for a customer tomorrow. He could still hear the voices from the tap room but now they were shouts of, "Goodnight," and, "Watch your step."

Having found what he was looking for, he locked up his storeroom. His father would be alone now. He knew he needed to speak to him before he saw Anna again. Perhaps now was a good a time to have a quiet word with him.

Fordy found his father damping down the fire in the tap room. Ben had continued to light his fire through the summer months. Temperatures dropped on an evening and he had found if he didn't offer some warmth, his customers would trickle away after a couple of pints. No one came out at night to sit and shake with cold.

"Early night tonight?" he said to his father, taking a seat on the settle that faced the fire.

"Aye," said Ben, turning to look at his son. "You fancy a dram?"

Fordy nodded, "I'd been wanting to have a word, Dad."

Ben got up from the fire and went to pour their drinks.

"What's up'?" he asked, handing Fordy a glass.

"We've always had one goal in mind… with the 'osses, haven't we?" stuttered Fordy.

"Aye," replied Ben, "but 'ave you another now?"

"I 'ad my eyes opened when I went to Yarm this time. There's going to be an explosion of enterprise and industry up there with the coal fields. I can't stop thinking we could do well there. The demand for 'orses will be endless. At best we could sell a couple of dozen a year down here to landowners and farmers but the need for horses from the canals and railways would be…" he tailed off.

"Are you thinking we might have a go at selling 'osses up there?" asked his father.

"Aye," said Fordy.

"So why so downhearted?" asked Ben, puzzled.

"It isn't what we planned, I thought you'd think I was letting you down, chasing after a bigger prize."

"If you can see an opportunity, we'd do well to think about it."

"You think it's a good idea?"

"It's certainly worth exploring, 'specially with this disastrous summer, there'll be starvation this year. There was a fella dropped in this afternoon, telling me things are even worse over the channel. Any meagre crops that have survived the harsh spring are now rotting in the ground," said Ben, swirling his whiskey round in his glass.

Fordy knew his father was right, cornfields that should have been turning yellowy gold were still green. Many were overgrown with weeds where the seed had failed to germinate. Other crops were failing too. Grass was sparse and short, potatoes were riddled with blight. The vital root crops, that saw man and beast over the winter months were stunted and struggling to fill out.

"What's goin' to 'appen when all the food supplies run out?" asked Fordy.

"Starvation, once the winter sets in it'll take the poorest and the sickest first, then work its way through all of us, even the wealthy will suffer if there's nothing to buy," said Ben.

"Maybe that's another reason to look at an alternative outlet for 'osses."

"Aye," answered Ben.

"I thought I might go and see Byers, he could have some contacts further north," suggested Fordy. "And His Grace? Would he have some idea of who to talk to?"

"He might but the bloody fella's not back yet. God knows when we'll see 'im again," said Ben, sipping on his drink, taking a few moments before continuing. "Is this what's botherin' y'? I thought you were maybe 'aving woman trouble again."

Fordy didn't reply at first. Ben sat quietly, waiting for his son to answer.

"There is a lass…but it's complicated."

"She's not wed, is she?" asked Ben quickly.

"No… there's other problems."

"There usually are where women are concerned," chuckled Ben.

"I may as well tell y'. I met her up at Kings Pasture."

"We have noticed your weekly visits take longer these days. Who is it? Anybody we know?" encouraged Ben.

"Not exactly, but you'll know the name."

"Come on lad, spit it out."

"Annabelle Stillerton… Sir Robwyn's daughter."

Ben stared at his son for a few moments. "By the saints, what have you got yourself into?"

"I know, it sounds bad, that's why I haven't told you. It started that night I went for the tea we used as payment for the drovers that took Mark Philpot up to Scotland. Her dog ran out in front of me and Dapple clipped it with his hoof."

"Don't tell me… and one thing led to another…" laughed Ben.

"It did," said Fordy shaking his head. "I find this as incredible as you, Dad. I've doubted the whole thing from the start… but I took her up to High Field Farm last week."

"Did you by God?" exclaimed Ben.

"She's been treated badly by her father. He has her locked up at Kings Pasture, waiting for her to come of age so he can get at her inheritance."

For the next hour Fordy and his father discussed Anna's predicament. Before turning in for the night, Ben had made Fordy promise he would bring Anna to Worlds End to meet Mary Ann and himself.

Content that he had shared his thoughts about expanding the horse breeding venture, Fordy was less sure about having told his father of Anna. While he kept her secret no one could interfere but once he had shared this news he knew that matters would be pushed along by others, mainly his father and Mary Ann.

He wanted to make his own way in the world, he just wished he could do it from the comfort of his familiar routine. A day with his horses may be physically exhausting but not threatening. He was less sure of himself when it came to the new challenges that increasingly cropped up in his life these days.

CHAPTER 16

The following week Fordy prepared for his trip to collect his goods from Kings Pasture and to see Anna. She would hopefully be pleased that he had spoken to his father about expanding their business but what words could he use to tell her that they had also talked about her? How would he explain that there was an invitation to spend an afternoon at Worlds End? The worry was not so much the telling but her reactions which were often the opposite to what he anticipated. Distracted by his thoughts, he had tripped over a skep of oats and banged his knee on the stone wall of the stables. Now, he realised, just in time, he was putting the wrong bridle onto Dapple.

"Here, lad, what a mess I'm makin' o' things," he chattered to the horse who pushed at Fordy with his damp nose then stopped and lifted his head, pricking his ears, giving a low whinny and looking out through the open stable door.

"What've you heard, old fella?" asked Fordy, straining to catch any noise from outside. Unable to hear anything, he moved to the stable door where he also caught the distant noise of bleating sheep. Drovers thought Fordy, but who was it? He finished saddling up Dapple, led him out into the yard and tied him up against the water trough before hurrying through the archway and out to the road. The sight gladdened his soul: it was Angus.

Over the poor summer there had been markedly fewer drovers moving animals around the country. Store stock was slow to fatten for market and farmers were reluctant to buy in more breeding ewes and cows for fear of running out of winter fodder. The result was a reduction in droving traffic. So this was only the second time Angus had called since Mark Philpott had been whisked away to safety.

Ben was already out in the road to greet the Scotsmen and Fordy joined in the welcoming banter.

"Never mind your moaning about poor trade, tell us how Mark is," said Fordy to Angus.

"You'd think the lad had been born into our family. He's fitted in grand. Never a moment o' complaint or misery fra' him," reassured Angus. "He's a good worker too. I reckon he can come down with us next year and see his family."

"There's no news about his father and brother," said Ben. "They're still down at York. We expected the case to come up before the bench a couple of weeks ago but word is it's been put back another week. Poor buggers, waiting in that stinking 'ole, not knowing what fate's in store."

"Well, you can tell his mother that Mark's doing fine. That might ease her mind on that front. Now, Ben, let me sort out m' lads and sheep. I'll grab a bite wi' 'em, then I'll be in t'sample your whisky. Although I've brought a wee bottle o'malt for ye t'try," said Angus, with a grin.

"He'll be bloody useless in the morning, Angus," remonstrated Fordy. "I'm leaving you to it." Fordy, shaking his head, walked back to his horse. As he was untying Dapple, Mary Ann hurried out towards him.

"You're definitely going to ask her?" Mary Ann fussed around him.

"I said I was," Fordy replied, trying to sound patient. Since she found out about Anna and the prospect of meeting her, Mary Ann had been unable to contain her excitement.

"I need to be away, Angus is out front wi' 200 hogs. Dad's with 'im."

"Oh," said Mary Ann, her happy smile dropped. "There'll be no work from him in the morning."

"Aye, he'll be nursin' a sore head till noon," agreed Fordy, as he mounted Dapple. "Have a quiet night to yourself, I should 'ave some pleasant news for you in the morning." He smiled kindly at her and watched her return to the house before flicking the horse's reins.

On his journey to Kings Pasture, Fordy's thoughts ran over the unremarkable events of the past hour. Every day was busy at Worlds End, they all had their jobs and knew what was expected of each other. Moving to High Field Farm would change all that, expanding the business would alter it even more. He could visualise that clearly enough but how Anna might fit into the situation was not so easy to picture. Could she be left in charge of the farm, should he need to travel away? Would she go down to Worlds End and help out on pig killing days over winter? How would they manage in the kitchen, could she run a busy household?

The stream of questions babbled through his head during the ride, ending only when he trotted Dapple into the stable yard, his final thought being that he couldn't contemplate life without Anna.

Fordy's business in the yard was brisk, he kept an eye out for Picard as always, but when he didn't see the Frenchman he assumed Higgins had him doing the donkey work in the stables. Fortunately Fordy hadn't come face to face with him since the incident in the trees at the entrance of Kings Pasture some weeks back.

Securing his load, Higgins approached Fordy, "Owt fresh, lad?"

"Not really, you'll 'ave heard I got High Field Farm?" replied Fordy.

"I had, well done, I bet the spot's a mess, awd Billy has never been one for looking after anything," laughed Higgins.

Fordy nodded, "Terrible state, it is. But we'll soon have it tidied up."

Higgins didn't reply for a moment and Fordy looked closer at him. Usually Higgins didn't have time for small talk. "Is everything alright?" he asked, bringing Higgins out of his silence.

"I wanted to tell you to be careful, Fordy," he said, moving closer.

"Careful of what?"

"I'm not rightly sure. I caught Picard and Rennie talking t'other day. Now my French isn't the best but I heard your name mentioned. I'd be happiest giving those two rogues the push but Stillerton won't hear of it. Between you and me, I've about 'ad enough of this carry on 'ere. Things aren't what they were. During the war there was a point to all this but now… well, I don't know… it just isn't the same. There's alus been plenty o' villains in this game but now…"

"It's alright 'Iggins, I'll keep an eye out," said Fordy, lifting himself onto Dapple.

"I've been offered another job o'er Leyburn way, if I'm not here next time you come, don't be surprised," muttered Higgins.

Fordy nodded in silence.

"And another thing, you be careful wi' y' visiting," said Higgins, nodding towards the back road that Fordy used.

Fordy snapped into high alert and bent to take Higgins sleeve. "You know about that?"

"Aye… like I said, watch your step," answered Higgins.

"Does anybody else know?"

"No idea but you don't want to be getting tangled up wi' Stillerton. If he suspected you were messing with his daughter…" confided Higgins. "He's ruthless… and greedy, as I know to my cost. He'd have a man's hide if he thought he could sell it." Higgins turned from Fordy, heading back to his work.

"Thanks," called Fordy, suspecting Higgins hadn't heard him. He pulled Dapple's head in the direction of the garden gates and encouraged the horse with a gentle kick.

This was the most unsettling news. If Higgins knew, who else was aware of his visits to Anna?

He totted up the weeks since he had first met her back in April. They'd managed four months without discovery, he was pushing his luck now. He remembered the other day at High Field when he almost asked her to marry him. With hindsight he knew that moment had been perfect to ask her. When would another opportunity arise? If only he had the courage to say those important words to her…but if she turned him down, what would he do?

He urged Dapple on and was disconcerted to find Anna waiting for him at the garden gate.

"Is everything alright?" he asked, as he dismounted.

"Yes, I was just feeling restless," she answered, wearily.

Bending to kiss her he could see she seemed frail and unsteady. He offered her his arm, which she readily took.

"You look pale, are you ailing summat?" he asked more roughly than was his intention.

She shook her head. "I thought we might sit outside this evening but I'm feeling the cold, can we go in?"

"Are you unwell?" he asked again in a gentler manner. Leaving Dapple tied up, they went into the shed and he guided her to a seat and sat down next to her. He wrapped an arm around her and pulled her close to warm her.

"Not really," she answered quickly, "it's the chill in the air that's got into my bones. She took his hand and gently ran her fingers over the back of it. "I do love your hands, so brown and strong, even the scars of where you hit yourself with the hammer," she murmured and lifted his fingers to her mouth to kiss them.

Fordy watched her. Did she know the effect she had on him when she did such things? He swallowed hard, trying to speak but his throat felt dry and rough. He sat still, speechless, as her simple act of kissing his hand aroused him.

"Enough of me, tell me your news," she said, keeping hold of him.

"I hardly know where to begin," he said, moving his thoughts on from his desire for her and settling into the couch, "I spoke to my father about the 'orses."

"Was it a favourable response?" she asked enthusiastically.

He nodded and went on to tell her of what had passed between them.

"So the final part of my news is I have to ask you to come up to Worlds End for an afternoon, sometime next week."

Her face crumpled as she broke into sobs and lifted her hands to her face.

"What's the matter? I thought you'd be happy." Fordy was exasperated.

"I am happy, Fordy. I don't know what's the matter with me, I seem to be crying all the time these past weeks. But these are tears of happiness."

"I can see that you're not your usual cheery self. Maybe we should put off your visit to Worlds End," he said worriedly.

"No, I'll be fine. I'm sure it's just a chill, I'll be back to normal tomorrow. Let me get up and pour us a drink and you can tell me all about the plans for next week."

In the warmth and safety of Anna's garden refuge they discussed her visit to Worlds End. Once again, at Anna's insistence, Fordy described the old place he called home and told her of his father's and Mary Ann's eagerness to meet her.

Concerned for her health, he suggested she return to the house earlier than usual. Together they locked up the garden shed and he walked with her a little way through the grounds. But he left her to walk the final stretch alone, he felt vulnerable in this garden.

He collected Dapple and walked out through the gates. Pulling them shut, Dapple gave a low snort. Fordy looked into the distance. Through the darkness he could see two lanterns swinging back and forth as they were being carried by walkers and heard the unmistakable guttural sounds of Picard and Rennie in their mother tongue. "Steady, lad," whispered Fordy to his horse, "that was a near thing. Let's be away." He quietly walked down the lane, waiting to mount Dapple until they were well round the bend of the track.

* * *

On the afternoon they'd agreed, Fordy once again collected Anna from the back lane at Kings Pasture. She had persuaded him to allow her to bring Jasper with her and, as he reached down to take the dog's basket, a shaft of sunlight warmed his face. He looked skyward and put his hand to his cheek. "It's the sun, a welcome visitor," commented Fordy.

"Never mind the weather," she said irritably, "my arms are aching holding this creature, take him."

He looked away from the sky and reached down for Jasper's basket. Her sharp words unsettled Fordy. Last time he had seen her she was pale and quieter than usual and today she seemed be annoyed with him. Was she regretting accepting his invitation to meet his father and Mary Ann? Or was she becoming bored, only spending time with him to fill her endless days? He wished he could be more confident of her and her feelings.

He put the basket in front of him then moved to the fence to allow Anna to climb up behind him. "Are you settled now?" he asked her.

"Not really, it's not that comfortable back here you know. I thought you might have brought a trap today, especially as I have Jasper with me."

Fordy realised his mistake instantly. What an oaf he was. No wonder she was mad at him.

"It never crossed my mind, I'm sorry," he said, weakly.

"It's too late now, let's just go," she said, gripping tightly onto him in readiness for Dapple to move off.

This wasn't the start that Fordy had hoped for; if this was an indication of her mood, the day was going to be a disaster.

Ben and Mary Ann were waiting for Fordy and Anna in the yard at Worlds End. Ben stepped forward to help Anna off the horse, then took the basket that Jasper was in. Fordy could see Mary Ann's excitement was getting the better of her. Once he had dismounted, he took Mary Ann's hand. "Anna, this is Mary Ann and, of course, my father," he said, turning to his father who was still holding the basket with the dog in it. Anna gave both of them a small curtsy.

"I'm so pleased to meet you," said Mary Ann, "come in and sit down, my dear. You must be exhausted after sitting behind Fordy on that 'orse." Mary Ann put her arm round Anna's waist and led her into the kitchen.

Fordy watched Mary Ann lead Anna away; the moment felt surreal. Would he wake from a troublesome night's sleep to find he was dreaming?

"Here, lad, you hold this dog and I'll 'ave Dapple," said Ben. "Don't stand there gawping, you knew Mary Ann would tek 'er in like any other waif and stray, never mind 'er fancy breeding."

Fordy chuckled. "Aye, I'd never thought about it like that," he said, lifting Jasper's basket from his father's grasp. "I think I might come over to the stables with you, give 'em chance to get to know each other."

"Coward," joked Ben.

After stabling Dapple and giving Jasper a run in the field, Fordy and Ben went in to join the women in the spotless kitchen. Mary Ann had been dusting and cleaning for days and her prized silver teapot and milk jug had been polished daily for a week, inviting the comment from Ben that the damned thing would disappear with so much rubbing.

The sight of the two most important women in his life in this unusually tidy kitchen sat at the table with a cup of tea at their sides added to Fordy's sense of disbelief. With their heads close together they were inspecting a piece of embroidery that Mary Ann had recently completed. They looked up at the noise of the men entering.

"Once we've taken a cup of tea, I'm going to show Anna my garden," announced Mary Ann. Fordy stole a glance at Anna to see how she was coping; he was rewarded with a beaming smile.

"Is Jasper alright?" asked Anna. "I hope you don't mind me bringing my dog but he so hates being left alone."

"He's right enough, he's out in the yard amusing 'imself with a mouse he's caught," said Ben.

Fordy knew this was all about the womenfolk. He sat back in his chair, awkwardly sipping out of a fine bone china cup that held no more than a thimble full of liquid and watched as these two individuals bonded. He observed Anna deferring to Mary Ann, allowing her to act the hostess, agreeing with her suggestions and opinions, showing her gratitude for Mary Ann's hospitality. It was like a game, both displaying their best side in the hope of gaining the ultimate prize of each other's trust and friendship.

"Are you finished your tea, my dear?" asked Mary Ann. Anna nodded. "If you are refreshed we could take a stroll," suggested Mary Ann.

Fordy and Ben followed them outside and sat on the garden wall, watching the two women chatter as they inspected Mary Ann's flowers and fruit trees.

"I 'ave to 'and it to you, she's a rare bonny lass… and kindly too… for her sort," said Ben.

"I know, I wasn't sure at first, but she 'as a natural way with her. She said she doesn't need all the refinements of gentle living, and I can tell you, the way that she is kept at Kings Pasture is terrible. Old Stillerton has only one thought: to get at her money."

"How much is the inheritance?" asked Ben cautiously.

"I don't know. I'm not sure she knows either."

"You sure the money isn't the main attraction?" probed Ben.

"No, to tell you the truth I'd fallen for her before I understood the terms of the inheritance. I assumed she'd be denied it if she married against her father's wishes. But it seems he has no say in that matter. Obviously, her mother's people were keen to try to keep Stillerton's hands off the family money. Her legacy wouldn't change my life. I admit it would make things easier, 'specially for her, but I need to work, doing nowt isn't for me."

"I'm glad to hear you say that, lad," said Ben, "but it wouldn't be right for Stillerton to rob his own daughter of her security so whatever it may or may not mean to you, think on what it means to Anna."

Fordy pondered his father's advice for a moment before replying. "Aye, well, it could take months or years for her to secure it. You know how bloody slow solicitors are," he laughed, getting up from the bench. "Mary Ann has monopolised Anna long enough, I'm going to show her the horses now."

Promising Mary Ann that they would soon be back for tea, Fordy led Anna to the paddock behind the house. They stopped at the gate and watched the horses. Nearest to them was Gilly and her eight-week-old foal. When the mare heard Fordy's voice she walked over to him. Fordy absently put his fingers on her nose. "What do you think of Gilly? She's the sweetest natured 'oss I've ever known," said Fordy.

"This must be Clover, she is gorgeous," murmured Anna with delight as the foal joined her mother at the gate, "I helped to choose your name, you little beauty. Can I go in and kiss her, you know, for good luck?"

"I've never heard that bit of superstitious nonsense before," answered Fordy.

"Oh, please. Surely you know that to kiss a new foal brings health, wealth and happiness."

"You're no better than Mary Ann with her fanciful ideas," he said, opening the gate to allow them to enter and for Anna to carry out her mystic ritual.

Fordy and Anna fussed over the two horses and the noise brought the other two animals in the field to the gate.

"Are you enjoying yourself?" he asked.

"More than you can imagine. Mary Ann is so kind, and your father is… well… I can't think of words to describe him. It's obvious his world revolves around you, you are so lucky to have that."

"What about this place, Worlds End?"

"It's wonderful, I can see why it means so much to you."

"Twenty years ago, before No Mans Moor was enclosed, this hostelry was the only safe place to take refuge for miles," said Fordy.

"Strange to think the area was so dangerous when today it feels so peaceful."

"I'm not a romantic but to me it's the most important place in the world."

She took him by the arm. "I do believe there is a soft heart in you, Fordy Robson, but where do I come in your life…after your horses and Worlds End?" she teased, kissing him quickly on the lips before he had time to answer.

Her sharp words and ill temper earlier in the day seemed to have been forgotten, to Fordy's relief. Still annoyed with himself for not harnessing up Mary Ann's trap and providing Anna with a more comfortable ride, he was pleased that the day was going well.

"Fordy, Anna, the food's on the table. Come on in," called Mary Ann from the kitchen door.

"We'd best do as she says." Fordy put an arm around Anna. "Here, kiss me again whilst no one is looking," he said, bending to meet her smiling lips.

Inside, the kitchen table was now covered with Mary Ann's best lace tablecloth and china. At the centre sat plates of the most carefully prepared food and, taking pride of place, was a freshly cooked ham, pricked with cloves and smeared in honey. Lucy hovered in the background fiddling with the new cap that Mary Ann had bought her and bobbing with nerves until Mary Ann gave her the command to pour out the tea.

"I don't suppose you've sat in a kitchen like this for a meal before," said Fordy, worrying that she might be thinking this sort of gathering beneath her.

"Of course I have, where do you think Mrs Dinsdale and I eat?" Anna replied brightly. "We take every meal at the kitchen table at Kings Pasture, apart from when I eat in the garden. Mary Ann, do you know Mrs Dinsdale?" Anna asked.

"No, she's not from round these parts, is she?"

"I believe not. But I can tell you, without her my life would be miserable, she's my only company… apart from Fordy of course."

Silence fell around the table; Fordy sensed his father and Mary Ann were discomforted by Anna's reference to her situation at Kings Pasture. He tried to think of something to say but took another bite of the ham instead, hoping that Mary Ann would save them with a friendly word or two.

"You like to ride?" asked Ben nonchalantly. Fordy glanced up at his father; perhaps he had misread the temporary quiet, maybe they hadn't felt embarrassed.

"I do, very much. I've missed being on horseback. Mary Ann, this food is delicious, I love this chutney, I think I could eat it with a spoon," Anna said, reaching for the bowl of Mary Ann's homemade apple and onion condiment.

Mary Ann smiled at Anna, acknowledging her appreciation of the spread.

"We'd maybe better see if we can't find an 'oss for thee," said Ben quietly. "I might know of one that'd just suit yer."

Fordy looked at his father in puzzlement, "Which 'orse is this Dad?"

"Never you mind, lad. I'm still capable o' doin' a deal with 'osses." He gave Anna a discreet wink.

"Thank you, Mr Robson, I don't know what to say. You are very thoughtful."

* * *

As the time approached for Anna to leave Worlds End, Fordy excused himself quietly. He reappeared with Dapple harnessed to Mary Ann's trap. "I should have been more considerate earlier," he admitted, when Anna commented on the appearance of a more comfortable ride home.

Anna climbed up the steps onto the trap. Once settled into her seat, Mary Ann passed her a small basket of scones and biscuits, insisting she accept the gift of food.

"We look forward to your next visit," said Mary Ann, clutching at Anna's hand.

With a profusion of thanks and promises to return soon, Fordy clicked Dapple on.

"We'd be here all night with Mary Ann fussing over you," chuntered Fordy, hiding his pleasure that his father and Mary Ann appeared to approve of Anna.

Contented with how the day had gone, Fordy felt more than ready to ask the question he had wanted to ask at High Field Farm. Anna slid close to him and he put his right arm around her, able to handle Dapple with the slightest of touches with his left hand which held the reins. He pulled Anna closer.

"Happy?" Fordy asked Anna as they travelled along No Mans Moor Lane.

"I've had a lovely day but I'm exhausted," she murmured into his ear.

"There's sommat I've been wanting ask. I should 'ave asked you t'other day at High Field Farm." He knew he was rambling and that his words should be gentler but he must try and get these words spoken. Despite his nervousness, he was determined to ask her to marry him.

"I know things are not easy for us and we 'aven't known each other that long, but… well… I was wondering… Anna?" he asked, aware that she wasn't responding. He stopped Dapple and looked down at her. She was asleep, still clutching Mary Ann's basket in her right hand.

Resigned to the situation, he made sure she was secure against him and he flicked the reins. He kept Dapple at a steady walk, ensuring Anna wasn't disturbed.

Fordy decided that he had no option other than take the trap down the lane that ran around Kings Pasture to the back gates of the garden. It wasn't ideal but he could hardly bundle Anna out on the roadside. Once they came to a standstill at the rear entrance and the movement of the trap stopped, Anna woke.

"Oh, I'm sorry, Fordy," she mumbled.

"Here, let me help you down," he said, jumping out to assist her. He lifted Jasper down and took the food basket from her then lifted her onto the ground.

"Have you enjoyed yourself?" he asked flatly.

"Of course. It was a wonderful day." She squeezed his arm and raised a thin smile. "I need to get back to the house… to bed."

"I can't leave you here, now," he pleaded. "There's so much I want to tell you… and ask you." Over the weeks they had been able to share so much time together but now, when he needed a few minutes to ask her to marry him, the opportunity was evading him.

He looked deeply into her eyes. Could she sense he was trying to propose to her? Was she flattering him with kindly words? Masking her disappointment over the realisation of his common situation? She may think his father and Mary Ann as kindly folk but had it dawned on her that these were the type of people she would mix with if she chose a life with him? Was she pretending to be tired to avoid an embarrassing situation?

"I know, but…"

"Anna," he whispered, holding her in his arms and kissing her. "Can we go into the garden shed, just for a little while?"

"I can't, I…" the words choked in her throat, "I'm exhausted. It must be that chill I caught, I'm so weary."

"If you insist," he said quietly, "but I'm going to walk you back up to the house."

He let Jasper out of his cage, checked Dapple was securely tied and picked up Mary Ann's basket before taking her arm. He didn't like this garden, the unfamiliarity caused his senses to sharpen. If Picard appeared he couldn't imagine what would happen. Anna was not in danger here but he was. As they came out of the shrubs and the house was in sight he stopped walking, "Anna, can you manage from here? If I'm seen with you, we could have terrible trouble."

"Of course," she nodded her head. "Please don't look so worried," she reached up and pecked him on the cheek then continued on her own over the grass that ran up to her home.

Leaving her here he felt cowardly and weak. His ride home in the trap was comfortable but he was far from happy.

On his return to Worlds End, Ben met him on the road.

"You get her back safely?" he asked Fordy.

"Yes, but she was exhausted. I was so concerned about her that I walked with her through the garden almost back up to the house." Fordy jumped down from the trap as Ben held Dapple's reins. He went close to his father, "There's something wrong with her. I can't work it out."

"Let me stable Dapple, Mary Anna's inside waiting to talk to you. I'll see you later, I have to get back to the tap room, I've got a bar full of drinkers," said Ben, giving Fordy no time to argue.

"What are you doing out here if you're busy with customers?" asked Fordy.

"They'll be alright for a few minutes, I thought it more important to warn you to brace yourself before Mary Ann starts on you," said Ben, grimacing.

Fordy's heart sank to his boots. What had he done wrong now? Perhaps she didn't like Anna. Swallowing hard, he walked into the house looking for Mary Ann.

CHAPTER 17

Fordy went into the kitchen and found Mary Ann busy at the sink.

"Ah, you're back. How was she when you left her?" asked Mary Ann, drying her hands on her apron. "I've got the kettle on, sit down, we'll have a pot o' tea. I think you and I need to have a talk."

Fordy sat down without answering; whatever was on Mary Ann's mind was about to get an airing.

While Mary Ann poured boiling water over the tea leaves Fordy glanced around the kitchen. The room had returned to its usual state, no longer the setting for an afternoon party. The white tablecloth had been removed and the delicate tea service was washed, dried and stacked on the dresser. Next to the china pots was her silverware, the tea pot, milk jug, sugar bowl and silver teaspoons, all waiting to be put back into their wooden box. Mary Ann was meticulous about storing these valuables out of sight; she worried about the number of strangers that visited Worlds End and liked to keep them hidden away. No one would think that the plain old box hidden at the back of her cupboard would contain her most precious items.

He sighed. If Mary Ann was going to criticise his relationship with Anna he didn't know what he would do.

Why were women so mysterious? He could never predict Anna's mood and he hadn't the faintest idea of what Mary Ann was going say. He watched her carry two mugs, put them on the table then sit down heavily opposite him.

"Dad said there was something on your mind," said Fordy.

"There is," she said, picking up her cup and taking a sip of the hot tea. Fordy could feel her eyes boring into him. Whatever she was going to say he wished she would get on with it. "How can you leave that poor defenceless girl at the mercy of her father?" she finally demanded.

"It's an impossible situation. If she wasn't so high born, I'd have asked her to marry me a while back but..." said Fordy, weakly.

"Her being gentry hasn't stopped you bedding her," snapped Mary Ann.

"How do you know that?" retorted Fordy, jerking his head up.

"She's carrying your child, that's how I know." Holding Fordy's gaze she shook her head. "You men are unbelievable, you really are."

"Are you sure?" he asked, taking a sharp breath. His stomach lurched at the thought of this possibility. "Is that what's the matter with her? She's been tired and irritable these last few weeks." Fordy's mind was racing. "I know I've dithered but I wanted to ask her to marry me tonight, back at Kings Pasture. She was so weary that she refused to talk, all she wanted to do was get back to her room and her bed." He hesitated as he tried to take in this news. "I've left her there, on her own. Why didn't I guess what's the matter with her?" he groaned.

Mary Ann didn't answer him. Her silence gave Fordy time to think through this startling news

What have I done? he asked himself. I've let her down, how could I not understand what was happening? How much trouble is this going to make for us? I'm not ready for this, he thought, struggling with the implications of Anna having a baby.

But what about her? This isn't all about me. She'll start to show soon and I have a duty to stand by her, whether I want the bairn or not. A child, maybe a lad… perhaps that isn't such a fearful idea after all. I could show him how to ride and tend the horses… the circumstances are still impossible… As he thought, Fordy's resolve hardened. A little one! He smiled as he pictured the bairn with Anna's eyes and his colouring. There'll be difficulties ahead but if Anna does love me and wants to marry me maybe things might work out after all.

I need to sort this out now, he told himself, I can't put it off any longer. God knows what her father will do when he finds outs. I must get to her before her father does.

"What a mess everything is," said Fordy. "The more I've tried to get things back on the level, the more my life has seemed to spiral out of control."

"Your problem is that you try to ignore what's in front of you. On this occasion that approach hasn't work," said Mary Ann, firmly.

"I know" he admitted, "but you have to believe me, I have been on the brink of asking her to marry me a couple of times, I just couldn't say the words. When I took her up to see High Field I was on the verge of spluttering out a proposal but I was terrified she was going to turn me down. Then tonight…"

"You can't see what's under your nose, can you? The girl loves you," exclaimed Mary Ann, "I hope I've shaken you into action." Taking hold of her mug, she got up and left Fordy sat at the table.

He watched her go to the sink. Why hadn't he spoken to Mary Ann about this before? Why had he continued in his same old ways of thinking he could laugh his way out of tricky situations? He knew he had kept everything to himself because he hated being told what to do, particularly by his father and Mary Ann, their advice often seemed old-fashioned and cautious. But this situation wasn't a difference of opinion over a trivial matter: he should have sought their help earlier.

That night in bed Fordy lay awake trying to work out what to do. Mary Ann's words rang in his head, 'How can you leave that poor defenceless girl at the mercy of her father?' How could he have been so blind and spineless?

Then there was the matter of the babe. Was he really going to be a father? Mary Ann could be wrong he told himself, with little conviction. Mary Ann was rarely wrong about such matters.

After hours of sleeplessness Fordy left his bed as dawn was breaking. He was first downstairs; the kitchen was quiet. He rattled out the stove and threw a few dry sticks onto the glowing embers; in a matter of minutes he had a good blaze going. He moved the kettle over to the hottest spot to boil. There was no point in going out to tend the horses, they were creatures of habit and he never went to them before six o'clock.

He made a pot of tea and drank it as he thought about the day ahead. As much as he wanted to jump on Dapple and go over to see Anna he knew it was pointless. He had to wait until the evening and hope that she might be in the gardener's shed. He would ask her to marry him without mentioning that Mary Ann had told him she was carrying his child. He didn't want her to think he was only asking her to be his wife because she was pregnant.

As the clock struck six he went to tend the horses. Most of them were out in the fields grazing the sparse grass that had shown itself this summer. It was unusual to supplement summer grass but Fordy threw a bit of last year's hay down for them. He didn't want them losing condition.

The morning dragged on. In no mood for talking he avoided his father and Mary Ann, walking over to the copse where he had buried the foal. The bare earthen mound was still visible and he kicked at a clump of dandelions that were growing there. Looking back at the house he thought of the contrast between yesterday's happiness, when Anna had stood next to him as they had watched the animals and stolen a kiss before going into the house for tea, and today's despair when all he could do was worry and wait.

His thoughts were erratic, jumping from images of her, considering the possibility of getting wed and the thoughts of a baby. There was no logical flow to his worries and concerns, they were all crushed into his head, rising to the top randomly, blurring together and losing clarity as the intensity of his feelings slowed his thought process.

He walked across the field to the fencing he had repaired earlier in the springtime and was reminded of that day when he'd smashed his fingers. It seemed an eternity ago but was only four months back. He lifted up his hand and inspected the fingers with their broken black nails. Breaking into his thoughts he could hear his father shouting, "Fordy, where are you?"

Fordy wasn't sure if he was imagining it or if Ben was really calling for him? He looked up to see his father and John Burgess walking towards him.

"John," said Fordy in surprise, "what brings you out here today?"

"Bit o' news I wanted to share wi' you," replied John.

Fordy glanced at his father, unsure whether John was happy for his father to hear what he had to say.

"I'll leave you fellas to talk, I've a couple o' jobs waitin' for me back in t'house," Ben said, gruffly.

"Alright, Dad," said Fordy, grateful that his father had made things easy for them. Fordy took a couple of deep breaths, trying to shake off his low mood but fearing John wasn't here to lift his spirits.

"What is it? Is this something to do with Adams?"

"Aye, things are moving fast," said John, hesitating for a moment, "and I wanted to tell you what's going on in case owt 'appens to me."

"Good God, man, tell me," said Fordy quickly.

"I don't know where to start. First thing this morning I heard that two blokes at Smeaton have been done over, one of 'em not likely to live."

"And?" asked Fordy.

"They'd put up a share to underwrite Adams's venture but when he went back and asked for more money, they turned 'im down."

"How do you know?"

"One of 'em is married to my wife's cousin, we got word through the family."

"You sure it was Adams's men?"

"Aye, the thugs that delivered the blows told 'em he had sent them."

Fordy sighed deeply. Both men leant over the railings and looked into the field.

"You think they'll come after you?" asked Fordy.

"Possibly. Adams has all of us smaller investors o'er a barrel, he threatens us with violence to get us to cough up more money. If we refuse, he has us murdered which means he will never have to reimburse us. Without Malbury around overseeing things Adams is riding rough shod over everyone."

"Where the bloody hell is Malbury, the bastard? He should be here…" exploded Fordy, glad of a reason to shout.

"I 'ad word from him that he will be back in Yorkshire at the end of August but I fear he'll be too late to stop Adams. But listen, I have more news. Couple of hours ago I received a message from Adams, tells me he's travelling over this way to meet up with Stillerton from Kings Pasture…"

"What?" asked Fordy, stepping back, his stomach lurching.

"You know, Stillerton that 'as Kings Pasture, where they keep the contraband in the stables…"

"Course I know who Stillerton is," snapped Fordy.

"Well, it seems Adams is meeting Stillerton there this week and they want me to go…"

"When? When is the meeting?" Fordy's mind was racing. Did this development affect Anna? Was he going to be able to get to her if Adams was at Kings Pasture? How difficult would it be if his henchmen were crawling all over the place? Fordy remembered the security that had surrounded Adams and his operation at Saltburn. A mouse couldn't move over there without being seen.

"I 'aven't been told. I'll be sent word. Now look, Fordy, I might not come out of this alive. No one knows that you put any money up and I'm telling you to keep your mouth shut. I've been stupid enough to get mixed up in this and even more foolhardy to drag you in."

Fordy nodded, relaxing slightly – if he moved quickly, there was time yet for him to get Anna out. He brought his thoughts back to John's situation. "Do you know what this meeting is about?"

"Not exactly but I heard on the quiet a few weeks ago that Stillerton's daughter is kept a prisoner up at Kings Pasture and –"

"You heard that?" gasped Fordy. He stepped forward and took John by the shoulders, involuntarily shaking him. "What has she got to do with this?" His voice came out as a high-pitched cry.

"Steady on old fella, what's got into you?" said John with an embarrassed shrug.

Fordy swung away from John, bringing his hands to his head. "Tell me why Anna Stillerton is involved in this?"

"She's sat on a fortune, from her late mother, her father is moving heaven and earth to get at it."

"I still don't understand," flustered Fordy. He thought her circumstances were private but if her situation was being openly discussed, even John knowing all this detail, what did it mean for Anna?

"My guess is Adams is in big trouble. Smuggling isn't as profitable as it used to be now the war with France is over. He's having to take greater risks to bring in expensive goods. He'll do anything to keep the money rolling in and if it means leaning on folks to put collateral up, then that's what he'll do. I reckon if Stillerton can get his hands on his daughter's inheritance he'll invest it in Adams's venture. Maybe Adams is putting pressure on him or Stillerton is a willing partner and has his eye on the potential rewards of this venture. Up till now Stillerton has been happy taking cash for providing a storage and distribution centre for the smuggling round here. It appears he's about to get in a whole lot deeper. You must know Stillerton is as much of a rogue as Adams and just as greedy."

Fordy leant against the fence, speechless, his thoughts firing off in all directions.

"What a bloody fool I've been." Fordy turned to the railings and leant heavily on them.

"Is there something you haven't told me?" asked John.

"Yes," muttered Fordy. "You remember I told you there was a lass I was seeing, well…"

Stood alone in the field at World Ends Fordy told the whole story of how he had met Anna and of their continuing courtship, even admitting he thought she was carrying his child.

Fordy had always relied upon John for sound sensible advice and he didn't fail Fordy in his hour of need.

"You need to rescue that lass from her father and get her down the aisle," said John.

"You're not going to tell me that I've been a dithering fool?" moaned Fordy.

John gave a grunt and grimace. "I'm the last one to say that after I've got us into this damned mess," he said, slapping Fordy's back. "I need to be away, I've got things to do and people to see and I suspect you have a few tasks that need tending to."

Fordy walked John back to his horse, watched him ride out of the yard then went in search of his father.

"What was all that about?" asked Ben.

"Adams is pressing for more capital to bring this consignment of goods into the country," explained Fordy. "Two fellas from Smeaton refused Adams's demand for more money. They've both been given a good beating, one's not expected to see the week out."

"Has John been threatened?"

"Not directly," said Fordy, "but he tells me that Adams is coming over to Kings Pasture to see Stillerton. John has had word that they want him to join them at Kings Pasture at some point…"

"What's going on?" asked Ben.

"I don't know but none of this news is good for us… or Anna," Fordy answered, processing John's news and what it might mean. He was reluctant at this stage to tell his father all of John's news and his own worst fears. If he voiced his worries it made them all the more real.

Ben coughed nervously, "Mary Ann's told me of her suspicions that Anna has a bairn on the way," he said, avoiding Fordy's eyes.

What?" asked Fordy, still distracted by what John had told him.

"Mary Ann thinks Anna's… you know… goin' to have a baby."

"Oh, yes," sighed Fordy, slowly. "That's what Mary Ann thinks. Now it's pointed out to me I think she's right, Anna has been acting strangely this past few weeks. I can't understand why she hasn't told me."

He waited for his father to say something but when he realised he wasn't going to reply, he continued.

"I'll go over tonight, see if I can find 'er…If Adams is already there I might not be able to see her. I was going to ask her to marry me but…"

"I hoped that was what you were going to do," Ben answered with a small, satisfied grunt. "I 'ave to say I am quite teken with her."

"Yes, Dad," Fordy managed a weak laugh, "so am I."

"Here, I've got something for you," said Ben, digging into his trouser pocket. He pulled out a little shabby box and thrust it into Fordy's hand. "It was your mother's. It's not much but I wondered if you'd like to give it to Anna."

Opening the stiff hinges, he found a simple gold ring decorated with three small pearls. Tears pricked in Fordy's eyes: he had never seen it before.

"Take it, lad. I bought it for your mother all them years ago. It took every bit o' cash I 'ad, but it was worth it to see the joy on her pretty face when she opened the box."

The two men stood silently. Fordy wished he could remember his mother wearing this ring but there were no memories to conjure up.

"It might not be what Anna's used to but if it's from you she'll treasure it," said Ben, choking up. He turned away but Fordy took his arm and pulled him back.

"Thanks, Dad. It's kind of you, I know she'll adore it. I'll give it to her tonight… if I can find her."

"What's your plan?" asked his father.

"If she says yes, then… Well, I don't know. What do you think?"

"Get her back here and go and get a license to be wed. But make sure that when she leaves Kings Pasture she brings some papers with her to prove who she is. Vicar'll want to see 'em for starters and she'll need as much documentation she can lay her hands on to prove her identity to claim her inheritance. Particularly if her father turns nasty."

Fordy nodded silently. His father's words piled on the pressure. How was Anna going to have the opportunity to collect together proof of who she was at such short notice, particularly if her father was already at Kings Pasture House?

The news that Adams was planning on going to Kings Pasture added to the urgency of getting Anna away from there as quickly and as efficiently as was possible. Who knew what schemes Stillerton had tucked away in his attempts to control his daughter and her fortune. Her days of languishing alone here would appear to be over. She had always known she was a pawn in her father's plans and John's words confirmed this. Fordy tried not to berate himself for his inactivity but it was to no avail. He knew he'd been a damned fool.

The day dragged by. Fordy busied himself with a few jobs round the yard, finding it difficult to settle to anything for more than an hour or so. The threat of Anna's father was a real one that couldn't be ignored any longer. He had known this for several weeks but with the news that John had brought there was a new desperation to the situation, never mind the baby that might be on its way.

He thought about the reality of marrying Anna and decided to go and talk to Mary Ann. The house was hers and Fordy had better check that she was content to let Anna live there, at least for a while.

Fordy found Mary Ann in the tap room washing some glasses.

"Hello, how are you?" she asked, kindly.

"I've been thinking that if Anna should agree to marry me, is it alright for me to bring her here?"

"Of course it is, she's a lovely girl and I'm glad you've found someone that will make you happy."

"Dad says I should go t'vicar tomorrow and get a licence..." said Fordy, hesitating, somehow fearful of saying this to Mary Ann.

Mary Ann nodded, "You'll be wed before the week's out," she said happily, "and a babe on the way."

Fordy sat down on the long settle. He knew he was fortunate to have his father and Mary Ann giving him so much support but he was aware his problems weren't over. He began to worry that Anna's father had arrived at Kings Pasture in readiness for his meeting with Adams. Had he left this too late? Was Anna going to be snatched away from him? What would her father do if he found out she was pregnant? It was too much for him. He jumped up.

"I want to go over there now, and get her," said Fordy.

"Well, why don't you?" asked Mary Ann.

"If I go with Dapple in the daytime, I'll be seen. I could go on foot but I'll have to take the horse for her to ride back. I know I must wait till dark but then there's the risk she'll be in the house. Plus there's the problem of her being able to prove her identity. Dad says I must be sure she brings papers with her. He says she'll need 'em to get wed because the vicar doesn't know her and, if her father starts cutting up rough, she might have to produce 'em to get her inheritance."

"You should have done this sooner," said Mary Ann.

"Don't I bloody know it," snapped Fordy, marching outside. In the yard he found his father talking to a small boy. "What's all this?" asked Fordy, as he approached them.

"This young lad 'as a note for you," said Ben, taking a crumpled piece of paper off the child.

"Missus said you'd pay us," blurted the boy.

"Aye, we will," said Ben, "just give us a minute to see what it says."

Fordy went to his father and took the note. Opening it out, he read:

Fordy,

My father has returned. Please do NOT come to Kings Pasture House.

He is here with two other men, they spend their time in the library discussing business-AND ME.

The plan is I am to marry the older one. We leave for London on Saturday.

I am being watched and there are men guarding every entrance.

Tomorrow we are going to the races at Richmond. Please be there.

Anna

Fordy crumpled the note in his hand, his heart was pounding. 'The older one'… it could be, could it? How much worse could things get?

235

"Give the lad a shilling," he barked at his father and ran over to the field calling for Dapple.

His father paid the lad off and was soon to Fordy. "What's in the letter?" he asked his son. "You look like you've a herd of 'osses stampeding towards you."

"It's from Anna, her father has already returned. He's at Kings Pasture." Fordy hesitated for a few moments, putting her news alongside the information that John had told him earlier.

"Dad, I'm fearful of what this letter really means. John said Adams was coming over to Kings Pasture. Now Anna tells me in this note that two men have already arrived along with her father and she has been told he expects her to marry the older one. If the plan is to force Anna to marry Adams it means they can get their hands on Anna's legacy."

"Bloody hell, this is the worst possible news. Does she name Adams in the letter?" asked Ben.

"No, I assume she doesn't know who he is. She warns me not to go to Kings Pasture but that I should try to see her at Richmond races tomorrow."

"That's probably your best hope," said Ben, weakly, "but I wish there was more we could do to get that lassie back here now."

"So do I, but we're up against some powerful and ruthless men. Three or four of us wouldn't stand a chance if we went to Kings Pasture and attempted to rescue her. I've got to try and get her away without them realising that she has gone. If I can get to her at the races and fetch her back here tomorrow can we keep her safe till we get wed?"

"Course we can," said Ben, eagerly.

"I'm going to see Abe an' Chalky. I was meant to be going to the races with 'em but I'd called it off. I need to tell them that circumstances have changed, that I will be going tomorrow… and that I'll need their help."

"Aye, you get away; I'll go in and tell Mary Ann."

Jumping onto Dapple, he kicked the animal into a trot as he left Worlds End yard. He had a mind to get down to Bedale as quickly as possible but once he was on the open road, he realised there was no need to hurry. Chalky and Abe would be working, if he wanted a quiet word with one or both of them he'd need to wait till they closed up shop. He had no idea what time it was and could be faced with quite a wait to talk to them. He pulled Dapple up and let the horse move on at a slower pace.

CHAPTER 18

Allowing Dapple to revert to a steady walk, Fordy made his way to Bedale. Alone, he was able to think over what had happened today. John had told him that Adams was getting desperate for more money and had instructed John to meet him at Kings Pasture House. This news alone was enough to make Anna's situation even more precarious but the letter he had just received from her, saying that her father had plans for her to marry was turning this situation into a nightmare. Assuming her intended bridegroom was Adams, Anna's welfare and safety were in grave danger. If Stillerton's plan to marry her off to Adams became a reality, Fordy found it difficult to imagine that Anna would be treated well. As her husband, Adams would have total control over her money, she would have no rights or say over what happened to it. Fordy dreaded to think what might happen when they found out she was pregnant.

Rage burnt in him. It wasn't right that Stillerton and Adams should treat Anna as a commodity, to be bought and sold at their will. He knew life was unjust, the wealthy wielded all the power, holding the defenceless and the poor at their mercy. As the son of a successful landlord he'd never found himself directly up against the brutal realities of that cruel, unfair system. But now any horror seemed possible.

There would be no honourable justice for Anna against her father; her only chance of freedom was in his hands. But the anger he felt for her tormentors was exceeded by the fury he felt towards himself. Had he acted sooner this dangerous situation could have been avoided.

It didn't matter how he looked at it, there was only one course of action to be taken and that was to get Anna away from Kings Pasture and her father.

He couldn't help but worry about John Burgess's predicament too. John had said that he was to be summoned to Kings Pasture at some point over the next few days. Whatever plans Adams had for John would be revealed and if John couldn't satisfy Adams's demands he would no doubt feel the fists of one of Adams's men, or worse. But if Stillerton could raise the money, John may not be under so much pressure to find more funds for Adams's venture. Although the only way Stillerton was going to have a chance of raising any capital must be through Anna marrying Adams.

As he worked through the possibilities he realised that if he saved Anna from her father and his scheming he may well be putting John in an even worse position. What punishment would Adams inflict upon him? He remembered John's words, he was aware that he was in danger from Adams, but Fordy knew John well enough to know that he would want Anna saving from this situation, no matter the cost. John was able to look after himself, Fordy reasoned.

On towards Bedale he and Dapple plodded until he reached the town. Passing the church he looked up at the clock. It was half past four; maybe he could get one of the boys out of the smithy for a word.

He jumped off Dapple as he turned into Wycar and walked the short distance to his friends' blacksmiths. He fastened the horse to a rail and gave him a reassuring pat on his neck before going into the forge to find Chalky and his father sorting through some old horseshoes.

"Now then," said Fordy, "you looking for scrap?"

Both men glanced ed up, "Alright, Fordy," said the older man, "we was just searching for an awd shoe that cam' off an awd cart 'orse we shod t'other day. I telt them lads to keep it safe but nobody listens to owt I says."

"That's just what me dad says," said Fordy, forcing himself to sound more cheerful than he felt.

"Tha'll be wantin' Chalky 'ere for a pint, I'm thinking," said Chalky's father.

"Can you manage, Dad?" said Chalky, getting up from the floor.

"Get yoursel' away, I'll put t'closed sign on t'door," said the old man.

Fordy walked outside towards Dapple and waited until Chalky appeared.

"Summat up?" asked Chalky.

"Aye," answered Fordy with a sigh.

"Over to t'Oak?" asked Chalky.

"Er, no. I think we'd better go somewhere where we can't be overheard."

"That's difficult in a place like Bedale, how about the graveyard?"

Fordy nodded. "Alright if I leave Dapple here?" he asked.

* * *

Seated on the wall that surrounded the church, Fordy began his story.

"You remember when I called in at your place that day I signed up for High Field Farm?" he asked Chalky.

"Aye, and you'd just bumped into Jane and 'er bulging belly," recollected Chalky with a grin on his face.

"Yes, and I told you I'd met a woman," he went on.

"I remember. Is this all about her?" asked Chalky, still appearing to find this situation amusing.

"It is, but you won't be laughing once you hear what I have to say."

Fordy told Chalky all about Anna, exactly as he had told John Burgess a few hours before. He told him how much he loved her, how she was trapped by her father and that she now found herself being forced into a marriage, possibly with Adams. He also told him of the dangerous position that John now found himself in with Adams.

"Well, I thought I had problems but they are of nothing compared with this," agreed Chalky. "What's your plan?"

"That we go to Richmond races tomorrow and bring Anna home with us," replied Fordy.

"I think we can manage that," said Chalky, thoughtfully.

"What's on your mind? I can tell you've thought of something. Is there a problem, is there something I have overlooked?" asked Fordy anxiously, jumping down from the hard stone wall.

"No, it's to do with me," said Chalky. "Adams has his poisonous claws into other folks' lives, as well as yours."

"Are you having trouble with him?" asked Fordy, finding it hard to believe that his steady reliable friend should have found himself in a difficult position with anyone.

"Not directly." Chalky fell silent.

Fordy stayed quiet, allowing him to continue at his own pace.

"There's summat I'm gonna tell you. You might reject me but I don't think you'll betray me," said Chalky in a downcast voice.

"Good God, man, what is it, what have you done?" asked Fordy.

"I don't know where to start… you remember Giles Redworth, you know, from Huntby?"

"Of course," encouraged Fordy.

"He's got Jim Adams on his back… blackmailing him."

"Bloody hell, the bastard. Whatever can Adams have over a gent like Redworth? A man with that much money and his connections could call Adams out. If I had his standing I'd square up to Stillerton and Adams."

"Aye, but you have nothing to be ashamed of, you've maybe courted a lass above your station and done a bit o' trading… " Chalky tailed off again.

"Has Redworth done something terrible?" asked Fordy in a whisper. "Has he killed somebody?"

Chalky shook his head.

"Come on, man, tell me what he's done?" urged Fordy, becoming impatient to know the worst but fearful of the facts.

"This is difficult for me, Fordy… Giles prefers the company of men to women… you understand what I'm saying?" said Chalky, quietly.

"You mean unnatural…?" Fordy whispered. In an instant he understood Chalky's reluctance to share this information.

Chalky nodded.

"They hang such men," gasped Fordy. "And Adams knows?"

Chalky nodded again.

"How did he find out?"

"It's a simple tale. Last year Giles went to a club in Durham, a place where such tastes are catered for. He only went a couple of times but he bumped into Adams there. They didn't know each other but Adams went out of his

242

way to find out who Giles was. Once he had discovered his identity he wasted no time in menacing Giles. Demanding money and threatening to tell his family and the law of his preferences."

"But what was Adams doing in a place like that?" cried Fordy.

"Adams is depraved. Giles tells me Adams will take men and women, even children."

"Are you sure? I've never heard of such things."

Both men fell silent again.

"If Adams can blackmail Giles, why can't Giles turn the tables on Adams?" reasoned Fordy.

"The authorities won't stand up to him, he has 'em all in his pocket. Anyway, who cares what Adams gets up to, folks that know him, know he's a bad 'un. That sort of behaviour no doubt enhances his fearsome reputation in the circles he mixes in. But for Giles... that's a different matter altogether. He may be wealthy but he's not rich enough to withstand a scandal of this nature. Then, of course, he has his parents' standing in the neighbourhood to consider," answered Chalky.

"What you say is true enough but I know that Adams is in big trouble with his trading, he's not making the vast amounts of money now we are no longer at war with France. I suspect he's using every means he can to supplement his income, he's as dangerous as a cornered dog now, desperately fighting to stay afloat and hang on to the power he has. One day he'll bully the wrong fellow and end up with a knife in his back."

"I didn't know that but he's still a mortal threat to Giles," said Chalky. "To avoid bringing his family down and facing the noose Giles has two choices, he either throws his lot in with Adams or leaves the country. The idea of associating with Adams is against everything Giles believes in. He may have this cursed vice but he is a good man so he's talking about going over to the continent. They're more tolerant of such things across the channel."

"That's probably the best idea, get away for a while. That's what young men like him do anyway, isn't it?" said Fordy, with a touch of jealousy in his voice. He knew Giles was the sort of man Anna would have been expected to marry under normal circumstances. If her mother was still alive, no doubt she would be encouraging her daughter to make an advantageous alliance with a wealthy man like him. Although he had no idea what Anna's mother had been like he found it difficult to imagine that she would have approved of her husband's behaviour and his treatment of their daughter.

"I 'aven't told you everything," said Chalky, sniffing loudly.

"Go on," said Fordy.

"Giles wants me to go with him."

"On his travels?" asked Fordy.

Chalky nodded.

"But why, does he a need a blacksmith?" asked Fordy.

Chalky didn't reply, dropping his head into his hands.

"I don't understand," said Fordy.

"For God's sake, Fordy, you must know what I mean. Surely you know I'm not one for the women either, they don't…"

Fordy sat motionless, he could feel his heart slowing, thudding in his chest, the pieces of information Chalky had given him started to slot into place. He felt his stomach turn and reached out his hand, putting it on Chalky's arm.

"You and Giles?" he asked.

Chalky nodded. His face was hidden by his hands but Fordy was sure Chalky was crying.

"Could you leave all this…?" asked Fordy. "Your family, the business and the town?"

"I think so, I've been more worried about Giles than myself over the past few weeks. He means everything to me."

Fordy couldn't answer him. How could he talk about another man like that? His initial reaction was revulsion at the thought of two men together but this was different… it was Chalky who was in trouble, he must put aside his own feelings and stay loyal to his friend.

"Why have you told me this now?" asked Fordy.

"My head has been near exploding, I've wanted to tell somebody but dare not for fear of the reaction. But now, when all of our futures are threatened by Adams, I took my chance. You see, if Giles decides to leave, it will be very soon and I may well go with him. I know I'm risking my life, and Giles's, by telling you this, and putting you in a difficult position. But you came to me in your hour of need and I thought that maybe you would listen…"

Neither man spoke for some time. Fordy's thoughts swirled. He was struggling with this news, although he already had enough on his dish to think about. As much as he cared about Chalky he knew his immediate concern was Anna and how to get her away from her father and Adams. But here was Chalky, in his own hell, reaching out for help. Damn the world, thought Fordy and all the crooked greedy men that make our lives difficult.

He thought of the dead birds that would pile up at the end of every cockfighting session. Disposable life, snuffed out in the pursuit of gaming and pleasure. We are as irrelevant as those crumpled lifeless animals in the minds of the powerful and wealthy men who control this country, he told himself.

He could hear Chalky's heavy breathing beside him. He knew he should say something… but what? They had both kept their own secrets close, too close. Now, together they sat on the brink, with no idea of how events might play out in the coming hours and days.

Chalky coughed and spat on the grass then wiped his eyes on the back of his arm. "Is that it?" he asked, with a touch of bitterness in his voice. "You'll be a friend as long as I'm the cheery dependable Chalky, always there for a laugh and beer, but not so welcome if I'm a filthy sodomite."

"Bloody 'ell, Chalky. Don't be so damned stupid. I'll not be the one to let you down. I was lost in my thoughts. I was just thinking, do you fancy riding o'er to Kings Pasture with me now? We could ride past the entrance, see if these fellows really are guarding the place. My guess is they are Adams's men. That day I went o'er with John to Saltburn Adams's place was fair bristling with lookouts."

"You still want my 'elp?" said Chalky, his voice croaky and weak.

"Course I do, mate, what do you take me for, a weak-minded fool? Your secret's safe with me and you're just the same to me as you alus was. Go and get your 'oss, we can talk as we travel up to Kings Pasture."

They walked back over the blacksmith's, Chalky saddled up one of their many horses from the stables at the back of the shop and the two men set off out of Bedale. Once they had crossed the river in Crakehall they swung right up the road towards Kings Pasture. Despite Fordy's suggestion they could talk further as they rode, both were quiet. Fordy felt he had spilt out all of his troubles and had little more to say. He glanced over at Chalky and guessed from his silence it was the same for him.

Taking the turning down Hollow Moor Road they pulled their horses up.

"I think there might be a lookout at the end of this lane if what Anna said in her letter is correct. I'm guessing there'll be others at the back entrance I use when I go in on a night to the stables and to see Anna. Then there'll be more at the main entrance. I suggest we go past them, give the fellows we see a curt nod and just keep on moving," suggested Fordy.

"Aye, sounds fine by me. There's no reason why they won't let us past, they can't kidnap everybody that 'appens to be using the road. Then if we keep going to Hackforth we can double back on the top road and return home without passing here again. We can't take on a bunch of rogues like this single handed."

"I agree, we're just checking this out but it might be useful to know exactly what precautions Stillerton has taken."

As Fordy predicted they found a couple of fellas stood at the end of Hollow Moor Road. Fordy felt apprehensive as they approached them but the men didn't bother them apart from an acknowledgment with the raise of a hand.

Chalky nodded and kicked on his horse. The road rose slightly as it curved around a slow bend. Once they were at the top of the rise they could clearly see the first small entrance into the grounds of Kings Pasture. Anna's words were correct. Stood in the drive were three surly looking men. Without hesitating Fordy and Chalky rode on past them, giving them a cursory glance and a nod. They continued on in silence to the main entrance and here they found half a dozen thugs pacing around the driveway. It suddenly occurred to Fordy that one of them might recognise him from his visit to Saltburn and he hunched his shoulders up in an attempt to obscure his face. Thankfully they hardly looked at Fordy and Chalky as they uttered incoherent grunts at them as they passed by along the road..

Once past the men Fordy and Chalky urged their horses on, eager to get home.

"Thanks for doing this," said Fordy, as they trotted along. "At least I know now that it's impossible for me to go back to Kings Pasture and get Anna."

Chalky nodded. "All still on for going to the races tomorrow?" he asked.

"Yes," nodded Fordy. "Shall we meet at Newton crossroads then we can ride up to Richmond together?"

"Aye," said Chalky, "you'll not mention what I told you earlier?"

Fordy shook his head. "I'll never tell a living soul, I know you've entrusted your life to me; I'll never split," said Fordy, moving Dapple nearer to Chalky. He reached out, took his friend's hand and held Chalky in a very firm handshake.

The men parted in Crakehall, Chalky bound for Bedale and Fordy for Worlds End. Once home Fordy explained to his father and Mary Ann that he was going to Richmond races the next day with Abe and Chalky and hoped to bring Anna back with him.

Ben was full of support for Fordy's plan and together they ran through how the next day might go until Ben was called away by a passing traveller who required refreshment. Fordy wandered into the kitchen where Mary Ann was busying herself with baking, Lucy was sat at the table chopping onions. When Mary Ann saw him come in she took him by the arm and led him back outside.

"What's the matter?" asked Fordy.

"There's something I have to tell you and I don't want Lucy to hear what I'm about to say. I'm fair worried about what might happen tomorrow. Yesterday the sun broke through the cloud but no sooner did it start to give off heat than three wisps of mist passed over its face. It's a sure sign o' trouble. Now, I've broken off a couple of leaves from my rowan tree, you must keep 'em in your pocket till you get Anna back here. There's no better way of keeping evil at bay than rowan."

Fordy was taken aback by her serious tone. He was used to Mary Ann giving mystical advice about inconsequential matters but he had never heard her give such a serious warning. He reached out his hand and took the offering.

"Thank you, Mary Ann. I shall take care. I promise."

She reached up, pulling his face towards hers and kissed him on his cheek. "You're more precious to me than any other living soul," she said, her voice choking.

"I know, Mary Ann, but think on this, I'll be bringing Anna back here tomorrow, and when the bairn is born that'll mean two more people for you to love and fuss over," he said, taking hold of her arm.

Mary Ann turned away. Fordy was sure he heard a sob but knew she wouldn't want him to know.

Fordy got no sleep that night as he played over in his head what might happen the next day. There was no doubt that tomorrow was going to be the most important day of his life, with no idea of how the dangers and obstacles he faced would play out. Whatever happened he knew both his and Anna's fate would be decided in the next few hours.

CHAPTER 19

After a sleepless night Fordy tended to the horses. Quickly seeing to their needs he returned to the kitchen. Over breakfast he reassured his father and Mary Ann that the intention was to bring Anna back from the races to Worlds End then to try to get a marriage license the next day and to wed immediately.

He had started the day with an air of optimism; if they could get Anna away from the racecourse without being apprehended by her father or any of his men, none of them would have any idea of where Anna had gone to. As far as Fordy knew there was nothing for her father to link him and Anna together. Once she was at Worlds End she should be safe.

But as the hours passed his anxiety grew. He repeatedly went through his plans, each time exposing another weakness. What if they couldn't find her at the races? She might be under close supervision and find it impossible to get away from her party. If Fordy wasn't able to make contact with her at the races what other chance would he have of seeing her and getting her away from her father?

In amongst his haphazard thoughts it struck him that she might be left at Kings Pasture, that her father wouldn't take her to Richmond. He might leave her at home under guard. Or what if the whole idea of going to the races had been called off by Stillerton? Even worse, had they left Yorkshire, already heading for London?

With all these worries spilling through his head, he rode to the crossroads where he had arranged to meet Abe and Chalky. His body was tense with worry as he ran his palm over his jacket; he could feel the small square box in his breast pocket that contained the ring that his father had given him. If all went well today it would be sat on Anna's finger before long. He had a romantic vision of getting down on one knee and gallantly asking her to marry him, although he found it hard to believe that such a moment would present itself if they had to leave the racecourse in a hurry. He slid his fingers into the pocket and pulled out the rowan leaves that Mary Ann had given him, rubbing his fingertips over their waxy surface. He had been sure to take them with him after Mary Ann's warning. Even though he wasn't superstitious he felt he needed any luck that might be on offer. Pushing the leaves back into the pocket, he laid his hand over his jacket again, checking that the box with the ring in was sat securely inside. He had a flashing moment of contentment, which soon disappeared as the weight of the day's tasks overwhelmed him again.

He reached forward to pat Dapple's neck, reassuring himself. "Thank God you're a steady 'oss," he said to the animal, then a new thought occurred to him. Should he have brought an extra horse for Anna to ride home on? Or would a horse on a lead rein drawn extra attention to him? Well, it was too late for that now.

The two brothers greeted Fordy in their usual boisterous manner. Fordy studied Chalky to see if there was any embarrassment after yesterday's admissions but there was nothing to pick up on. Fordy was relieved for a number of reasons. He hoped it meant Chalky trusted Fordy and realised he hadn't judged him harshly. More importantly, the last thing Fordy wanted was any awkwardness when they had such an important task ahead of them. It also occurred to Fordy that Chalky was so used to putting on a good show that it came naturally to him to brush aside his inner feelings and pretend that all was well with the world. Something that Fordy would have to do himself if he didn't want to attract attention at the races before rescuing Anna.

Together they set off for Richmond, riding over the high ground towards Scotton, Fordy had been keen to go this way as he felt sure the Stillerton party would take the slightly longer but more comfortable route up Leeming Lane then cut across country, approaching Richmond from the east. He assumed they would be travelling in a carriage but wanted to take no chances of being recognised by any of the group, particularly if Picard and Rennie were travelling with them as protection. Fordy knew Picard would have no hesitation in calling Fordy out. He had never understood why Picard disliked him so much. Was Picard the type of lout that hated everybody or did he hold a grudge against him for dumping Jane? If Jane's bairn was Picard's perhaps his anger stemmed from his disappointment that Fordy wouldn't pick up the pieces. If Jane had led him to believe that Fordy would stand by her, he was a fool. Thank God he'd not bedded her and felt he was obliged to marry her.

Such thoughts scrambled through Fordy's head as they rode along in the unseasonal cool weather.

"Have you got a plan?" asked Abe, breaking the silence.

"Not really, I don't know what we are going to be up against," admitted Fordy. "I'm assuming Chalky has told you everything."

"Aye," said Abe, laughing loudly. "I love a good adventure particularly if it involves you and a woman."

Fordy sighed and looked round at Abe; he found it hard to believe that there was any humour in this fiasco. Would he have found it amusing if this was happening to someone else? He thought on that for a moment. Probably he would but did Abe understand that Stillerton could force Anna to marry against her will... that she could be lost to him forever, never able to see her again... or their unborn child?

Fordy then looked miserably over at Chalky, who took the cue.

"It's maybe amusing at first, Abe, but I think there's a lot at stake here for Fordy and this lass," said Chalky.

Silence descended on the group again. Leaving Scotton behind they made steady progress over the wide-open area known as Scotton Moor. This stretch of road was usually deserted, with the odd farm steading dotted here and there. Today, however, there was more traffic, mostly small groups bound for the festivities in Richmond.

"Look who's heading our way," said Abe, pointing up the road.

"Who?" asked Fordy.

"It's that fellow Edwards we did that work for, miserable beggar hasn't settled his account," said Chalky.

"I'll have a word him," said Abe. "You two keep on going, this won't take long."

Fordy and Chalky didn't argue. They gave Edwards a nod in greeting as they passed him, leaving Abe to tackle the late payer.

"Now then, Edwards, I'm glad I've bumped into you..." said Abe, his voice disappearing into the distance as he was left behind.

"Shall we stop here for a minute, let him catch up when he's finished with Edwards?" suggested Chalky, once they were out of earshot.

Both men pulled on their reins, bringing their horses to a halt.

"I'm glad of a moment alone with you, Fordy. I couldn't speak in front of Abe," he said hurriedly. "I wanted to thank you for listening to me yesterday. I know you've plenty to handle just now and I'm here to help you. But I wanted you to know that I've decided to go with Giles, get away from here. If Adams is struggling to keep afloat, he may not be around for much longer. I haven't spoken to Giles yet but I think knowing what you told me yesterday about Adams, it's easier to make a decision. Probably go away for a year or so till all this dies down."

Fordy listened silently to his friend, nodding occasionally.

"It'll be a shock to my father and Abe but I can't live like this anymore and…"

"Look up, here comes Abe," interrupted Fordy. "I don't care how busy you might be I shall expect you and Abe to be at my wedding once I get Anna away from her father," he went on in a loud voice, changing the subject from Chalky's intimate secrets.

"Any luck?" asked Chalky, when Abe was nearer.

"Says he'll call in to settle up next time he's in town. I told him I'd give 'im a week then I'd be back up here to see him," said Abe, with a chuckle. "He was fair dropped on when he saw me."

"Fordy was halfway through asking us to his wedding," said Chalky, cheerfully.

It struck Fordy again how easily Chalky moved from distress over his complicated life to putting on a show of relaxed comradery.

"I'll be there whenever it is," replied Abe, "no doubt your father'll have open house to celebrate. One of the benefits of owning your own hostelry."

With the prospect of a wedding and a party they exchanged banter and jokes, the mood lightening for a while although Fordy's spirits were still subdued, keeping his real worries hidden, as he knew Chalky was too.

As they neared Richmond the roads became busier and the threesome carefully picked their way down the steep Slee Gill road. On their right the ruined castle towered above them but their eyes were fixed on the road as it narrowed over the bridge that took them over the fast-flowing Swale. They pulled up their horses to the left of the road to confer.

"Shall we take a pint at Mr Martin's Pit or would you rather go straight up to the racecourse?" Chalky asked Fordy.

"I know we'd normally stop here for a drink and watch a couple of cockfights," said Fordy, nodding towards the road that went off to the right between the banks of the river and the high ground where the castle stood. Three hundred yards further, sat on a piece of flat ground outside the castle walls, was the infamous Mr Martin's cock pit. It attracted crowds from far and wide every week of the year; on a race day it rivalled the racecourse for popularity and for the amount of money that changed hands in both wagers and prizes.

"I'd rather head straight up but if you lads want to stay down here for a couple of mains I'll go on my own," offered Fordy. The racecourse was situated on a piece of high ground, known as Gallow Fields Pasture, about a mile north of the town.

"No," said Chalky, "We're not leaving you, anything could 'appen."

"Aye, we're here to help. Bugger t'cocking today," agreed Abe.

Fordy looked at Chalky who nodded in agreement. Despite the problems Fordy was facing he wondered about the words that Abe had just used and if they took on a deeper meaning for Chalky. But Fordy didn't have time to dwell on Chalky's predicament for long.

"Bloody 'ell, there's Picard and Rennie coming down t'street," alerted Abe in a low voice.

Fordy looked up the road ahead that came down from the town centre and saw the two thugs approaching.

"Let's go along past the cock pit and climb back up into the market square by another route. I bet they are heading for Mr Martin's pit, we just need to keep well ahead of them," said Abe, already turning his horse down the lane that ran around the foot of the castle. Fordy and Chalky quickly followed him without looking back. With the river tumbling past on their right, they trotted on towards the cockpit and through the crowds that were spilling out on the road, then climbed back up into town and came out into the marketplace.

"In a way it's a good sign Picard's here, it probably means that Stillerton is here too… and hopefully Anna," said Fordy. The small group pulled up their horses to take stock of the situation.

Dozens of stalls filled the crowded town square and they carefully rode by the traders and their customers, stopping for a moment to let a couple of performers on stilts cross their path. As they left the marketplace the clock struck twelve. "We'd better get a move on or the day'll be over and we'll 'ave missed our chance," called Fordy.

They made their way to Gallow Gate and began the steep climb out of town. The road was heaving with people both mounted and on foot making for the same destination. Occasionally a coach or trap would try to push its way through, the drivers bellowing and shouting for folk to get clear, only serving to increase the congestion and inflaming tempers. The hill was a challenge for man and beast alike.

Once the climb was done it took a while to get onto the familiar racecourse; the entrance was narrow and restricted by two tall stone posts. Fordy remained alert all the while, looking out for a carriage that might be Stillerton's or the familiar figure of Anna. He was relieved when they finally got to the area reserved for coaches and horses. After checking their animals were securely tied up, they made their way to the westerly end of the course where the newly built Judges Stand sat opposite the magnificent two-storey grandstand. This course was situated on a high flat stretch of land. On a clear day it was said the coast was visible but today, as with most days of this summer, the sky was shrouded in murky haze.

As Fordy pushed through the crowds his senses were heightened, looking around for both Anna and danger, ready to take whatever action was necessary. In the past a visit to the races was a day of merriment and fun, taking too much ale and backing a few horses, usually the wrong ones. But today, Fordy knew his future happiness was at stake: and Anna's safety.

"I think our best chance of finding her is here," said Fordy, coming to a halt opposite the grandstand. "I can't think Stillerton would want to mix with the riff-raff out here, he'll want to be in there, with t'gentry."

The three men stood for a moment or two staring into the area reserved for distinguished guests. High railings separated the occupants from the common folk but it was still possible to observe the finely dressed racegoers socialising and enjoying themselves. Many were at tables at the front of the building and others were stood on the open balconies that ran along the first storey. Fordy looked for Anna but was cautious, aware that if Adams was in the enclosure he might recognise him; the last thing he wanted was to draw attention to himself. He was safe in the knowledge he was unknown to Stillerton and that Picard and Rennie were down in the town for now and under no circumstances would two such ruffians be allowed into the grandstand.

"Can you see 'er?" asked Chalky.

"No," answered Fordy, "shall we walk around for a while and see if I can spot her?"

The brothers agreed and together they pushed their way through the crowd and around the imposing structure. For a fleeting moment Fordy thought he saw a couple of faces he recognised from his trip to Saltburn. Were they Adams's men? But they disappeared into the crowd before Fordy could get another look at them. He knew this was a risky operation, the key was to stay vigilant and not let his guard down. Abe and Chalky stuck close to Fordy, they didn't know what Anna looked like so the small party was reliant on Fordy finding her. Their search proved fruitless and Fordy's frustration grew. He wondered if they would be better standing still and watching the occupants in the grandstand more closely. Before he could suggest this the sound of horns could be heard from the other side of the field. Everyone stopped in their tracks and looked over to see what was happening.

"What's going on?" asked Fordy, "I can't see."

"There's a line of fine carriages making their way onto the course from the west entrance. It must be the Kirklands and their party, here to watch the big race," said Chalky, craning his neck to see over the heads of the people.

"She won't be with that lot, will she?" asked Abe.

"I doubt it," said Fordy, "let's get near the entrance of the grandstand, we might have a better chance of seeing in when they open the gates for this group to go in."

It seemed everyone else had the same idea, folk were keen to catch a glimpse of the wealthy aristocrats. The three men pushed their way through the tight mass of folk to the gates of the enclosure, Fordy straining his eyes looking for the familiar figure of Anna. But still no luck. For a few moments he was distracted by the two open carriages that pulled up at the grandstand. He watched as the finely dressed ladies and gentlemen descended and walked into the enclosure. He noted their aloof manner, neither looking left or right at the hordes of people who were watching them. "God bless his Lordship," a voice called out from the crowd. No one acknowledged the greeting apart from the oldest man in the party who looked up and returned a friendly greeting with a raised hand in the direction of the man who had shouted out.

Fordy didn't know anything about the Kirkland family other than they were very prosperous and bred high quality horses. He was in no position to make a judgement of what he had just seen. He knew that if the Duke of Malbury was in such a setting he would probably have exchanged a word with people he knew, sharing a tip about a horse or commenting on the weather. Not that that made Malbury any better or worse than these folk. Fordy's anger flared up; Malbury had neglected his duties and responsibilities up here in Yorkshire. He might well be affable and friendly when he was in the neighbourhood but didn't appear to care a damn about what was happening while he was away. Was he aware that Adams was pressing people for money and spreading violence and fear in the area in an attempt to prop up his business ventures? Malbury seemed content to set these business ventures in motion but didn't have the interest or commitment to see them through. Fordy also believed that Malbury had enough influence to intervene in the Philpot case, should he wish to, but had admitted to Fordy and his father that he had other problems brewing.

Typical of the upper classes, happy to help as long is their actions didn't compromise their own comfortable lives.

"I don't know what to do," said Fordy, turning to Abe and Chalky. "I have no idea whether she is here or still at Kings Pasture. For all I know she could already be in a coach on her way to London."

"The smell of them pastries is fair bothering me," said Abe, gesturing towards a brightly adorned stall with trestles piled up with pies and pasties of every shape and size. "Let's go over to and get food…"

"Aye, and a pint," agreed Chalky. "We can still keep looking for 'er."

Dispirited, Fordy nodded in agreement and they made their way over to the stand selling refreshments.

"You keep a look out and we'll get the food," said Chalky. Fordy agreed and while he waited for the boys he turned his attention to his surroundings. The racing hadn't started yet and the noise of the racegoers continued to grow in anticipation of the afternoon's sport.

Today's race was one of the most important in the northern racing calendar, although the most prestigious event of the year was held in October when the Gold Cup was at stake. Yorkshire was the unrivalled centre of thoroughbred racing and this town had an abundance of local wealthy estates that spent huge amounts of money breeding and training horses. The competition at Richmond was of the highest calibre. Fortunes and reputations could be made or broken today.

This track was particularly challenging. Although circular, the course was elliptical and had two tight corners at each end. One circuit was just over twelve furlongs and the horses went round three or four times for most of the races. The jockeys' ability to control their horses and navigate the bends made the races here exciting and dangerous, sometimes fatal for both horse and rider.

Around the track were stalls selling a variety of food and drink along with offerings of knick-knacks and gifts. Near the starting gates were two lines of touts, some calling out the odds and others chalking them up on blackboards for those who could read. The atmosphere was loud and exhilarating but Fordy felt detached from his surroundings. He was there as an observer, not to participate in the jollity and thrill of the proceedings. He wasn't able to relax for a moment, cautious of losing contact with Abe and Chalky while he waited for them queuing for the food and drink; he continued watching the crowds, hoping to spot Anna.

Fordy felt someone pull at his arm. He tensed and turned to see who was taking hold of him, fearing that Picard had caught up with him. But it was a woman, her head wrapped in a brown shawl.

"Fordy, it's me. Take my arm, I don't want to lose you now I have found you," she said breathlessly.

Fordy gasped and did as Anna bid, startled and elated that she had found him.

"Are you alright?" he asked, bending to kiss her. She lifted her head to return the greeting. He saw her eyes were swollen and red.

"Have they harmed you?" he asked quickly, after meeting her lips.

"No," she answered. "I daren't remove this covering for fear of being recognised by my party," she explained.

"Where did you get this raggedy old thing?" he asked.

"I found it in one of Mrs Dinsdale's cupboards. I thought it would be a useful disguise if I got the opportunity to slip away. When the Kirkland party came into the grandstand everyone stood aside to let them in and to greet them. With that distraction I took my chance and made my way out of the enclosure."

A wave of relief and desire swept through Fordy. It had been four days since he had seen her; her resilience and fortitude was just as reassuring and appealing as it always was. He pulled her to him and hugged her tightly.

"Oh, Anna, what a mess I've made of things. I wanted to ask you to marry me after you visited Worlds End on Wednesday but you were so tired," he said. "Actually, I've been wanting to ask you for weeks but dare not in fear of being turned down."

"I'm sorry too, I should have let you come into the gardener's shed. We should have talked more that day about… us," she hesitated.

"I know about the babe," he said, gently.

"You guessed?" she asked, looking up at him wide-eyed.

"Not really, Mary Ann told me, but now I know why you have been so tired. We haven't much time," he said, aware that at any moment they might be seen and that Anna could be snatched away from him.

"I have a plan… Will you come with me now? We can go back to Worlds End and we can be wed tomorrow." He stopped, swallowing hard, "That is of course, if you'll marry me."

He stepped back from her a little and looked into her eyes.

"Will you marry me?" he asked again.

She nodded, tears flowing down her cheeks.

"Will you come away with me now?"

She nodded again and began to sob. He held her close for a moment before being interrupted by Abe who was walking towards them, his hands full of tankards of beer.

"Fordy, come on, we've got pies and drink," called Abe, stopping in his tracks, his jaw dropped.

"Bloody 'ell," he exclaimed, his eyes widening with excitement. "Is this 'er?"

"Yes," said Fordy, taking Anna's arm as Chalky appeared behind his brother. "Let's get out of this crowd and away from the grandstand."

The four of them moved quickly away to the boundary of the field and found a low wall to lean against.

Fordy introduced Anna to Abe and Chalky. The brothers had already started to eat the food they had just bought; despite the urgency of the situation for Fordy, they weren't going to let this freshly baked treat go to waste. Unable to speak as their cheeks bulged with pastry and meat they acknowledged her with enthusiastic nods and beaming grins.

"When I got your note," said Fordy, "we thought to come here... as you suggested and try to rescue you. I've been a fool, can you ever forgive me?"

"Yes, of course. It doesn't matter now," said Anna, "but we must get away from here immediately. Once my father realises I have gone he will send out a search party for me. We haven't got much time."

"Before we go, I need to know something. Do you know the name of the man your father wants you to marry?" he asked, desperate to know but fearful of the answer.

"He's called Jim Adams," she answered, close to tears. "Please, do not speak of him, just get me away from here."

Fordy's worst fears were realised but now was not the time to dwell on it. Action was required now.

As they hurried over to the lines of tethered horses Fordy pulled Chalky close to him. "She's told me her intended bridegroom is definitely Adams," he whispered to Chalky who nodded silently. Neither man needed to say more.

Walking towards their animals they were met by a familiar figure striding towards them. It was Giles Redworth.

"Well, hello there," he called to them as they neared him. Despite the desperate situation Fordy was in he couldn't help but notice how cheerful Giles was. Was he like Chalky, having to put on a show that all was well with the world? But he had no time to dwell on such matters.

Chalky rushed forward to Giles, "We have an urgent situation here. Fordy must get this lady away from the course at all speed. She is Annabelle Stillerton, Sir Robwyn's daughter, there are plans to marry her to Adams this week," he said quickly.

"Jim Adams?" asked Giles, horror crumpling his face.

"Yes. I'll explain it all to you later. But our hurry is to get them away," answered Chalky.

Fordy watched Giles react to this news. The happy confident man disappeared, his shoulders slumped, his face lost all its colour. "Is Adams here?" he stuttered.

"Yes, you must stay here with us. But please help us get Anna and Fordy off before her father sends a search party out for her," said Chalky.

"Of course," said Giles, turning to Anna and giving her a deep bow, "Ma'am, your servant."

Fordy watched Anna return a small curtsey. Even in this most dire of situations their upbringing and manners prevailed, stealing precious moments away from the immediate task of making their escape.

"It's good to see you, Mr Redworth, but we must leave with all haste," said Fordy, grabbing at Anna's hand and making his way to Dapple. Fordy was now faced with the problem that he had considered earlier that day.

"I haven't got an extra 'orse, do you think you'll be alright on the back of Dapple?" he asked her, knowing that this was less than ideal. It was a long way home for anyone to ride as an extra passenger on a horse but in her condition it was almost impossible. "If we didn't have to hurry, I would happily walk beside you and let you have Dapple," he said.

"Here, Fordy, take my 'orse," said Chalky. "I'll find my own way 'ome, it's more important for you to get Anna away."

"Thanks, Chalky," said Fordy, immediately accepting the offer.

"We'll find a way of getting him home," added Giles.

Chalky handed over the reins of his animal to Fordy.

"Why don't you have Dapple?" suggested Fordy to Anna, "and I'll ride Chalky's horse."

"Alright but I can't sit astride a horse in this dress, it's too tight," she told Fordy, pulling at the material around her legs. "I knew this might happen. When I dressed this morning I put on a roomier outfit but Father insisted I wear this thing. Fortunately I found a pair of men's britches, I have them on underneath.

Fordy looked at her, "You're wearing that bonny yella' dress," he stuttered. His thoughts were taken back to the night in the orchard when they first knew each other.

"Do have you a knife?" she asked, urgently.

"Here," said Chalky, pulling one out of a pocket in his jerkin.

"Is it sharp?" she asked, snatching it from his hand and turning her back to their group before Chalky had chance to answer her. Fordy saw the men turn their heads away from Anna but Fordy watched her plunge the blade in the fabric. She began to saw round the skirt, taking it off above the knee.

"But your dress," spluttered Fordy.

"Hang the dress, at least I have room to move," laughed Anna. "It's too tight anyway, now that I'm filling out."

Fordy swallowed hard. "You look just as lovely," he whispered, glancing at the tight fabric pulling over her breasts, her pale flesh spilling over the low-cut bodice.

"Help me, I can't reach round the back," she told him. He took the knife and continued her work. Lifting his eyes for a moment he saw his friends still had their backs turned. Fordy wasn't sure if it was from discretion or whether they were watching out for Stillerton and Adams. Once he had worked the knife round the dress the material fell to the ground, Anna kicked it aside.

Fordy stepped forward, putting an arm around her, "Where do you get your bravery from?" he asked gently.

"I'm not sure, maybe from you…"

"Come on, you two, there'll be plenty of time for soft words once Anna is safely away from here," interrupted Abe. "I'm going to come with you, Fordy, give you a hand if we meet with any trouble."

Not giving Fordy time to argue, Abe then turned to Chalky. "You sure you're alright staying 'ere?"

"Course," said Chalky, "stop y' yattering and get away. I'll keep an eye out for anyone approaching us while you get yourselves mounted," he added, stepping away from them and looking back out over the racecourse.

Abe held Dapple and Fordy cupped his hands for Anna as she stepped up onto his horse. Dapple stood perfectly still as his master's most precious cargo made herself comfortable in the saddle.

"Do you feel safe?" Fordy asked awkwardly, adjusting the lengths of the stirrups for her and pulling at Dapple's girth, checking it was securely tightened.

"I'm fine, ready to get off," she said. Their moment of tender exchanges gave way as practical necessities took over.

Fordy and Abe jumped onto their own mounts. Fordy had never ridden Chalky's horse before but a strange animal wasn't a problem for him as he settled into the unfamiliar saddle and took the measure of the beast.

"All clear?" Fordy called to Chalky and Giles.

"As far as I can see there's nobody making their way over here. I think the first race is about to start, everyone's milling around the start line and the edge of the track," called Giles.

"We'll be away then," said Fordy. "Thanks for your help and the loan of your 'orse."

"Thank you, Chalky and you too, Mr Redworth. I hope I shall get to know you both soon," said Anna.

Chalky took his cap off and gave a small bow to Anna, "It's my pleasure, miss," he said. Giles gave a small nod of the head and mumbled something that Fordy couldn't hear.

"I'll see you tomorrow, Chalky. I almost forgot, Anna and I hope to marry in the next few days, I shall expect you at the wedding, along with Mr Redworth," Fordy called out as Chalky's horse paddled in uncertainty, unused to its new rider.

"Come on," shouted Abe, "we must leave." He reached down for Dapple's bridle and encouraged the horse to walk alongside him. "See you tonight," he called back to Chalky as they headed for the gates.

CHAPTER 20

They left the course the same way that they had entered it and made their way steadily down the hill into Richmond. The town was quieter than it had been a couple of hours earlier, most folks were now up at Gallow Fields for the racing.

"We'll 'ave to keep an eye out for Picard and Rennie," said Fordy, as they rode through Richmond.

"With any luck those dullards are still in Martin's pit with so much ale in them they're legless," said Abe with little conviction in his voice.

Anna remained silent as the two men chattered between themselves whilst keeping an eye out for trouble. Once over the bridge Fordy allowed himself to relax a little. Thankfully there were plenty of travellers on the road and they were never totally alone. It would be a brave man who dare to kidnap Anna with so many witnesses, Fordy tried to tell himself.

Fordy pulled up beside Anna. "Are you still alright?" he asked, noticing Abe had pulled back, probably to allow them a few private words.

She looked at him and smiled. "Yes, I can't believe we have done this, I have been so frightened, terrified that I would never see you again. At first I didn't understand what was happening when my father arrived with all those men. Initially a handful of them went into the library, I crept downstairs and could hear raised voices and lots of arguing. The house was surrounded by horrible surly fellows, Mrs Higgins and I were terrified. I was called into the drawing room by my father, he told me I was to marry a man he had chosen for me. Then he called this awful creature into the room. He never spoke, just stared at me with indifference, a cold smirk on his face. That was the first time I met Jim Adams," she said with a shiver and a sniffle. "I think he has something to do with smuggling and the dealing that goes on in Father's stables…"

"You are right, Adams masterminds the whole smuggling enterprise in Yorkshire," interrupted Fordy. "I've met him a couple of times, I was afraid he might recognise me up at the races, if he'd seen me and drawn attention to my presence, we could've had problems…"

"How do you know him?" she asked.

Fordy thought quickly, reluctant to expose his connection to Adams, partly because he felt foolish for having become so entangled with the rogue and because he didn't want to cause Anna more worry. "Someone once asked me to deliver a message to 'im. You remember that time I went up to Yarm, I met 'im there. But all of that doesn't matter now. I want to talk about us getting wed. Mary Ann says I can get a licence and we could be married tomorrow or the day after. How does that sound?"

"Perfect, but there's something else," Anna paused.

"What?"

"I have some papers that I might need. I'm sure my father will try to withhold my inheritance. There's a letter from my mother's solicitor explaining that her money has been placed in a trust in my name. I found it in my father's study a few weeks ago and took it. I also have a few pieces of correspondence that prove my identity. After hearing how my father has been talking these last few days, I fear he would even deny that I am his daughter. He is desperate for my money. He intends investing with this man Adams." She paused.

"You remember I told you this morning I had dressed in a bulkier dress, more suited to riding a horse?"

Fordy nodded.

"My plan was to secrete half a dozen documents in my petticoats. It would have been difficult but I was sure I could manage it. But when my father saw what I was wearing he commanded me to change into this frivolous day dress and I had nowhere to hide anything. I even thought he was going to take this old shawl off me until I insisted I needed it over my knees when we travelled in the coach. As we readied ourselves to leave I managed to slip out of the house and take the documents down to the garden shed. I thought I had a better chance of keeping possession of them if I got them out of the house."

Fordy's heart sank at this news. But he realised she had already risked a great deal. At least she'd had the forethought to get these vital documents out of the house.

"I've packed a few clothes too, they're in a bag, also in the gardener's shed. I thought if I couldn't find you at Richmond that I might try to escape in the night and I reasoned that if I left my papers and belongings in there I could escape down the back lane and over the fields to avoid all of those men guarding the place."

Fordy nodded in silence, realising he would have to go round by Kings Pasture immediately, before the party returned home.

"There's another reason…" she hesitated.

"What?" asked Fordy.

"Jasper… he's in the shed too," she grimaced.

"Bloody dog," muttered Fordy, thinking for a moment. If these documents weren't so important he wouldn't go at all, certainly not for that damned dog, or her clothes. He pulled up his horse and waited for Abe to catch up with them.

"Abe, I've got to go to Kings Pasture. Anna has left some important papers in the gardener's shed…" he petered out, his mind racing. "Can you escort her back to Worlds End?" he added, nodding towards Anna. "This shouldn't take me more than an hour or so."

"Fordy, I'm sorry. Will you be safe?" cried Anna.

"Of course I'll be safe, they don't know that it's me that has taken you from your father. Apart from Picard having some irrational grudge against me there's no reason for them to bother with me."

"But if they see you with Jasper and a bundle of papers they will…"

"Nonsense," interrupted Fordy, "there's nothing to fear. They'll still be at Richmond, looking for you. But, I must get there with all speed," he reassured her, although he knew there was substance to her fears.

"Can you do this for me Abe?" he asked, looking over at his friend.

Abe nodded and moved his horse towards Dapple.

"You're a good man," said Fordy. He leant towards Anna and took her hand. "Go with Abe, my father and Mary Ann are expecting you. I'll be as quick as I can but tell me where the bag is with your things."

"Both the papers and my clothes are under the settee, in the shed, I didn't lock it," she said, beginning to cry. "Oh, Fordy, do hurry,"

"Don't upset yourself, I will get back to you at Worlds End," he said. As he reached forward to kiss her, the aroma of her Lily of the Valley perfume came afresh to his nostrils and he drew in the smell of her familiar scent. He hesitated for a moment, how he wanted to go with her and forget about having to go for those documents.

Dismissing these thoughts, he pulled the head of his horse round and cantered off in the direction of Kings Pasture House.

* * *

He travelled so quickly he hardly had time to consider what he was doing but, as he neared Kings Pasture his senses heightened, looking out for men and listening for the sound of approaching horses.

He wondered how long it had taken Stillerton to miss his daughter and how much time would they spend searching for her at the racecourse. If Adams and Stillerton's deal was reliant on Anna going through with this arranged marriage, Adams would be as keen to find her as her father. No doubt Adams's men would have been sent out to search for her around the racecourse. The big question that was occupying his thoughts now was how many men Adams had left here to guard Kings Pasture House and how difficult was it going to be to get to the garden and back out again unseen?

He was relieved to find there was nobody stood guarding the end of Hollow Moor Lane and he turned left towards the back entrance of Kings Pasture, the one he used when he came to collect contraband and visit Anna. There was still no sign of any watchmen but he knew he needed to move as quickly as possible whilst staying alert for danger. How he wished he had Dapple at this moment as he drew up outside the garden gates. His own horse knew the routine and would have quietly stood, waiting for Fordy but Chalky's horse was unsure of what was expected of him. Fordy took valuable minutes fastening the horse to the

272

gates which he discovered were locked. He felt vulnerable in the broad daylight, a sitting target if he was noticed, but reasoned it should be a simple matter to skim over the garden wall, dash into the shed, collect Anna's bag and the dog, then exit quickly and quietly through the garden gates.

He got over the wall with ease and landed quietly in the grounds of the garden. He stayed crouched down as he checked the area for movement. All was quiet and still. He walked stealthily towards the shed, the only noise was the thudding of his heart. Reaching the garden shed door he turned the handle and gently pushed at it.

"Damn it," he hissed. The door was locked. She said she hadn't locked the door. He looked behind, checking no one was there. Either she had made a mistake or someone else had come along and secured it. Either way he could easily kick at it and break the small lock, but what about the noise he would make?

There was no time to consider other alternatives, he raised his leg and kicked at the handle. The door swung open easily but with a loud crack. Fordy turned round to check if anyone was watching him. He saw nothing and could hear no sound of anyone approaching. Breathing rapidly, he charged into the familiar surroundings of the room. He dropped to his knees to search under the settee: the leather travelling bag was there along with a satchel that he guessed had Anna's paper's in. Grabbing them he dashed from the confines of the outhouse. Then he remembered the dog and turned back into the building.

"Jasper, are you there?" he whispered, looking around for the animal. "Damned dog," he hissed, "Jasper, here boy," he repeated, trying to sound friendly and encouraging. With that, Jasper ran out from behind a chair and scurried into the garden. Fordy followed the dog, cursing under his breath. It had disappeared into the undergrowth. He wasn't going to go any further into the garden, the dog would have to fend for itself. With luck Jasper would wander out of the grounds and Fordy might be able to find him later for Anna when things had died down.

Looking about him he was relieved to see he was still alone. His heart thudding against his chest, he took a deep breath; the most difficult part of his job was done. A quick run over to the gates and he would be away from the dangers of this place.

He slipped through the garden gate, diving out onto the back lane that led to safety. With a final glance back towards the stables he heaved a sigh of relief: there was no one in sight. He undid Chalky's horse and led it a few yards down the track that he had used a few minutes ago. Holding Anna's bags in his left hand he tried to mount the horse but before he got one foot off the ground a shout went up and the horse started, backing away from Fordy. He looked up and saw two men running towards him along the road that led to the rear exit from the grounds. It was Picard and Rennie, and they were blocking Fordy's escape route. As they approached Fordy they continued to bellow at him, Chalky's horse becoming even jumpier, tugging his reins out of Fordy's hand.

Another quick decision was needed; if the horse wasn't going to provide Fordy with a speedy means of exit his legs would have to. He dropped the travelling bag, keeping securely hold of the satchel, and ran, leaping from the path and darting into the trees.

Then a thought occurred to him; Higgins would be down in the stable block. If he could get to Higgins, he would be safe.

Sprinting down the lane he saw the entrance to the stable yard, he could hear his pursuers calling after him but they were having difficulty keeping up with Fordy's young legs.

"'Iggins, are y' there?" called Fordy, gasping for air. He listened for a familiar shout, but none came. He ran to the entrance of the building where the contraband was distributed.

"'Iggins! It's me, Fordy, where are you?" Fordy shouted again, looking round for any sign of life. The place was deserted. Where was Higgins? Maybe he'd gone to the races. In desperation Fordy went into the stables. He had never been in here before. Boxes and barrels were piled high, straw and hay that was used for packing lay scattered over the floor. To his right was a tall desk with a large ledger laid open; Fordy guessed it belonged to Higgins.

This wasn't the refuge he had hoped for, if he didn't get out quickly he risked getting trapped in here. A new plan came to him – if he went around the stable block, he could get across the fields and run towards Bowbridge Lane at the other side of Kings Pasture. It would take him ages to get back home to Worlds End but he could skirt round this place over land that he knew, avoiding these idiots that were after him.

Swinging round to leave the stables, he saw he was too late. Picard and Rennie were on him. They flattened him to the floor.

"Where's 'Iggins?" shouted Fordy.

"Gone," sneered Picard, lifting Fordy to his feet. "Thought your friend would save you? He's bin packed off, he's a rogue, 'ad 'is hand in Stillerton's pot."

"You're the rogue, Picard, I wouldn't trust you…"

Picard punched Fordy in the face, the speed and power of his clenched fist splitting Fordy's cheek and sending him staggering backwards, dropping Anna's bag. Struggling to keep his feet, Picard was on him again. Fordy was surprised by the quickness of the thug, who he had always thought of as a blundering idiot, not a nimble assailant. Still trying to recover from the blow he felt Picard yank at his arms, then coarse rope bit into his wrists.

Fordy was immobilised, his arms and legs were bound and he was left to lie on the compacted earthen ground. He was expecting a beating but both men walked away, leaving him laid on the floor. What was going to happen next? When had these two returned from Richmond? Fordy would have put money on them staying all day and night in the town. And how long before Stillerton came back? Would he have Adams with him?

Fordy edged himself towards the wall and adjusted his position in an attempt to find a more comfortable one. The change of perspective also allowed him to look around the stables for a chance of escape. But his discomfort grew, the restraints on his hands and ankles had been pulled tight and he could feel his limbs going cold and numb, making it hard for him to concentrate on finding a way out of this mess. He forced himself to take a deep breath, pushed the ache in his hands and feet aside, and looked around for anything sharp that he might use as a tool to cut through the rope. He spotted a knife hung up on a low beam but he had no chance of getting to it. He knew he had limited time in which to make an escape and continued to search round the room with his eyes. Over in the far corner he could see a scythe laid on the floor, if he could get to it and position himself properly, he might be able to work through the sisal.

He began to caterpillar himself over the floor, moving a few inches with every awkward and painful shunt, but before he was halfway across four silhouettes appeared at the open doorway. Fordy looked up to see the familiar sight of Picard and Rennie. With them was Jim Adams and a stranger who Fordy thought must be Anna's father.

Stillerton marched into the stables. "Who the hell are you?" he bawled at Fordy.

Fordy didn't answer.

"It's zat bastard Robson I was telling you 'bout," answered Picard, in his heavy French accent.

"Who?" bellowed Stillerton.

"Robson," shouted Picard, tugging on the rope that held Fordy. The sisal that bound him tightened to a burning rasp and Fordy let out a stifled groan.

"He's ze one who 'as bin sniffin' round your daughter," sneered Picard.

"Do you know where she is?" screamed Stillerton, marching up to Fordy and raising his arm, as if to strike.

Fordy remained silent.

"Answer him, you dog," spat Picard, pulling sharply on the rope again.

"I know our friend here," said Adams, stepping forward. "Fordy Robson, John Burgess's trusty companion if I'm not mistaken."

Fordy saw the cold smile that Adams invariably wore and wondered if he could use his acquaintance with Adams to get out of this.

"Mr Adams, sir, there seems to have been some sort of misunderstanding," he spluttered forming the thought just a second or two before the words. "I'm only here to collect a couple of bags of tea and a few bottles of brandy."

"I haven't time for him, we need to find Anna," yelled Stillerton, marching around and waving his hands in the air.

"Enough," said Adams quietly. "Our operations here are totally compromised now. You've been fool enough to lose your daughter, Stillerton. I suggest you go and find her. Rennie, go with him, Picard, stay here with me."

Fordy watched Stillerton and Rennie shuffle out of the stables. Once they were gone Adams and Picard came closer to Fordy. They both crouched down on their haunches.

"What was that you were saying about our friend here and Annabelle Stillerton?" Adams asked Picard, in a quiet menacing tone.

"He iz always here, visiting her when he collects his goods," grunted Picard.

"Is that so? I'd lay a wager that you know where she is now," hissed Adams, glaring into Fordy's face.

Fordy held his mouth tight, all he had to do was keep quiet. Once they realised they couldn't find her they would forget about him and he should be able to make his escape.

Adams gave Picard a nod. The ruffian grabbed at Fordy's arms, the bindings on his wrists biting into his raw flesh. He gritted his teeth, not wanting these thugs to know how much pain he was in.

"Now," said Adams slowly, "we haven't much time. I'm going to give you one chance to tell me where the Stillerton girl is."

With that, Picard's fist thumped into Fordy's stomach, pushing the air from his lungs. He gasped involuntarily. Then another punch landed which sent him reeling backwards.

Dazed but still aware of his surroundings he gulped quickly to fill his lungs and shook his head to reorientate himself. His eyes were watering and he lifted his bound hands to rub them dry, hoping to clear his blurred vision.

Fordy knew he must remain silent, aware they would have to act quickly, both to find Anna and to avoid being discovered here. Adams was a man who liked the shadows, he was in strange territory here and had obviously come for a purpose; Fordy calculated he would want to be back to the safety of Saltburn with all speed. He gambled that staying quiet was the best way to end this ordeal. As long as they didn't notice Anna's bag he should be able to talk his way out of this.

Fordy watched Adams prowling up and down, he had stepped away while Picard dished out his violence, no doubt hoping that Fordy would start talking soon. But Adams was no longing looking at Fordy; he was staring at the floor.

"What's that?" he barked at Picard, pointing at the ground. "Fetch it here."

Fordy couldn't see what Adams had spotted until Picard scuttled over and picked the item up.

It was Anna's satchel. Fordy's heart sank to his boots as he watched Picard hand it to Adams.

Fordy's pulse pounded in his head as Adams undid the buckles and grabbed at the papers in it. He watched as Adams quickly scanned a couple of sheets before thrusting them back into the bag. Adams returned his eyes to Fordy, gave a grunt of fury and threw the bag back at Fordy. Despite the state he was in Fordy was able to grasp hold of the bag, pulling it close to himself.

"So, we have ourselves a couple of starry-eyed lovers, have we?" said Adams, his face almost lit up with malicious humour. "About to make a run for it?"

Fordy didn't answer.

"No wonder she was proving to be a reluctant bride," said Adams thoughtfully, he turned away and walked outside leaving Picard standing over Fordy.

"Picard, out here," shouted Adams.

Fordy watched Picard obey the command, both men were now out of view but still within earshot.

"I'm closing this place down. We sent 'Iggins packing this morning so there should be no one asking questions. I want you back to Saltburn by sunrise tomorrow so get anything valuable out of here," Adams barked.

As Fordy listened to these words, a glimmer of hope rose in him. He might have to take a couple more punches from Picard but if that meant this ordeal was over…

"Then deal with him, understand?" commanded Adams.

Picard grunted in reply to Adams's instructions.

Fordy's rising hopes were dashed. Did Adams's words, 'deal with him', mean, kill him? Surely there must be a way of escape, thought Fordy, his mind racing.

Picard came back into the stables and without uttering a word yanked Fordy up. He came to his feet with a loud groan, somehow still hanging onto the leather satchel. Picard clutched onto the rope that dangled from Fordy's arms then bent to slice through the twisted cord around Fordy's ankles.

"I'm not carrying you," grumbled Picard. "Go over there," he added, pushing Fordy towards an opening in the floor. Fordy twisted and struggled free from Picard's grip. Shoving his captor aside he turned to run out of the stables. But before he was through the open doorway he was stopped by a loud crack and a burning punch in the back of his leg. Fordy fell to the floor. He struggled to get to his feet but his right leg was like tripe, he had no control over it. He moved his bound hands to the pain in his thigh. His leg was wet and warm, he knew it was blood, nothing else felt like it. He saw Picard rushing towards him, holding a pistol in his hand. Fordy cowered, expecting Picard to discharge the weapon again.

Picard took hold of Fordy's collar and dragged him back across the floor then pushed him through the hole in the ground. Fordy tumbled down the wooden steps that led into a cellar. As he landed on the floor the trap door slammed shut above him and the room went dark. Somehow, he had managed to keep a grip on Anna's satchel that held her papers.

In the blackness, as the pain from the bullet-wound shot through him, he could only guess at his surroundings. He tried to console himself; it shouldn't be long before someone found him here. As long as he wasn't bleeding too badly it would all be fine. Anna would soon be back at Worlds End and his father would come looking for him. Stillerton wouldn't dare set his thugs on his father; he couldn't start assaulting the whole neighbourhood, even if he was gentry.

Fordy shuffled himself across the floor until he hit a wall. He wedged himself up against it hoping to find more comfort. The pain in his leg was intense and the cut on his cheek throbbed. He tried to steady his breathing, drawing in deep breaths through his nose but his stomach churned and he spewed up over himself. Heat burned through his body, the smell of his vomit rose to his nose before he slumped back into deeper darkness.

* * *

The world he woke to was confusing. Weak shafts of light glittered through the wooden planks above him. Smoke filled his nostrils and rasped at the back of his throat. Slowly, then suddenly, he remembered; Picard, the cellar, his leg, and realised a fire raged above him. If he could tuck himself into a corner away from the burning falling debris, he had a good chance of surviving this. The smoke would rise and once the fire had burnt out, he would be able to climb from this hole.

But with his injured leg, hands tied and his eyes useless in the darkness, movement was difficult. Any effort to get to shelter brought new pains to his leg. He ran his hand over the wound, it felt sticky and his flesh was burning hot. Reaching out to his left he felt what he thought was a barrel full of liquor. He shuffled himself close to it hoping for a small degree of protection. Breathing heavily, he rested back, waiting for this nightmare to end. He pictured Anna at Worlds End, telling his father of what had happened. He imagined Mary Ann cosseting her and reassuring her that all would be well. He remembered the ring his father had given him and felt inside his jacket for the box. It was still there, he had forgotten to give it to her. His fingers also felt the crumpled rowan leaves that Mary Ann had given him, not that they had done him much good.

Through the noise of the fire he could hear Anna's voice calling for him. "Fordy, hurry."

What if he couldn't get out of this place? What would happen to Anna…and their unborn child? What if Adams and her father found her at Worlds End and forced her to go through with that wedding?

He pulled the bag that contained her papers tightly to his chest. How would she manage without proof of her identity?

"Anna," he called, "I will get back to you, I promise." His world went dark.

HISTORICAL NOTES

The inspiration for writing this story came from an offhand remark that my husband made in the car some years ago as we drove along No Mans Moor. He commented on the wide grassy verges and said he had always thought that this was an old droving road. The width allowed animals to move freely along the route.

Then I came across the Jeffries map from the 1770's which highlighted No Mans Moor and a place at the eastern end of No Mans Moor Lane called Worlds End. Three miles away near Hackforth sat Kings Pasture House.

Today, Worlds End goes by another name, although I have taken the liberty of moving its location a couple of miles westward, up the road. There is now no sign that a house sat on the site where Kings Pasture House is marked on the Jeffries Map at the junction of Hackforth Road and Bowbridge Lane.

Using real placenames and historical facts I have attempted to recreate life in the rural North Riding of Yorkshire in the early nineteenth century. With the backdrop of the newly ended Napoleonic Wars, The Year without a Summer of 1816, the continuing enclosures of common land and the introduction of the Corn Laws life was uncertain and precarious. Hunger loomed every winter.

Every generation thinks times are hard and it is not difficult to relate to these people 200 years ago who felt they were living through an unprecedented age.

I have stayed true to the spellings on The Jeffries Map where possible.

ACKNOWLEDGEMENT

My writing journey has been a long one.

There are so many people to thank.

Thank you to all of you, you know who you are.